In the Midst of Darkness

In the Midst of Darkness

▼

Colleen Rice

Writers Club Press
San Jose New York Lincoln Shanghai

In the Midst of Darkness

Writers Club Press
an imprint of iUniverse.com, Inc.

For information address:
iUniverse.com, Inc.
5220 S 16th, Ste. 200
Lincoln, NE 68512
www.iuniverse.com

Cover Photo by Liam Lyons
Author Photo by Michael Romanos

ISBN: 0-595-15906-0

Printed in the United States of America

Introduction

ULSTER, IRELAND 1756

Under the English enforced Penal Laws, the Catholic O'Dowd farm is confiscated and turned over to the Presbyterian Campbell family, newly arrived from Scotland. Hugh Campbell, feeling an instant affinity to the widower Padraic, and in total disregard for the law, quietly shares the work and the profits from the farm. Anna Campbell raises the mother-less Seamus along with her own son, Donald.

ULSTER 1771

The young man lay in a bed tucked into a corner of the small kitchen, barely breathing, eyes fastened onto the rough door, dimly visible in the glow from the turf fire. Had he dreamed it, he wondered. Then it came again— a soft knocking. Throwing back the patchwork quilt, Donald Campbell slid his feet onto the cold earthen floor. He slipped the bolt off the door and peered out into the darkness. Only the maize fields, barren in the autumn night, and beyond, the empty road. Not a sound even, except for crickets and the harsh wind that pushed against him and whistled around his bare legs. He glanced nervously around the tidy yard. Things were the same as always.

"I must be hearing things." He shrugged and started to close the door, when it was pushed inward, nearly knocking him off his feet. A rawboned figure hurried inside, pulled two books out from underneath his shabby coat and handed them over to his childhood friend.

"You frightened me half to death, you rogue," Donald whispered, and replaced the books on a rough wooden shelf beside the small window on the back wall.

Seamus swung aside a large black pot, poked up the fire and held his chapped hands out to the heat. "I had to wait till the moon went behind a cloud, didn't I?"

"I'm just grateful you're home safe."

"So am I, Donald, so am I."

"The soldiers came looking for you a fortnight ago, Seamus," he whispered.

Seamus, blue eyes too old for his face, spun around. "What?"

"Your Da told them he didn't know where you were."

Seamus's breath whooshed out in relief. "Precisely why I keep my own council concerning my whereabouts."

They huddled together on stools in front of the fire, talking softly.

Donald clasped his hands between his knees. "Do you think the cursed laws will ever be lifted so you can come home, instead of having to hide out in the hedgerows to teach?"

Seamus dismissed the question with a wave of his hand. "I've no idea. I try not to think about that too much. Not to change the subject, but how are your own studies coming along?"

The boy's gray eyes lit up. "I'm especially fond of mathematics." Then he ran a hand through his thick, black hair. "But I feel that guilty, going off to school, leaving father and your Da to do most of the work."

"Well, that's the way they'd have it, isn't it?"

"I suppose." Donald jumped up and got a bowl and a spoon out of the dresser.

"There's some bannock left from supper and mother made some barley soup. Here, let me fetch you a bowl." He broke off a piece of the flat

Chapter 1

▼

County Mayo, March 1786

Her naked feet ached with the cold as she sloshed down the coast road, through freezing puddles towards Ballymullian. She silently cursed the rules that forbade the removal of one's shoes from the big house until they were paid for. While she trudged barefoot to Crofton House in the damp of this March morning, Reanna's shoes were tucked tidily along with her apron and mop cap in a cubbyhole inside the servant's entrance on the other side of Ballymullian. There they would remain until the cost of them had been exacted from her wages.

She pulled her threadbare shawl closed against the chill wind of Innislow Bay and slid a hand into the pocket of her shift. Her icy fingers clutched a dog-eared letter as though it were a lifeline.

"Now that I know where you are, Siobhan, nothing will keep me here," she vowed to the swirling mist. Her words echoed back to her and gave her courage. She'd had Alex read the letter to her so often she practically knew it off by heart. *My dearest Reanna,* her cousin had written, *I hope that after all this time, you will have forgiven me for not bringing you along when I left Mayo. Now that you are fifteen, I pray that you understand my reluctance, when I had no idea what awaited myself in Dunbury. I think of you often and hope you are well.*

Reanna had understood her cousin's reasons for leaving, for in spite of being a spinster of twenty-six, Siobhan had never been further away than the town of Castlebar. But the fact of the matter was, they were supposed to leave together. Reanna's throat ached as the old feelings of abandonment resurfaced. Siobhan had been the closest thing to a mother she'd ever known and she missed her terribly. When Ma snatched Reanna's hard-earned wages to buy the drink for herself and Reanna's layabout brother, Fergus, Siobhan had lifted her cousin's spirit with dreams of the day when they would go away from this place together.

Then, the worst of all things happened. Siobhan's parents died of 'the cough' and Siobhan, practical as always, went away by herself, leaving Reanna with a promise to return and fetch her when the time was right. Siobhan's dear face swam into view. Soft, brown hair and steady eyes.

Reanna escaped once more into the warmth of her cousin's letter. *As I did not receive a reply to my letter of one year ago, sent in care of Father Meehan, I can only imagine two reasons why you haven't replied. You either haven't forgiven me for leaving you, or my letter hasn't gotten passed on to you, as you've not been to Mass, which would seem an ungrateful thing to do, now that we can attend in the open and in front of the eyes of the world.*

Scalding tears spilled over and coursed down her cheeks as she recalled what had happened to that ill-fated letter, and cursed Father Meehan afresh for the miserable thing he had done to her.

It had been almost a year ago. After celebrating Mass outdoors on top of Slieve Rathmill, Father Meehan had beckoned to her with a jerk of his head to come forward.

She'd walked slowly toward him, heart in her mouth, convinced that he was about to read her the riot act, but for what, she had no idea.

He pulled a letter out of his pocket and slapped it rhythmically into his other hand. "I've received this letter from up north," he said,

"Dunbury in Ulster to be exact. It has your name on it. Do you have any idea who would be writing to the likes of you from up there?"

Reanna's heart soared. "Indeed I do, Father," she answered. "It must be from my cousin Siobhan." She hopped from one foot to the other in anticipation. "Please, would you read it to me?"

"Siobhan Leary, is it," he muttered. "So that's where she ended up." He shook his finger in Reanna's face. "Bad cess to her, taking herself off to that Catholic hating place, and her poor dead parents still warm in their graves." He fingered the letter open with exasperating slowness. His two eyes frowned at its contents as he read aloud.

When he'd finished, he proclaimed in a thunderous voice, "So now miss high and mighty Leary is conversing in English, Irish not being good enough for her now that she's joined the ranks of the Protestants and is living in mortal sin with a man."

"I don't believe that's it at all, Father. Siobhan had to speak English in order to get a job and didn't she say she was there to look after Mr. Campbell's ailing mother?"

"A likely story," he sniffed. He shook the letter in Reanna's face. "She's a wicked turncoat and in danger of losing her immortal soul. I forbid you to answer this letter or to have anything further to do with the likes of her."

"But it's mine," she mumbled under her breath. She screwed up her courage and held out her hand. "Could I please, Father, have my letter?"

He swiped at her outstretched hand, put his hands on his hips and leaned down into her face. "Do you not understand what I'm saying to you?"

She twisted her red hair around her finger. "Yes, Father, I do," she whispered, "but…"

"Well then," he said, "you'll be having no more need of this." He tossed the letter containing Siobhan's address into the open turf fire.

Reanna cried out and fell to her knees beside the flames, where her salvation curled into ashes before her very eyes. She burst into tears as the flames licked at her hands. Father Meehan picked her up by the scruff of her neck and propelled her toward the stony path that led down the mountain. All the way down the steep, treacherous path she cursed 'that miserable old wretch' for having robbed her of her only link with Siobhan.

Something hardened in her heart after that encounter. She was finished with those who would hold her down. She would continue to attend Mass only in the hopes of receiving another letter from Siobhan. On that day, she vowed to leave this place and never return.

*   *   *

It had been a long year's wait until another letter had arrived—last Sunday it was, to be exact. That old hypocrite, Father Meehan, letter in hand, had hailed her on the road.

"I took the liberty of opening it," he'd said. "I prayed for that shameful girl and you'll be pleased to hear that she has redeemed herself in the eyes of Almighty God." He read the words aloud to Reanna and then offered to write a reply for her. She thanked him and with the lie between her teeth, said she would return later. He handed her Siobhan's letter. She had not let it out of her sight since. *I have wonderful news,* the letter went on, *Last year, I met and married a lovely Catholic man by the name of Seamus O'Dowd. He is a schoolmaster. The political climate being what it is in Ulster, he cannot get a teaching job, but we are hoping that will all change in the near future. But the best news of all and the reason for my writing, is, that I am expecting a child in September. I pray that you receive this letter and will respond in kind.*

With love,
Your cousin Siobhan.
PS Be brave Reanna. Your turn will come.

Reanna walked along with Siobhan's news singing in her ears. A wee baby. Think of it!

*   *   *

The bell on the Protestant church chimed six times as she made her way over the small wooden bridge into Ballymullian. In town, the wind from Innislow Bay gave way to an early morning fog that swirled down the street in front of her. She peered into it as though by sheer power of will, her eyes could penetrate its depths. She turned the corner onto Shop Street and trod carefully on the slick cobbles, past limestone flats, whose candlelit windows cast their light onto the wet street. She made her way to the little millinery shop where Alex lived with his Aunt Mae.

She agonized over how was she going to break the news to him that she was leaving. Since Siobhan had left, Alex had been her saving grace. Reanna had lived day by lonely day, till he'd come to work in the stables at Crofton House. He'd run away from his father's tailor shop in Paris to live with his aunt in Ballymullian. The lonely girl and the rebellious boy became fast friends, sharing confidences and dreams. Now their friendship seemed on the verge of blossoming into something deeper, a fact that Reanna found disquieting, somehow.

Her heart skipped a beat as she spotted Alex's slim figure standing in the light of the lamppost, hands scrunched in his pockets to ward off the cold. He raised a hand in greeting and fell into step beside her.

"I have something to tell you, Alex," she began, "but you have to promise me that you won't tell a soul."

He crossed his heart. "I promise." He blew on his hands to warm them and took her hand in his. They walked along in silence, then Reanna screwed up her courage.

"I'm going to run away to Siobhan."

He stopped short and turned his yellow eyes on her, his voice thick with emotion.

"Why Reanna?"

Reanna lowered her eyes. "Siobhan needs me, what with the new baby coming and all."

He raised her chin and made her look at him. "What about your family? What about me?"

She snorted, "Ma and Fergus? They give me no reason to stay. Let them look after themselves for a change." Her voice softened. "I will miss you, Alex, but I have to leave."

      *   *   *

As they climbed the hill that led out of town, the fog thinned and a soft rain began to fall. Reanna pulled her thin shawl close around her neck.

They walked along in silence. Alex said, his voice breaking, "It's a far piece, Dunbury."

Reanna took his hand in hers. "I know."

"It will take you the better part of a week to get there. How will you manage?"

"I'll walk, same as Siobhan did."

"How about food and shelter?"

"I have a nest egg hid underneath a rock near Crofton House. It'll get me there."

He stopped and wrapped his arms around her. He murmured into her hair. "I don't want you to leave, Reanna. I thought we'd always be together."

She almost gave into the emotions that were threatening to overcome her good sense. Then, she bit her tongue. "I must, don't you see? I don't want to be scrubbing pots for the rest of my life and end up living in some hovel like my mother. If there's a better life to be had in Dunbury, I mean to have it." She tossed her head. "In any case, I won't be leaving for at least a fortnight."

      *   *   *

Later that night, in the scullery of Crofton House, Reanna, slight arm muscles straining under the weight of a full bucket, sloshed steaming water over the dishes that filled the wooden sink. She rubbed a cloth over a large square of yellow soap and proceeded to scrub the plates clean and lay them on the drainboard for drying. Earlier, she and Maire, the gap-toothed scullery maid had helped themselves to a generous cut of leftover porter cake from Lord and Lady Dalton's anniversary party. They drained the dregs of sherry from twenty pewter goblets into a chipped cup and salvaged enough wine to wash down the cake. It was grand fun and they fell down laughing at their cleverness.

Now, at almost eleven o'clock, weariness had taken the place of good humor. Reanna's waterlogged fingers were etched with wrinkles. She rubbed her aching back. Earlier, she had spilled water down the front of her apron, and now her damp shift felt cold and clammy against her skin. And, it would start all over again tomorrow.

Since Lady Margaret's death six months ago, Reanna had been passed around Crofton House, doing for no one in particular, just helping out wherever she was needed, carding wool, spinning fleece. The fact of the matter was, apart from Alex, her only reason for staying in Mayo at all, had died with Lady Margaret.

*   *   *

That first day, twelve-year-old Reanna had stood outside Lady Margaret's bedchamber receiving her instructions from the head housekeeper. Hester cautioned Reanna that her Ladyship was in a great deal of pain and exceedingly cranky. She'd found fault with everyone sent up to clean her bedchamber, and had banished all but her nurse from her sight. The hope was that she would be kinder to a child.

Reanna had crossed herself for luck before opening the door. She walked directly to the window, pulled aside the heavy wine colored draperies and secured them to the wall with gold tiebacks. She felt the old woman's eyes boring into her back. To cover her nervousness, Reanna pretended that it was her room and she belonged here. Humming softly, she cracked open the tall narrow windows to air out the room. Then, she swept out the slate hearth and straightened the brocade chair that faced the window. Her daydream faltered when she approached the high mahogany bed. She lowered her eyes and stepped up onto the stool. She removed the feather pillow that was circled with perspiration. Reanna covered another pillow with fresh linen and placed it gently under the sick woman's head. She barely appeared to be breathing. As Reanna straightened the covers and draped a white lace spread over the wine wool coverlet, she stole another look at the austere face on the pillow. Thin nose in a waxen face, stubby lashes against sunken cheeks. Reanna laid her hand gently on Lady Margaret's forehead. It felt clammy. She wrung out a cloth in the lukewarm water from the washbasin against the wall, sponged off the sick woman's face and patted it dry with a square of linen.

She felt the older woman's eyes on her as she moved her attention to the marble- topped bedside table. She carefully dusted the gold shade on the oil lamp, and closed Lady Margaret's book, making sure the bookmark was in place. She didn't want to upset nurse, either. Lastly, she retrieved a tin of red lozenges from the drawer of the bedside table.

A petulant voice startled her, and the lozenges scattered onto the table.

"Fetch me a fresh glass of water," Lady Margaret demanded, "and stir a little of that laudanum into it for me."

Reanna took the small brown bottle from the drawer of the dresser. She wrinkled her nose in distaste at the cloying smell that emanated from it as she pulled out the stopper. She fixed the drink and held the glass to Lady Margaret's lips while she drank. She hastily gathered up the spilled lozenges and made her way toward the door.

Lady Margaret's hoarse voice stopped her. "What's your name girl?"

Reanna turned on her heel and curtsied. "Reanna, milady."

"Well done Reanna," she croaked.

From that time on, except for nurse, Reanna had worked exclusively for Lady Margaret. The pain-ridden old woman had insisted she wanted no one else to do for her or touch her things.

*   *   *

With a sigh of relief, Reanna dried the last plate and placed it in the sideboard alongside the others. She hung her laundered apron and wet dishcloths close to the hearth to dry. Tonight's celebration also marked the end of the family's six months mourning period. After Lady Margaret's death, her room had been kept exactly as it was when she was alive. Tomorrow, life was expected to return to normal. After Reanna aired out the sick room, and gave it a thorough spring-cleaning, it would be turned into a guestroom.

She would miss it so. The time she spent daydreaming that it was her room and she belonged there had made her living conditions at home at least bearable. Someday, she promised herself, she would have a room like that to call her own…her haven, her safe place.

She wanted to soak in the atmosphere of that orderly, serene room, one last time.

"Maire," she breathed, "I'm going up to Lady Margaret's room. I forgot my duster up there, and I don't want Hester all over me when she makes her rounds in the morning."

"Be careful you don't run into his nibs," Maire warned, "you know how grabby he gets when he's had a snootful."

Reanna ignited the wick on the candle. "Aah Maire, I've managed to stay out of his way this far. Besides, I'm sure he's tucked in long ago."

Maire snorted. "Maybe so, but be watchful in any case."

"I promise."

Reanna slipped out of the scullery and groped her way up the narrow staircase, pewter candlestick in hand, and the familiar odor of beeswax in her nostrils. Heart thumping, she opened the servant's door to the family's sleeping quarters and peeked around it. The double doors of Lord and Lady Dalton's suite loomed forbidding at the end of the long corridor. She sheltered the candle's flame with her hand and tiptoed across the corridor on cat feet to Lady Margaret's room.

Once inside, she placed the candlestick on a small table beside the wardrobe and eased open its double doors for one last look. She lifted a linen nightdress from one of the drawers, held it against her cheek. It still held the fragrance of the dried rose petals and orange pomander balls that lay among Lady Margaret's personals. Unable to resist the temptation, she held the ivory colored garment up in front of her and stood in front of the mirror that hung on the inside of the wardrobe door. She took off her mop cap. Her copper colored hair spilled out onto her shoulders. She smiled at her reflection. In the dim light of the candle, she twirled from side to side in admiration at what she saw.

A movement behind her reflection in the mirror almost choked her with fear. She dropped the garment to the floor and whirled around to see the rotund figure of Lord Dalton rise from the chair in front of the window and stagger towards her.

He took her by both her arms and shook her roundly. "Here," he said, "what do you think you're about, sneaking around at this time of night?"

"I was just finishing up in the scullery, milord," she babbled, "from the party. Then I realized I forgot my duster up here." She added, "I'll just get it and leave. I wasn't doing any harm."

"Duster, is it," he muttered, running his hands up and down her arms, eyes fastened on her bosom. "More likely looking for something to steal, eh?"

Reanna looked around frantically. He had backed her up against the small table and she was dangerously off balance. Fearful thoughts ran crazily through her brain like mice, trapped in a bag.

She'd heard terrible stories about him from the other servants that he'd forced to do his bidding and dreaded the day her turn might arrive.

"No," she cried, her voice rising hysterically, "I wasn't stealing anything, leave me be." She tried to twist out of his grasp.

He grabbed her by the throat and squeezed. "Be still," he whispered hoarsely, "don't you put on airs and graces with me, you Irish slattern. You ought to be grateful I'd even look at you."

His grip on her slackened as he attempted to unbutton his trousers. Reanna fell backward into the small table, dislodging the candle. The flame extinguished itself as it hit the floor. Lord Dalton grabbed her again, forced his hand up under her shift and pushed her to the floor. She threw herself about in a frenzy to escape from under his smothering bulk as he lunged into her, but her struggles seemed only to fuel his excitement. So, she lay still, with her eyes squeezed shut to escape the sight of that slack red face that hovered above her, expelling his foul breath into her face, and glazed eyes that looked right through her, intent only on his twisted wants.

When finally he collapsed on top of her, Reanna went mad. She groped for the fallen candlestick, found it and brought it down on the back of Lord Dalton's head. He slumped into a dead weight on top of her. She wriggled out from beneath him and rose to her knees. He weaved from side to side as he tried to get up.

Panic-stricken, Reanna raised the candlestick. He raised his arms to ward off the blows. She continued to beat on him, time and time again, like he was a loathsome bug that refused to die. When he lay still, she stood over him, gasping, fist in her mouth, trying to stifle her cries. The horror of what had happened washed over her in waves of nausea.

Shaking like a crazy person, she fled silently through the hall and down the back stairs and burst through the scullery door. She heard Maire call out in alarm to her as she threw open the back door and stumbled into the stable yard. She sped out the gate and down the road to where she'd hidden her run away money. She removed her shoes, tucked her stash of coins into their toes and tied them by their laces

around her neck. She flew back down the road, like the hounds of hell
were after her, past the big house, north to Dunbury and Siobhan.

*   *   *

Hour after hour she tramped the road northward, till the dark clouds
of night faded to a murky dawn. Exhausted and seeking refuge from the
punishment of the road, she trudged reluctantly past mud-walled cabins that dotted the countryside. Devoid of greenery, they would afford
her little sanctuary. As well, she was too terrified to seek shelter within.
Around a bend in the road, at the foot of a rolling hill, she found what
she was looking for. A tenant farm spread out here, edged in by a rock
wall. Yellow gorse bushes grew in profusion the length of the inner wall.

A forbidding stone house stood sentinel at the end of a long lane. She
continued on her way until she was out of sight of the gate, then quickly
clambered over the sharp wall, hurdled a muddy ditch and crawled
between two gorse bushes, taking care to avoid the thorns that pro-
truded from its shiny branches. Peering through the thicket, she saw a
rickety stable and a huddle of rundown windowless cabins, of the sort
rented out to Irish farm workers in exchange for their labor and little
else. Nonetheless, Reanna gazed enviously at a wisp of smoke that trick-
led from the chimney of a dark cabin and longed for the warmth of the
hearth inside, but fear of discovery made her stay where she was. She lay
listening to the stamping of horses in the stables and the soft snuffling
of a penned up pig, before fatigue took its toll and she fell into a deep
and troubled sleep.

*   *   *

A short time later, a loud cawing startled Reanna awake. A large
raven blinked malevolently down at her from his perch on a gorse
branch above. Heart thumping, she skidded herself backwards out of
the damp briers, prying her colorless shift free from the clinging thorns

and dislodging the large bird from his perch. With an angry screech and a flap of his wings, he took flight to the top of a hawthorn tree, where he continued his harangue.

A mixture of relief and anger took hold of her spirit. "Get out of it, you cheeky devil," she whispered hoarsely, and put her arms around her shivering body. She looked at the blood that ran freely from the scratches on her arm and her body was seized by a terrible fury as though trying to shake itself free from the horror of the previous night. Lord Dalton was dead, she told herself and she, Reanna O'Neal, had killed him. In her mind's eye, she saw again the scarlet stain infuse his mouse-colored hair, as he lay still on the floor, but a mortal fear that he would rise and wreak a terrible vengeance on her had impelled her to keep hitting him till he lay still.

Panic clawed at her throat and the urge to run almost overpowered her. She forced herself to stay put until the panic subsided and she could think clearly.

The authorities would be on her trail now, she told herself. In her haste to escape, she had left her shawl in her cubbyhole at Crofton House. Her bare head would surely draw unwanted attention. She had to change her looks somehow. Scooping up some mud in her fingers, she smeared it onto her face and pulled the rest of it through her dark copper hair. She reached back under the bush and picked up her shoes, momentarily comforted by the stash of coins they held and tucked them inside the top of her shift.

Her eyes darted down the road, first one way and then the other. Cold, black mud oozed between her toes as she jumped short of the ditch and scrambled up and over the fence to the road. She recognized nothing of the countryside, but knew only that the road she followed led north to Dunbury.

*   *   *

Reanna tramped the roads through a cold pounding rain, over rolling hills, through little hamlets and past long stretches of bog. By midmorning, the wind picked up and shifted the clouds. The sun broke through in a blaze of light. Seduced by the warmth on her back and half-asleep with exhaustion, she trudged along with bowed head, watching her feet move under her. A shout from behind brought her hurtling back to the present and sent her scurrying to safety on the side of the road. A post boy on horseback, mailbags secured to his horse's side, clattered past her on his way to the post town of Castlebar to deliver the mail.

As the watery sun rose higher in the sky, the road Reanna trod filled up with people on their way to market. She passed weavers, pulling two-wheeled carts filled with webs of linen, and spinners who trudged along carrying bulging bags of raw wool and knitted clothing to sell. A young lad, pulled along by a trotting pig on a tether, ran out of control down the middle of the road, almost upending a young girl, carrying a nest of eggs in her apron. Reanna hurried by a toothless old woman, wrestling with a blindfolded hen that seemed bent on escaping from underneath her arm.

Reanna's stomach rumbled at the sight of a farmer, wheeling a barrow of potatoes. She secretly retrieved a coin from her stash and caught up to him. He sorted carefully through the wheelbarrow and selected the biggest and best potato he could find and handed it to her with a flourish. She wiped the dirt off as best she could and ate it out of hand, peel and all as she approached the market square. Her gaze wandered over the crowd. A man she recognized from Ballymullian stood in line, chatting with another weaver, in front of the brown linen market. Her throat tightened in panic. She lowered her head and edged her way slowly through the crowd, desperate to get away, but aware of the danger of calling attention to herself by hurrying. She spotted a rag picker set up on the side of the road. She quickly lifted a coin from her shoe and in the blink of an eye, walked away, head and shoulders enveloped in a large square of faded blue wool. She melted back into the crowd and was soon on her way out the other side of Castlebar, wrapped in a shawl that was none too clean and smelled like a wet dog.

*　　　　　　　*　　　　　　　*

After five grueling days on the road, Reanna was nearing exhaustion, but fear that she might be only a step ahead of the authorities kept her on the move. On dry nights, she slept under bushes away from prying eyes, but when the rain pelted down and the wind howled, she rapped on friendly doors at suppertime and offered to pay for a bite to eat and a scrap of daub floor to sleep on.

Earlier in the day, she had crossed the border into Ulster, not knowing what to expect, but fearful of being challenged. It didn't appear to be much different from Mayo, aside from seeing more cabins alongside the road. Now that she was two days away from Dunbury and Siobhan, a new worry beset her. What if she wasn't made welcome by Seamus? She quickly dismissed that fear as foolishness. Of course she would be made welcome. Siobhan wouldn't marry anyone who wasn't at least as good-hearted as herself. Besides, her cousin was expecting a baby wasn't she? Couldn't she use the extra help, with her working and all?

As it was not Reanna's intention to spend any more of her life in service, her wish was that Seamus could be persuaded to teach her to read and write. Then she could get a job in a shop. She thought about her shoes, tucked inside her shift. They would clean up nicely and the coins she had in her pocket, although disappearing at an alarming rate, would still be enough to buy her a decent set of second hand clothing. This would be a new start in life for her and she intended to make the most of it. She would marry herself a good man as Siobhan had done and he would take care of her. Someday, she would have children as well.

As she saw the bustling market town of Kilkelly laid out before her, she breathed a little easier. Maybe she would make it to Dunbury safely after all. She had met all sorts of people on the road and had seen no one who appeared to show any undue interest in her.

Reanna thought of the questions Siobhan might have when she turned up unannounced on her doorstep. She'd not tell her the truth, certainly. That was past and the memory of it brought on the horrible quaking in her body that she couldn't control, and so she smothered the memory deep inside herself and refused to think about it. She would only allow good things to become memories in this new life, she told herself, as she worked her way through the crowd in the market place.

Her newfound confidence lasted until, lost in her own thoughts, she bumped into someone and was flung rudely aside. Her ankle gave way and she tumbled in the dusty street. Her ears burned with humiliation as she looked around for her tormentor. The angry words she'd been about to fling froze in her mouth.

A foppish British officer stood looking down his nose at her with contempt in his bulging eyes. "Look where you're going," he shouted hysterically, brushing off the scarlet sleeve of his spotless uniform, where it had come in contact with her.

Fear clawed at her stomach as she raised herself quickly to her feet. "A thousand pardons, sir," she babbled in English, "I was looking for my lost hen. It got fair away from me as I was bringing it to market and I didn't see where I was going. Is yourself all right then?" she asked in false humility.

"Yes, no thanks to you," he replied disdainfully. He turned on his heel and minced away from her on skinny legs encased in white stockings.

Reanna hobbled over to the side of the road, her ankle stabbing in pain at every step. She eased herself down onto a patch of grass by the side of a livery stable and gingerly massaged her ankle

A stocky young man, dressed in a blue frockcoat and breeches, approached her. He squatted in front of her and set his carpetbag beside him on the dusty street. His gray eyes showed concern. "Are you all right, lass?"

She nodded yes and lowered her head.

He removed his hat and bent his dark head toward her, trying to catch her eye. "Are you in some kind of trouble, then?"

Reanna's heart stopped. She couldn't speak from the fear of it. She raised her tear- filled eyes to meet his and said nothing.

"Where are you from?" he inquired kindly. When she didn't answer, he went on, "I'm not trying to frighten you, miss, but I heard you speak to the officer and I did notice that your accent was not from around here."

Reanna looked up at him in bewilderment at his remark. He didn't sound Irish himself, or English either, for that matter. His words sort of rolled out of him. But, he did have kind eyes, she felt, and so she decided to trust him.

"My name is Reanna and I'm on my way to Dunbury."

"My name is Donald. Dunbury is a long way from here, Reanna. How are you going to get there?" When she didn't answer, he pointed at her foot. "May I?"

She nodded.

He picked up her foot and examined it. "You'll not get far, walking on that ankle." He stood up decisively, took hold of her hands and lifted her to her feet. He pointed across the street. "Do you see that building over there with the three arches?"

"The linen market?"

"Aye," he answered, "that's the one. I'll be working over there all day. I'm a draper, you see. You come and sit by me and rest. When the market closes at four, we'll see what we can do about your ankle."

"Thank you, sir," she whispered. Tears of gratitude stung her eyes.

"There's no need to thank me." He picked up his bag and took her arm.

"But I do, in any case."

*　　　　　*　　　　　*

All day she sat beside the kind man called Donald and watched him while he worked. He stood on a stool inside one of the arches as a queue of weavers, with webs of linen cloth to sell, passed by in front of him. Donald inspected the sheetings carefully, struck a bargain and stamped with a seal, the corners of the ones he wished to purchase. Then he made notes in a ledger.

Reanna's ankle was throbbing. As well, she was dying of the hunger and wished with all her heart that some nourishment might be forthcoming, but Donald seemed to have need for neither food nor drink. When the pealing of the bells on the Anglican Church tolled four o'clock, and the last of the weavers had gone, he placed the ledger in his bag, stretched his arms over his head, then wiped a hand over his eyes.

He smiled kindly at her. "How are you now, Reanna?"

She shrugged. "My ankle still hurts if I move it."

He bent down to where she sat on the ground and probed gently at the puffy skin. She yelped in pain.

Donald shook his head in dismay. "A good night's rest will do wonders for the swelling. I have a room at the Fife and Crow down the street," he offered. "You're welcome to stay there with me tonight."

Reanna's ears burned with shame at his proposal. Lord Dalton's unjust remark came back to her. "You ought to be grateful I'd even look at you, you Irish slattern."

Anger made her want to strike out at this stranger and his proposal. She was not like her mother—she wasn't. But, instead, the futility of her situation engulfed her and she wrapped her arms around her knees and rocked back and forth, trying vainly to stifle the sobs that threatened to burst from her throat. She wiped away angry tears with a grimy hand.

Donald noted the change that came over Reanna at his offer of shelter. He stood up.

"You've not had lunch, have you, lass?"

She shook her head dispiritedly. "Indeed I haven't."

"You must be quite famished, then."

Hunger overcame her fear for the moment. She raised her eyes to his. "I am."

He raised her to her feet. "Well, come along, then." He picked up his bag, took her arm and they walked slowly down the street toward the inn.

Reanna took comfort in the support of his firm grip on her arm. She allowed herself to lean against his stocky body for support as she hobbled the last few feet towards the door of the inn.

They paused inside the tavern entrance of the Fife and Crow. Reanna's mouth watered at the savory smells that filled the room, and she saw its source, a tray of hot kidney pies and flagons of beer. It floated above the wooden tables, in the hands of a dark haired serving girl with flushed cheeks. Reanna's fingers itched to snatch one of the pies off the tray and shove it whole into her mouth. The serving girl set down the tray of food and drink at a table of boisterous weavers. They pushed aside their bolts of cloth to accommodate their supper.

Donald plucked at Reanna's sleeve for attention and led her towards a stuffed deer head with an enormous rack of antlers that hung over the double doors to the lobby. As they passed the bar, a small man, dressed in tabby tweed, caught Donald's eye and raised his flagon of ale in a discreet salute. Donald appeared not to notice. He picked up his room key from the clerk and helped Reanna climb the flight of narrow stairs. They walked down a dimly lit hallway to a corner room.

Donald opened the door and helped her inside. A shaft of light from the lone window fell across a narrow bed that was made up with a red and white patchwork quilt and two pillows, one beside the other. Reanna was ecstatic. She had never slept in a bed before. At home, she slept on a pallet of bags on the dirt floor, curled up in a ragged, filthy blanket alongside her mother and her brother, Fergus.

Donald put down his bag and helped her over to a dun colored horsehair armchair that was pulled up to the hearth. She had never seen anything approaching this luxury, except at Crofton House, but of course, she told herself, Crofton House was much grander.

Donald eased her down into the chair. "You rest now." He bent down and lit the turf fire in the fireplace. "I have to go downstairs to pay the weavers and load up my linen wagon. I'll be back in a wee while." He removed a tin box from his bag, picked up his ledger and left.

"And still not a bite to eat," Reanna groaned aloud. A large mouthed white pitcher with a red and blue design sat inside a matching basin, on a washstand in the corner of the small room. She hopped over to it, found a cup, dipped out some water and drank deeply. She studied her image in a small looking glass that hung by a string above the washstand. Frightened eyes, a dirty face and mud-streaked hair looked back at her. She undressed down to the bare buff, filled the basin with water, picked up a cut of yellow soap and bathed herself from head to toe. She washed her shift, wiped her shoes clean with her shawl and then scrubbed it between her hands till her knuckles were raw. She wrung out her clothes and hung them over the back of a chair in front of the fire. Her stash of coins, she shoved back into her shoes, limped over to the bed and wrapped a woolen blanket around her slight body. She sat cross-legged in front of the fire, ankle forgotten, easing the tangles out of her damp curls and dreaming of her reunion with Siobhan, when a sharp rap sounded on the door. She froze to the spot like a frightened animal, her heart pounding in her chest. She heard a clatter and then footsteps receding down the hall. She opened the door cautiously and saw the retreating back of the serving girl from the tavern downstairs. She was swinging an empty tray at her side. Reanna looked down at her feet. A dish of brown-crusted kidney pie and a mug of fragrant, steaming tea, sat on the floor outside the door. Reanna bent down, slid the food inside the door and fell upon it like a starving dog.

          *   *   *

Later that night, Donald returned to his room. He removed his frock coat and hung it on a hook on the back of the door and lit the oil lamp. He chuckled softly at the sight of his charge, swaddled in a blanket, curled up in the chair by the hearth, fists under her chin and snoring softly. He lifted her gently out of the chair and deposited her, still sleeping, into the bed and pulled the quilt up around her shoulders.

He placed another clod of turf on the smoldering embers in the grate and poked it to life. He removed Reanna's supper dish from the table. It had been licked clean. He drew a chair up to the small table, and set to work. He removed two ledgers from his bag and proceeded to copy some figures from the first ledger to the second. When he had finished his bookwork, he stood up and emptied the remaining bills and coins out of the tin box into a pouch, which he deposited in an inside pocket of his waistcoat. With a sigh, he stretched out in the chair, covered himself with his frockcoat, blew out the candle and slept.

*   *   *

Next morning, Reanna woke up with the sun shining in her face. Donald was nowhere to be seen. She sat up in the strange bed. He must have put her to bed, she reasoned, but where did he sleep. Not here, for the other side of the bed was still made up. Well done Reanna. First time in a real bed and you slept through it.

She tucked the blanket around herself, stepped gingerly onto the floor and tested her weight on her ankle. It still felt a little catchy. She limped around on the cold floor, gaining strength in her ankle. Only gray embers remained in the hearth. She stood in the shaft of sunlight that flooded the long narrow window, reveling in its warmth. The street looked quieter today. Market day over, everything back to normal, she thought to herself. Fewer horses tied up in front of the livery stable down the street. A young couple with a small child stood chatting outside her window. Donald was nowhere to be seen.

She limped over to the mirror and stood in front of it. She undid her braid and combed her hair with her fingers until it fell softly in dark copper waves to her shoulders. Her cheeks flushed with pleasure at her appearance. Things would work out now, she told herself. She slipped her shift over her head, dropped her stash of coins in the pocket and slid into her shoes. Her shawl was still damp. She shrugged and tied it over her shoulders anyway.

Then she noticed that all of Donald's belongings were gone. She chewed on her knuckle apprehensively, and paced the room in indecision for a few minutes. Then she decided to ask the hotel clerk if he'd left.

She walked down the stairs and into the lobby. The front door opened and a youth entered with a bundle of newspapers. He pushed the top one through the cubicle to the clerk and dropped the rest on a bench in the lobby.

"Another house burning spree last night," he said. "Keep that up, and we soon won't have a papist left in the whole county."

The disgruntled clerk looked over his spectacles at him. "Wouldn't that be a terrible disgrace?" He looked up at Reanna briefly, dismissed her as not worthy of his attention and went back to his newspapers.

She'd been on the verge of asking after Donald, but the conversation she'd overheard prompted her to avoid the clerk altogether. She hobbled out the back door into the courtyard. Stablehands scurried around, helping out of town merchants get on their way with their weekly purchases. Horses stood hitched up to wagons, munching oats out of nosebags, ready to go. Reanna spotted the back of a horse-drawn wagon loaded with linen sheetings clattering its way out of the porte-cochere into the street. The driver was already out of sight. She hobbled across the courtyard and shouted at him to stop. The wagon shuddered to a halt and a leathery-faced stranger turned to face her.

"What is it you're wanting, miss?"

"I'm sorry," she stammered. "I thought you were someone else." She limped dejectedly back to the lobby of the inn. The smell of food drew her into the tavern. It looked like a different place in the morning light. Where last night, it had been all conviviality and food and drink, in the morning light, the tavern looked forlorn and wore an air of neglect. Only a handful of people sat at the tables, eating breakfast. The stale odor of yesterday's ale hung strong in the airless room and dust motes floated in the light that filtered through the leaded windows. The bar was devoid of customers, but vestiges of spilled drink still ringed the dark wood of the bar. A mouse skittered around on a long table at the back, eating the dregs of someone's supper that had been left overnight on a plate.

Reanna chose a table that gave her a view of the lobby. She ate slowly, relishing her breakfast of wheaten bread and a mug of hot tea laced with milk, hoping Donald would turn up. He didn't. When the shovel-faced serving girl cleared the dishes off the table, Reanna paid for her breakfast and left, bitterly disappointed at being deserted.

*   *   *

She limped along on her swollen ankle, stopping frequently to rest, until the sun faded. Clouds filled the sky and a lashing rain turned the road to an oozing mess. Footsore and weary, she began her search for a scrap of floor to sleep on out of the rain and a bite to eat. Down a rutted side road, she spotted a scurvy cabin with a curl of smoke drifting out of the chimney. She hobbled towards it gratefully and let herself in through the broken gate that hung on one hinge. She dipped into her pocket to select a coin and pulled out a slip of paper. In the fading daylight, she saw words she could not read, but assumed it had to be from Donald. Maybe he hadn't deserted her after all. Maybe he was looking for her right now, and she off the road in pursuit of her stomach. The thought of going back to the main road to look for him was tempting, but the pain in her ankle would allow her to go no further. By noon it had swollen over the top of her shoe, forcing her to go barefoot. Coin in hand, she rapped hesitantly on the rough door.

A slatternly woman with a caved in mouth and ferret eyes peeked around the half-opened door. "What is it ye want," she inquired with a suspicious glance.

Reanna held out the coin to her. "I was hoping to come in out of the rain for the night and have a bite to eat."

"Not a chance of it," the woman replied emphatically, "we've no room for strangers here." She was about to close the door in Reanna's face when she spotted the coin.

"Well, all right then," she said grudgingly, snatching the coin from Reanna's outstretched hand, "ye can come in, but ye'd best be gone by early morning before the mister wakes up."

Reanna walked into a one-roomed cabin, dimly lit by a single candle jutting out from a crude sconce on one wall. Two grubby boys sat in front of the hearth, quarreling loudly over a stick that was shaped like a soldier.

"Shut yer gobs," the woman yelled and boxed their ears for their clatter. "Here," she waved a grimy thumb at Reanna, "sit yerself down beside these two ruffians."

Reanna eased herself down onto the daub floor. The hard packed dirt felt cold and clammy under her thin shift. Her eyes took in her surroundings. Barely a step up from the O'Neal household in Mayo, she concluded.

The woman took some boiled potatoes out of a three-legged pot that sat over the fire and put them into a basket. She set it on the floor in front of them, placing a bowl of buttermilk and a dish of salt beside it. Then she sat her fleshy bulk across from Reanna. With a large knife, she cut the potatoes in chunks. The boys snatched the hot potatoes with grubby hands, dipped them by turns in buttermilk, then salt and popped them into their mouths, swallowing them whole. Their ma wielded the stick that was shaped like a soldier as a deterrent to grabby fingers that would take more than their share.

Reanna followed suit, picking up the hot chunks of potato with her fingers and dipping them in the milk and salt. They slid down her throat with great ease.

The woman motioned accusingly to Reanna with her potato-studded knife. "What is it yer doing out in the dark and the rain, anyway?"

Too tired to think, Reanna answered, "I'm from Mayo and I'm on my way to Dunbury."

"Mayo," the woman shrieked, ferret eyes widening in fear. "A bloody papist, is it ye are?" She dropped the knife, stood up and pointed to the door. "Get out while you can still walk," she warned. "If the mister comes home and finds a papist under his roof, he'll break yer head for being here and mine for letting ye in."

Reanna stood up and held out her hand. "I'll take my coin back then," she said, her anger barely under control. "I paid for food and lodgings, as I remember."

A sly look came over the other woman's face and she gathered together the colorless hair that streeled over her shoulders and twisted it into a knot. "Aye, well," she said in a wheedling voice, "but then, on the other hand, what he don't know won't hurt him, will it? Crawl on over into the corner there. When he comes home, just pretend yer asleep. I'll tell him yer thickheaded and I let ye in out of the rain. But ye better make sure to be up and on yer way before he wakes up in the morning."

Reanna curled up next to the wall, ears still burning with resentment, but not willing to go back out into the pouring rain. She listened to the rain pinging on a tin bucket outside the door, until her eyelids grew heavy and she slept.

She heard 'the mister' roll in sometime during the night, smelling of fire and the drink. Through slitted eyes, she watched a round pudding of a man plop himself down beside his wife on the floor. The small cabin soon reverberated with his snores.

Things here were not so different from Mayo, Reanna decided. Aside from not letting on you were Catholic, it seemed much the same as far as she could figure. She fell back into a fitful sleep. The next time she woke up, the rain had stopped. She crept to the door and left.

Chapter 2

▼

Ulster, April 1786

The heavy April downpour that had assailed Dunbury since early morning eased off into a fine rain by the time Reanna arrived in late afternoon. A damp wind blew in off the Glenna River, straight up High Street, seeped through her thin shift into her bones and sucked all the warmth out of her. She walked barefoot down the cobbles of High Street, clutching her shawl closed at the throat and coughing the deep croupy cough that had plagued her since yesterday. Her shoes remained warm and dry underneath her shawl, to be kept in good condition for a job that was sure to follow.

As she passed the *Dunbury Guardian,* she looked longingly through the glass at the men working inside. Dry they were, and probably going home to their families soon, where the paid help would cook them a hot meal. She vowed once more that she would make something of herself. Her stomach grumbled with hunger. Visions of Siobhan and a warm place to stay, spurred her on to find Biggens Alley.

A wizened little man lounged under a tavern sign that was shaped like a whistle and hung over the street on an iron rod. She crossed over and approached him, raising her voice so's to be heard over the squeaking of the sign as it swung in the wind.

"Pardon me sir, would you be familiar with a place by the name of Biggens Alley?"

He took measure of her and pointed down the street towards the river. "Go down past the Highbury Inn…" he began in a wavering voice.

Reanna inwardly cursed again her inability to read. "Which one would that be?" she asked.

The little man waved his arm impatiently, as though it had eyes on the end of it. He raised his voice, spacing his words out as though being ignorant, she was deaf and thick headed as well. "Down there on the other side of the street—by the corner. D'ye see it—the black building with the wee panes of glass." He wagged a warning finger at her. "But you don't want to cross the street. Keep walking on this side until you reach the park. Then keep on going till you come to a block of warehouses—Buffen Street that'll be. Turn to your left, and you'll see the boatyard and some tenements. It's down there."

Reanna walked down High Street, past tenements with lace curtains on the windows and shops with pots of red geraniums outside. As she neared the Glenna River, however, these were replaced by empty fields and neglected buildings with broken-out windows. A faded sign tacked on the side of an abandoned warehouse announced to the world it had arrived at Buffen Street. A jumbled boatyard took up most of Buffen Street on the riverside. Workmen hammering home beams, crawled like bees over a partially constructed sailboat that sat up on crossbars in the middle of the yard. A row of planks lay alongside it, covered in sawdust. A tow headed youngster noisily scraped barnacles off a fishing boat in dry-dock. A man wearing heavy oversize gloves dipped a wound up rag on a stick into a kettle of boiling tar and applied a thick layer to the seams on the bottom of a sailboat. Reanna's eyes smarted from the pungent fumes.

Across the street, a ragged creature lay huddled on the crumbling stoop of a dilapidated tenement next to a lane. He roused himself at her approach and held out a begging hand.

She bent forward, hands on her knees. "Could you tell me where I might find Biggens Alley?"

He looked at her out of rheumy eyes. "Yer standin' in it." When no handout was forthcoming, he closed his eyes again.

Reanna entered the alley, ducking under strings of dripping laundry that hung like grimy fingers between the tenements. The stench of poverty hung thick in the air. She approached a straggly line of barefoot children waiting to fill their pots from a lone water tap.

"Does the schoolmaster, Seamus O'Dowd live around here?" she asked no one in particular, hoping against hope that she was in the wrong place.

An emaciated girl with pale sullen eyes looked Reanna up and down. She pointed at a decrepit door halfway down the alley. "In there," she said, "top floor."

As Reanna approached the door, a young lad burst through it. Close on his heels, reeled a drunken man, fists clenched and spouting oaths. He made for the terrified lad, who hid behind a scraggly woman in the water line. Reanna stood frozen in fear. Her heart thumped in her chest till she thought it would burst. Then her head went all queer and the quaking in her limbs started up and she feared she would die from it. She wheeled around and ran back out to Buffen Street and stood trembling with her back against a tenement wall. It was her father all over again.

*   *   *

She was ten years old the last day she'd seen him. Brought home after a drunken brawl to their wretched hovel by two of his like. They dumped him through the door, where he lay broken and bleeding in his own filth, till the next morning, when he up and left and never returned. That very day Reanna's ma had hauled her off to Crofton House and secured her a place in the scullery, scrubbing pots. Since then she'd given over almost every penny she earned to her ma, who in turn gave it to her brother Fergus, the layabout. What ma herself earned lying down in the bog for anybody who asked her, she spent for the drink.

                    *   *   *

Go back in the alley, Reanna chided herself. *You've come all this way and there is nowhere else to go. Find Siobhan and everything will be all right.*

She pulled herself together and returned to the alley, keeping her face averted from the water line.

She stepped over the teeming gutter, into the broken door of the tenement. Her feet moved quickly up the stairs, sidestepping naked toddlers who reeked of urine and vomit. She averted her eyes from a pair of grubby youngsters, glued in an embrace against a back wall. She stepped around a missing board on the landing and climbed the remaining stairs to the fourth floor attic room where the child at the tap had said Siobhan and Seamus lived.

She stood outside the scarred door, knees knocking, heart hammering in her chest, hesitating to rap on the door, but feeling too weak to go any further. She screwed up her courage and knocked hesitantly on the rough boards.

A rawboned man with bushy brows opened the door and peeked his face around it.

"Are you Seamus?" Reanna asked through chattering teeth.

"I am indeed." He opened the door wider. "Come in, come in."

Relief at his words of welcome made her weak at the knees and her head spin. "Are you all right, miss?" she heard him ask, as she fell.

Reanna came to inside the flat, lying on the floor, supported by Seamus's arms. Siobhan knelt beside her husband, rubbing Reanna's hands and trying to feed her hot tea with a spoon. Reanna's eyes drank in her cousin's presence; tawny hair parted in the middle and drawn softly back over her ears, framing her broad face. Reanna sat up and with a happy cry, threw her arms around Siobhan and hugged her as though she would never let go.

Siobhan removed Reanna's arms from around her neck, held her at arm's length and looked worriedly into her cousin's face. "What in the name of God are you doing in Dunbury, Reanna? How did you get here at all?"

In spite of Reanna's intentions to say nothing of why she fled Mayo, the moment her older cousin fastened her clear eyes onto her own, the truth came tumbling out and she unburdened herself of the awful secret she held. It had always been so, as though Siobhan's direct gaze laid Reanna's soul bare.

When Reanna had finished her tale, Siobhan enveloped her cousin's cold hands between her own and rubbed warmth into them. Her voice trembled with remorse. "I should have sent for you sooner."

Reanna nodded her bowed head. "But I'm here now, and I'll be fine. Please don't worry, Siobhan."

Siobhan's voice trembled. "Are you certain that you killed the man, Reanna?"

Reanna fell into another fit of crying. Between shuddering sobs, she replied, "I'm not certain. He was on the floor. There was blood on his head."

"Does anyone know you're here?"

Reanna shook her head. "No one."

"Did you not go home, then?"

"I didn't, no."

Siobhan cast a worried glance at Seamus. "What are we to do, Seamus?"

He shrugged his shoulders. "There's nothing to be done, but take our chances. We can't send the child back out into the cold. She'll just have to stay here and hope for the best."

*　　　　　　*　　　　　　*

At daybreak, a frightful din awakened Reanna as she lay curled up on the floor. Children bickered on the landing outside the O'Dowd flat. Doors slammed, feet pounded on the stairs, fretful babies cried. In the alley, the noise of too many people crowded in too small a space, intruded through the open window. Poor Siobhan, to have ended up here. She'd had such high hopes when she left Mayo. Reanna glanced around at the wretchedness of the flat. A tin pail of water with a dipper in it sat on an upended wooden crate in front of the small window. At the gabled end of the room, dying embers from the hearth cast flickering shadows on the sloped walls. Nearby, Siobhan and Seamus lay curled up together on the floor, spoon fashion. Beside them sat a burned down candlestick and two books, one of which was opened.

Reanna lay on her side, plagued by guilt for being here, and resolved to find work and another place to live as soon as possible. By the looks of things, they barely had enough for themselves without another mouth to feed. It was not surprising that Siobhan had neglected to send for her.

Last night, when Reanna had voiced her concern about the dark circles under her cousin's eyes and her pale, drawn face, a grief-stricken Siobhan told Reanna of her miscarriage…her second one in as many years. It seemed they'd enough troubles of their own without hers to add to the mix.

Reanna stilled her thoughts as she overheard a mumbled conversation from across the room.

"Maybe it is God's blessing that Reanna landed in when she did, Siobhan. She can look after the Campbell place for a short while until you are better."

"I hate to ask her favors when she's only just arrived Seamus, and her with that bad cough and all. I'm sure I'll be up and around in another day or two."

"Not a bit of it. You need your rest. If you like, I'll ask her myself."

Reanna rose to her feet and squatted beside Siobhan and Seamus. "I'll be happy to do it, Siobhan. It's little enough for the troubles I've visited on you."

"If you're sure you wouldn't mind, love. It will only be for a few days. I'm sure I'll be right as rain by then."

*   *   *

Later that morning, Reanna and Seamus walked up High Street on their way to the Campbell flat. She breathed a sigh of relief to be out of the alley, if only for a little while, and resolved to get out that awful place, no matter what the cost and the sooner the better.

The damp, clean air refreshed her soul as they walked past the park, with its banks of purple and white crocuses and spoke like paths, all leading to a central bandstand. On both sides of High Street, tradesmen plied their wares. A tinsmith broke the quiet of the morning with a clatter of pans, as he removed them from a shoulder pole and set them out on the ground in front of the armory. A cobbler stood, ropy arms folded, not a bit delighted to see the visitor set up in front of his shop, a red-faced old man with sparse white hair and a pink scalp, who held court with a pig on a rope. A burly ironmonger sat in front of a grocery store surrounded by big black pots. Picking absently at a burn mark on his arm, he gawked at a group of maids who were giggling and gossiping together.

Reanna spotted a peddler with second hand clothing for sale. She ran over and picked through the piles he'd placed on the ground around him. She found a navy blue dress with petticoats, form fitted sleeves and a wealth of creamy lace on the low cut bodice. It had a matching hat with peacock feathers that cascading over the wide brim. It took her breath away. Why would anyone give up anything so grand, she wondered. On examination, she discovered a jagged tear in the bottom hem, which was filthy from sweeping the cobbles. She placed the hat on her head and held the dress up to her slight frame.

"I know it's much too long, Seamus, but I can shorten it and remove all the damaged bits." She turned to him with a timorous smile, "Do you like it?"

"Indeed I do. You look grand, Reanna."

With a happy smile, she struck a bargain and walked away loaded down with her purchases.

They turned off High Street onto Keeley, into a neighborhood of well-maintained limestone tenements with raised stoops. They passed *St. Andrews Anglican Church,* which was constructed of gray stone, with a high steeple. They turned at the next corner onto Henry Street. Seamus left her in front of the shiny black door of the Campbell tenement with a promise to return by six o'clock to walk her back home.

She ran over Siobhan's instructions in her mind as she stood on the stoop and watched Seamus's retreating back. She mentally listed the household tasks to be done and what food Siobhan had instructed her to buy and prepare for her employer's supper. Satisfied that she had it all straight in her mind, she opened the door and walked into the Campbell home. She loved it from the moment she saw it. It smelled of camphor and beeswax and only the ticking of a large clock in the hallway disturbed the silence.

She hung up her shawl on the hall rack that sat at the bottom of a flight of stairs, dropped her bundle beside it and fluffed out her hair in front of the hall rack mirror. She glanced down the hall into the open door of the kitchen. She poked her head into a sparsely furnished parlour that led off to the right of the front door. A spinning wheel sat on a faded rug in front of the hearth. The grate was laid with coal, but it looked unused. The window was partially opened to let in the breeze. The fluttering lace curtains had knocked over a framed picture that sat on a table in front of the window. It was a likeness of a robust man with his hand on the shoulder of a frail looking woman. Reanna replaced the picture on the table, closed the window and lit the fire in the hearth.

She walked through the double glass doors into a bright breakfast room that led off from the kitchen. She helped herself to the remains of breakfast that sat undisturbed on a table in front of the window. Chewing on a piece of bread, she pulled open the drawer of the green sideboard and checked to make sure that it contained the small coin purse with the marketing money. She poked the kitchen fire to life and went upstairs to gather laundry and straighten up before tackling the downstairs chores.

$$*\qquad\qquad *\qquad\qquad *$$

Later on that afternoon, she returned from market and prepared a simple supper, following Siobhan's instructions from memory, but not very well, she'd concluded. She heard the front door open. Thinking it was Seamus, she tripped down the hall to greet him. Instead, she saw the faintly familiar figure of a stocky man with his back to her, hanging up his tan frock coat on the hall rack. He placed his hat on a hook and turned to face her.

His gray eyes frowned at the sight of her. He looked beyond her, down the hall. "Who are you? Where's Siobhan?"

She recognized him as the man from the road. "Siobhan is ill. My name is Reanna."

Recognition lit up his face. "So it is." He took both her hands in his own and looked down at her shod feet. "I didn't think I'd ever see you again. Your ankle, has it mended, then?"

"It has indeed," she stammered, removing her hands from his, but still feeling their heat.

"My cousin Siobhan asked me to take her place."

He interrupted her. "Siobhan? Seamus O'Dowd's wife Siobhan? Is that who you came to Dunbury to see?"

"Yes," she answered, "but she's been taken ill, you see, and has asked me to take over for a few days, if that's all right, sir."

"Of course it's all right, and my name is Donald, remember?" His face took on a worried look. "It's not the babby again, is it?"

Reanna hung her head. "Sad to say, it is. She's lost it, you see."

His face fell. "Aah, such a shame."

"I expect it was God's will," Reanna murmured.

"In any case," he said, "tell Siobhan to take as long as she needs."

He followed Reanna into the kitchen and pulled a chair over to the hearth. She could feel his eyes on her as she bustled around setting the table.

"I waited for you all morning at the Fife and Crow. Did you not get my note saying to wait for me, that I had to leave for a while? You looked so peaceful lying there, I couldn't bear to waken you, so I put the note in the pocket of your shift so you'd be sure to find it."

Reanna's face burned in embarrassment at her ignorance. She'd never regretted her inability to read as she had at this moment. "Yes, yes sir, I did," she said, making it up as she went along, "but I was that anxious to get to Dunbury, and a kind man in the lobby offered me a lift on his cart, so I took it."

"Well, in any case, you're here now, aren't you, and that's fine." He lifted the lid on the cooking pot and took a sniff.

"I'm not a very good cook," Reanna offered, "but I made you some supper. I'll just dish it up and be on my way. Seamus should be picking me up any time now."

He smiled and pulled out a chair for her. "Well then, sit down until he comes for you. He knows where the door is." He took another plate from the green sideboard and laid it before her.

Reanna spooned out some mutton stew onto their plates and sat across from Donald.

"I think I may have scorched the meat a wee bit." She watched in anticipation as he ate the first mouthful.

His gray eyes widened. "Well," he said, "well now." He rubbed his hand across the back of his neck and then picked up a pinch of salt between his fingers. He sprinkled a fine layer up and down and across and over the whole of his meal. He ate the top layer and continued the salt layering process until his plate was empty. Then he wiped up the bits with a crust of bread.

Reanna ate her stew as it was and relished every bite of it.

When they'd finished their meal, Donald wiped his mouth with his serviette and picked up his teacup. "So, Reanna," he asked, "are you and Siobhan from the same place in Mayo?"

"Yes, we are," she replied. "Well, not in the town itself— more on the outside, in the country, near Innislow Bay."

As she drew herself back into the past, a vision of Lord Dalton lying prone on the floor swam before her eyes. She felt sweat break out on her forehead, shook her head clear of the sickening memories and turned his question back on him. "And yourself, were you born here?"

"No." He hesitated. "My parents came from Scotland when I was just a lad. We were given a farm outside of Dunbury." He went on, choosing his words carefully. "That's where Seamus and I first met. It was his family's farm we were given."

His strange answer took her aback. She hadn't realized that Donald and Seamus were even acquainted. Neither Seamus nor Siobhan had mentioned this fact, and now here was this stranger talking about someone giving away farms.

She wanted to pursue the matter, but Donald's words seemed to have upset him and he sat looking out the window into the darkness. She decided to question Siobhan further when she returned to Biggens Alley.

Uncomfortable with his silence, but not knowing what else to say, Reanna pushed herself away from the table and proceeded to tidy up the supper dishes.

When she'd finished, she hung up her apron on the hearth. "I'll go and see if there is any sign of Seamus. He should be here by now."

She opened the front door, stepped onto the stoop and looked up the street. A lone lamppost shone dimly into the inky blackness of the April night. Seamus was nowhere to be seen. The cool night air smelled sweet and fresh. She drew it deeply into her lungs. It caught in her throat and she doubled over in a fit of coughing.

At once, Donald was at her side. He slipped her shawl over her shoulders. "You'll catch your death out here, Reanna."

His gentle words touched something deep in Reanna's heart. She'd never had anyone treat her with such care and her eyes filled with gratitude for this kind man.

He offered to walk her back to Biggens Alley. "I'll just see for myself if they need anything." He shook his head, sadly. "It's such a shame, that. They were so looking forward to that child."

*   *   *

She felt his hand tremble on her elbow as they walked down the empty street. Could it be possible that someone as grand as Donald might actually like her. That being the case, she must learn to read and write as soon as possible, for certainly he could never like an ignoramus such as herself. Her hands tightened around the bowl of mutton stew that Donald had insisted they bring along for the O'Dowd's supper.

His grip tightened protectively on her arm as they neared the river end of High Street. Reanna recognized Seamus's rolling gait as, book in hand, he turned out of the alley onto Buffen Street.

The two men shook hands in greeting. Donald inquired after Siobhan's health.

"As it happened," Seamus apologized, running a hand through his sandy hair, "she needed me at the precise moment I was on my way out—that's why I'm late. Otherwise, she's on the mend, thanks be to

God." He handed a bound copy of Gulliver's Travels to Donald. "My pupils ate this up." he said, face creasing in a smile. "Some of the younger ones still have trouble understanding the English words, but listening to a grand story keeps them asking questions and coming back for more."

Donald handed Reanna's bundle to Seamus. "Does Siobhan have everything she needs?"

"Indeed she does," Seamus replied firmly, with a nod of his head.

"Well, in that case, you needn't leave her at all tomorrow. I'll walk Reanna home and bring another book along. Will Aesop's Fables do?"

Seamus smiled. "I'll have to pick and choose through the stories for the younger pupils sakes, but yes, that'll do just fine."

Reanna sensed Donald's eyes on her as she walked into the alley on Seamus's arm.

*　　　　　*　　　　　*

Later that evening, after Seamus and Siobhan had eaten supper, Seamus read aloud by the light of the candle. Reanna lay with her fists under her chin, mesmerized by his words.

When he'd run his hand over his eyes and closed the book for the evening, Reanna asked, "Seamus, did you teach Siobhan her letters and numbers?"

"Indeed he did, and I'm still learning." Siobhan answered for him.

"Do you think you could teach me, Seamus?"

"Isn't it what I do? We can start tomorrow, after you come home from the Campbell place." He stood up and stretched his arms over his head. "If there's nothing else then, I'm off to sleep."

"There is one more thing, Seamus. Donald—he told me to call him that—said that when you were lads, your farm was given away to his family. Why was that?"

Noting the shocked look that Seamus and Siobhan exchanged, she quickly added, "it's really none of my affair in any case—I was only wondering—"

Seamus answered slowly, "It all happened a long time ago, Reanna, and the telling of it will change nothing."

"I'm that sorry, Seamus, it just happened to come up."

Siobhan smiled. "It's fine, love. We're only surprised that Donald mentioned it, is all."

After that, the conversation dried up. Reanna was puzzled. People up in Ulster were peculiar altogether, she told herself.

*   *   *

During the next week, she found herself consumed with thoughts of Donald and joyously anticipating his arrival home each day. He'd made a point of bringing home little treats, sometimes a sweet, or a bit of lace. After she mentioned in passing, her knowledge of spinning, he brought her a gift of carded wool and offered her the use of his mother's wheel. When they ate supper together nightly, Reanna could almost believe that this safe house was her real life and the horror of the past had only been a nightmare. This daydream would last until she had to bid Donald goodbye and return to Biggens Alley.

And then the day arrived when Siobhan had regained enough strength to return to work at the Campbell home. By then, Reanna had given up all ideas of pursuing employment in a shop. The mere thought of it filled her with dread. So many new faces and almost certainly, questions to answer about her background. She had found her place of safety and it was here in Donald's house. And now, loyalty to Siobhan would compel her to walk away from it.

Reanna reluctantly told Donald that she had to leave, as Siobhan would be returning to work the next day.

He appeared taken aback. "Do you want to leave, Reanna?"

She hung her head. "I don't," she whispered.

"Well then, there is no need for it."

Reanna raised her eyes. "There isn't?"

"Truth is, Siobhan will need your help for a time until she regains all of her strength, and the wheel is at your disposal as well. It's wasted, sitting there unused."

*   *   *

In the following weeks, Reanna was the happiest she'd ever been in her life. She had Siobhan with her all day in a lovely warm house. They cleaned and did the marketing together. Siobhan taught her how to cook Donald's favorite meals. Reanna continued to spin daily at the flat, in the warmth of the hearth fire. Each Thursday she brought her yarn to market to sell. Donald provided some rejected linen from the Davenport bleaching house, which she and Siobhan turned into two simple shifts. What Reanna couldn't make herself, she purchased second hand with her savings.

*   *   *

One afternoon, they'd been dyeing yarn, and sat down for a cup of tea in the kitchen.

Reanna poured the tea into her cousin's cup. "Tell me now, how is it that Donald's family came to own the O'Dowd farm?"

Siobhan nailed Reanna with her eyes. "It's not my story to tell."

Reanna picked up her spoon and vigorously stirred her tea. She wished that Siobhan were a little more given to gossip. She kept her own counsel to a fault.

Reanna tried once more. "How did you meet Seamus, then?"

"Aah that," Siobhan said, taking a sip of her tea. "Now there's a story."

Reanna sat forward in her chair. "It wasn't long after I'd come to look after Donald's poor mother. I answered the door one day and there he was, big as life. I'd seen him at Mass of a Sunday in Biggens Alley." She poured them some more tea. "Introductions were made and there you are."

*   *   *

Sunlight filtered through the tree outside of Donald's bedchamber window. It danced over his face as he lay sleeping. He opened his eyes and rolled away from the sunlight, stretched sleepily and lay on his back, awake now, arms cradling his head.

He rolled her name around on his tongue. "Reanna O'Neal." He smiled to himself as he said her name aloud. When he first met her on the road, he considered her a waif who needed help, nothing more, but when he returned to his room at the inn, his heart had melted at the sight of her little self, curled up in the chair. Now, he could hardly wait to get home every day to see her face light up when she saw what he'd brought home. Aside from Siobhan, Reanna was the only female company he'd been privy to since his mother had passed away. After she'd gone, the heart had gone out of him as well.

Now, Reanna had brought life back into this house. You're almost twice her age, and you're acting like a schoolboy, he chided himself. If only she weren't so reluctant to give out about herself, though. After almost two weeks of conversation, he still knew nothing of her past or her family, although he had volunteered that after the deaths of both their fathers ten years ago, he and his mother had moved to this coastal town of Dunbury and Seamus had joined them later. He'd plied Siobhan with questions about Reanna's past, but for some reason, she seemed as reluctant to divulge any information as Reanna herself.

Today, he and Reanna were going for an afternoon stroll down to Warden Quay. Donald determined that he would not be put off with any more half answers. He jumped out of bed in anticipation. She'd insisted that she had something to drop off at the flat and they could leave from here. He suspected that shame at living in Biggens Alley, had fueled Reanna's insistence. He didn't like the idea of her living there either when his mother's room sat empty upstairs. But, they'd not known each other nearly long enough to suggest such a thing.

When Seamus and Siobhan married, he'd offered them the use of his mother's old room, but Seamus had stubbornly refused to budge from the alley.

"Sure, I lived in a hell of a lot worse than Biggens Alley during the laws, when I had to teach on the run," he'd said. "Hiding in the hedgerows in the bitter cold was not exactly the Highbury Inn."

"But could you not teach from here, Seamus?" he'd asked. "It'd be that grand to have you and Siobhan for company."

"Thanks all the same, old friend," he'd answered, "but my pupils live in the alley and to gain their trust, I need to live among them."

Donald had always fought a running battle with Seamus to accept any help at all. Siobhan, with high good humor, was in her own way, just as intractable as her husband.

*   *   *

On their walk, Donald and Reanna passed St. Andrew's church at precisely noon as the bells began to peal. The doors opened and groups of people, clad in their Sunday best, emerged and stood chatting in the middle of the road. Donald took Reanna's arm and steered her through the crowd and crossed over High Street.

They stopped in front of the Dunbury Guardian, with the tall narrow windows upstairs and decorative parapet on the roof. Donald read tomorrow's front page that was on display in the small paned bay window. Reanna wandered off down the street. She watched fascinated as the sun shot sparks off the red, green and amber globes of water that hung by brass chains in the window of Goodwins Apothecary. When Donald caught up to her, Reanna exclaimed in admiration at a green velvet hat with an upswept brim that sat on display in the millinery shop window next door to Goodwins.

They strolled down into the park, then on down toward the town dock, which split High Street in two at its foot and extended itself down towards the Glenna River. When they reached the dock, Donald took her arm and they veered right and began the descent to Warden Quay that ran south to Bevins Bridge.

He couldn't take his eyes off Reanna. In her finery, he thought her quite the most beautiful sight his eyes had ever seen. She was certainly unrecognizable from the waif he had rescued barely a fortnight ago. He appraised her costume with a practiced eye. She wore a sapphire linen dress with a creamy lace bodice and a flowing skirt that brushed the tips of her shoes. Copper hair smoothed up off her neck into a coil on top of her head and tucked underneath a matching hat. Breathtaking altogether, he concluded. Her clothing although not new, still had to be bought, and he wondered where had she gotten the funds to pay for it.

As they neared the quay, a gust of wind lifted Reanna's wide brimmed hat from her head and it skittered across the road and down the hill toward the water, followed closely by Donald.

Her hat came to rest against one of the pilings that lined the dock. Donald snatched it up. He turned around in triumph to see Reanna bent over in spasms of laughter. He must have been a sight, he told himself—hunched over, gray coat tails flapping in the wind, legs in white stockings, kicking out on either side of his outstretched arms. Red-faced, he walked back toward her, brushing the hat off on his sleeve.

He presented it to her with a flourish. "Here you are lass, good as new."

She wiped the tears of laughter out of her eyes, swept her hat in front of her and bent her knee in a deep curtsy. "Thank you kindly, sir." She walked by his side, swinging her hat by its brim.

Donald clasped her other hand in his own. The brilliant April sun turned her hair to fire. He itched to take the pins out of it and run his fingers through its length. The sea breeze whipped their clothing around their bodies and outlined Reanna's trim figure.

No time like the present, Donald told himself. He took a deep breath and jumped into the fray. "How does your family feel about your living so far away, Reanna?" he began cautiously.

Her eyes slid away from his. "My family are all dead, Donald," she answered evasively.

The sun disappeared behind a cloud and the air turned chilly. Reanna took her hand out of Donald's and hugged herself for warmth. Then she turned his questions back on him.

"Your own father, Donald," she began cautiously, "what did he die from, then?"

Caught off guard, his throat burned with the need to tell her the truth of it, but he'd said too much already. He wanted to say that his father didn't just die; he was murdered. He and Seamus's father, Padraic O'Dowd; both murdered in their beds for flaunting their partnership in the face of the law—the cursed Penal Law, that forbade a Catholic to own anything worth more than five pounds, and was the reason that the Catholic O'Dowd farm was turned over to Donald's father, a Scottish Presbyterian in the first place.

He could only say aloud to Reanna, "He died very suddenly in his own bed."

She placed a consoling hand on his sleeve. "I'm that sorry, Donald."

They walked along in silence except for the rhythmic sounds of the waves slapping against the hull of a fishing boat tied up at the quay and the screeching of seagulls as they swooped and jockeyed for position to catch scraps that a fisherman jettisoned over the side of the boat.

Reanna put her arm through his. "How is it that you didn't stay on the farm?"

His voice thickened in spite of himself. "I couldn't—I wanted to, but I couldn't." He wanted to tell her everything. That after their fathers were murdered, the Campbell and O'Dowd families were thrown out penniless on the side of the road and the farm was turned over to someone else. It was then that his mother began her slide into madness. After the move to Dunbury, she got queerer and queerer, asking where Hughie was and when he was coming home. After Siobhan moved in as caretaker, she told Donald that his mother would close herself up in a cupboard for hours at a time, in fear of the murderers return. And then the insult of it, when two years later, Catholics were given the privilege of owning property again if they swore allegiance to England. This, when every Catholic-owned piece of property had already been confiscated by them.

Donald's bitter memories upset him all over again. He clasped his hands behind his back so Reanna wouldn't see them trembling. He watched a seagull swoop towards him from Bevins Bridge and land on the choppy water nearby.

"After we moved to Dunbury," he said, "…to the flat on Henry Street, I started to work at the Davenport Bleaching House as an apprentice. Then sadly, my mother's health failed. That's when Siobhan was kind enough to move in and take care of her."

The sun reappeared from behind the clouds. Donald shielded his eyes with his hand as he tried to get a closer look at a white sailboat on the horizon.

Tasting the bitterness of old injustices rising to the surface, he attempted to change the subject and try for a little levity. "And you, mystery girl," he began, "whom did you kill, that you won't tell me about your past?" He heard a hard edge to his voice even as he spoke. He could tell she picked up on it too and that his clumsy attempt at humor had fallen flat.

Reanna's face paled. She stopped short and in a shaky voice said, "Donald, I have to leave now."

He stood by helplessly and watched her as she picked up her skirts and hurried off back the way they came. Her stiff posture made him fear that he had lost her forever.

*   *   *

Donald agonized all the next day at work, thinking of ways to make it right with Reanna again. At seven o'clock, he entered the flat with his speech ready. Siobhan walked up the hall to greet him. He smiled distractedly at her and moved past her into the parlour. With a sinking heart, he saw that the spinning wheel sat unoccupied and the grate unlit.

"Has Reanna been and gone?"

Siobhan answered in a puzzled voice. "She's not been here today, Donald. She said she had studying to do at home."

He tried to hide his disappointment from Siobhan, but he went to bed heartsick that night. After a week of trying to convince himself that Reanna just needed one more day to get over his faux pas, he couldn't bear it.

Saturday, he asked Siobhan to deliver a note to her. In it, he apologized for his heavy handed humor and asked her to please come back. He spent a tortured Sunday in the flat waiting in vain for a knock on the door.

When he arrived home from work Monday, Reanna was at her usual place in the parlour, spinning wheel humming, flames dancing in the grate, acting as though nothing had happened. But Donald had learned his lesson well and never questioned her again.

*　　　　　*　　　　　*

After a fortnight of an uneasy truce, the fear of losing her altogether, prompted Donald to propose marriage to Reanna. To his great joy, she agreed to be his wife.

At that time, he mentioned to her his wish that Siobhan continue on as their housekeeper. He confided to Reanna that the wages Siobhan earned provided the means for Seamus to continue his work in the alley. Without it, Donald's generosity would be considered charity and would not be accepted. Reanna agreed to this arrangement with gratitude. To continue to see Siobhan every day was more than she could have hoped for.

As a marriage between a Catholic and a Protestant was illegal, Donald, with Reanna's connivance, concocted a story for the Presbyterian minister that her baptismal papers were burned up in a fire. Almost one month from the day of her arrival in Dunbury, Reanna and Donald became husband and wife in the eyes of God.

*   *   *

One day in late April, Siobhan arrived just after Donald had left for work. When she entered the flat, she heard strange noises coming from upstairs. She sped up to Reanna's sleeping room and found her bent over the washbasin, slight shoulders heaving.

"Reanna, ansa, what is it?" Siobhan cried, rushing over and putting her arms around her cousin.

Reanna wiped her mouth with the back of her hand and raised her pale face to Siobhan.

"I don't know," she said, eyes wide in fright, "but it keeps happening and I'm afraid something is terrible wrong with me."

Siobhan's eyes traveled from her cousin's worried eyes down to her stomach. "Are you eating?"

Reanna warded off Siobhan's words with an upraised hand. "Och, dear God, no. The mere thought of food turns my stomach."

Siobhan's own face paled at Reanna's answer, but she said nothing, just searched Reanna's eyes with her own.

"What is it?" Reanna asked, frightened at the look on her cousin's face.

"I'm only after thinking, it sounds to me like you're having a baby, but—"

Reanna's eyes lit up in hope, but when she saw how upset Siobhan looked, her face blanched. She covered her eyes with her hands and shook her head violently from side to side. To admit, even to herself, that the child she carried inside her body might be the result of that terrifying night was more than she could bear to think about. "No, not Lord Dalton's baby. It can't be, Siobhan. It's too cruel."

Siobhan put her arms around her and patted her on the back. "There, there now. Maybe it's not that at all," she soothed. "Sometimes, we know right away when we're expecting, you see, and that's probably the case with you."

In the end, Reanna told Donald only that they were expecting a baby and filed her secret fears in the back of her mind with the rest of her baggage. To make up to him for her deception, she determined to be the best wife and mother of which she was capable.

*　　　　　*　　　　　*

On Christmas day, 1786, Reanna, with Siobhan in attendance, gave birth to a baby girl, whom they named Erris, a name that meant faith in Mayo Irish. She had hair as dark as the night, a rosy complexion and she followed the sound of their voices with eyes as blue as cornflowers. She was perfectly formed, except for a spatulate thumb on her left hand. Reanna was convinced that it was God's punishment delivered on herself for not admitting to Donald, her suspicions about Erris's parentage.

*　　　　　*　　　　　*

The following day, Siobhan prepared dinner for them and extracted a promise from Reanna that she would tell Donald the circumstances of Lord Dalton's assault on her and admit her suspicions about Erris's parentage.

Reanna's eyes were big in her face. "—and what if he puts us out into the street? What then? I can't take that chance."

Siobhan was insistent. "You must, for if he finds out on his own, he'd never trust you again. Wouldn't that be worse?"

*　　　　　*　　　　　*

After Siobhan left for home, Reanna lay in bed, palms sweating, going over in her mind, again and again, the words she would use in explanation to Donald on his arrival. As she heard the front door open, her bowels clutched in fear. She heard footsteps running up the stairs and a moment later Donald burst into their bedchamber, still dressed in his outdoor clothes and smelling of the cold.

"How are my girls?" he said with a broad grin, unbuttoning his coat. He sat on the bed, kissed Reanna softly on the mouth and pressed a sweet into her hand. He draped his coat and hat over a chair, blew into his hands, rubbed them together to warm them, and then bent over the baby's basket.

Reanna's good intentions wavered as she watched Donald joyously enfold his new daughter in his arms. Whatever the circumstances, they belong together, she told herself. No question about it. She put it off telling him for another day. And so it continued.

*   *   *

In the following months, as the love between father and daughter strengthened, Reanna's resolve weakened, until one day, she knew she had waited too long. Her confession now would crush both of them. Her own procrastination would be the secret punishment she would carry alone, eating like maggots into her very soul, and along with her other baggage, strangling her in a tissue of lies.

Chapter 3

▼

Ulster, December 1787

Donald reached into his pocket and retrieved a folded slip of paper. It was a note from Siobhan. Puzzled, he crossed to the window for the light. She'd written: *Donald, I'm hiding this note in your pocket to be out of sight of Reanna. She'd be upset if she knew I was interfering. But Donald, I'm that worried about her. I know she hasn't been herself since Erris's birth, but lately, I find her actions worrisome.*

She's not been out of the house for weeks, not even to market, which she formerly loved to do. I'm unable even to persuade her into a stroll. I thought you ought to know.

Siobhan.

Donald, shaken now, crossed over and sat on the side of the bed. He'd been through his own mother's madness. He knew the signs, why had he not paid more attention to Reanna's mental state? He'd been so caught up with his own intrigue that it had blinded him to conditions within his own walls. He felt an urgent need to confess to Reanna about his double life, before it was too late and the decision was taken out of his hands. He felt that he was on a very slippery slope indeed, with the bottom nowhere in sight.

At the sound of footsteps in the downstairs hall, he rose from the bed and shoved the note back into his pocket.

Reanna's voice floated up the stairs to him. "Your breakfast is ready, Donald."

"I'm coming love."

        *   *   *

Donald sat at the breakfast table, hands cradled around his tea cup, trying to conceive a way out of his dilemma, without sending Reanna off the edge altogether. She sat across from him now, fiery hair bathed in the pale sunlight from the tall window behind her. She held Erris on her lap, patiently attempting to feed the fidgety baby a spoon of porridge. Erris's dark curls, the match of his own, down to the cowlick, bobbed from side to side in an effort to evade the spoon. "Eat up your breakfast ansa, there's a good girl."

Donald cast his eyes down to his plate and fiddled with his soft-boiled egg, breaking the shell off bit by bit and placing it in a neat pile on the plate beside his eggcup.

"Is something wrong with your breakfast, love?"

He raised his head, distractedly. "No, no, it's just fine." He dutifully picked up a slice of brown bread from the flowered plate in front of him. He broke off a piece, absently dipped it into his egg and began to eat. While he chewed, his eyes wandered over to the narrow chiffonier with the oval mirror that sat against the wall. His family's future security sat inside the locked drawer, in a tin box with brass hinges. Beside it, in three ledgers from the Davenport Bleaching House, lay his own undoing. He'd have to come clean with Reanna about his embezzlement. That was the first step. "Some things around here need clearing up."

Reanna's spoon clattered to the floor. "What?"

He hadn't meant to speak those words aloud, but since he had, he pressed on. "We'll discuss it tonight," he said softly. "I have some settling up to do."

He watched his beloved wife shrink into herself.

No need to have put things so bluntly, he chided himself, and scurried around in his mind, looking for the right words to ease her distress. Before he could find them, she'd gathered up Erris and hurried her through the glass doors into the parlor. He followed her, teacup in hand, feeling helpless. She deposited Erris in front of the window and gave her a bracelet of wooden beads to play with. Then, she escaped to her spinning wheel, which sat in the corner like a cornered animal, flanked by brimming baskets of wool for spinning and yarn to be dyed. Face strained, she set to work, feeding the wool to the wheel. She appeared to have nothing more to say to him. He returned to the kitchen.

He swallowed the last mouthful of his tea, brought his cup and saucer over to the drain board, and walked down the hall to get his hat and coat. He stuck his head in the parlor. Reanna sat at her spinning wheel, face pale, her limbs moving rhythmically.

"I'm leaving now," he said.

Erris toddled towards him. He scooped her up in his arms, buried his face in her warm neck and made grunting sounds. She giggled with delight. He put her down and held out his arms to Reanna.

She returned his embrace distractedly, and kissed him on the cheek. "Off to work with you, now," she said softly.

*　　　　*　　　　*

Donald waved to Erris and Reanna in the window, then made his way past neighboring tenements toward High Street. In the beginning, he reflected, his choices had been so simple. Just he and his beliefs. Now, with a family to consider, it seemed that his choices became more complicated daily. Every move he made led them all down a path from which he felt there was no turning back.

"Good day, Donald." Siobhan's voice shook him out of his reverie.

"Good day to yourself. I didn't see you coming."

"I was aware of that. Did you get my note?"

"I did, thank you, and I was hoping to run into you. I wonder would you do two things for me?"

She nodded her head. "I'll do what I can."

"Would you tell Reanna that I'll be late coming home and not to wait dinner for me, and would you ask Seamus to meet me in High Park at quarter past seven this evening?"

"I will."

            *   *   *

A short time later, Donald stepped carefully down High Street, wearing a wide rimmed hat that sat high on his head and showed the dark hair that curled over his ears. Although it was a cold morning, his pale skin wore a sheen of perspiration. What steps would Reanna take when she learned of his crime and the sort of people he was involved with? Might she take the baby and return to Ballymullian? He'd just have to take that chance.

He turned the corner and stood underneath the sign that hung over the street in front of the Tin Whistle. Scanning both sides of High Street with a jaundiced eye, he crossed the cobbles. The shop windows held pretty ribbons and fancy hats for all to see but only the privileged few to buy. The owners themselves, he knew, would live a spartan existence in a tiny room above the shop.

A bowlegged old farmer set down a rickety wheelbarrow by the side of the road. It was heaped with cabbages and root vegetables with the dirt still on them. The old man licked his stub of a pencil, wrote the price of the produce on a scrap of paper, ran a stick through the top and bottom of it and jammed it in between the mounds of potatoes.

Donald's lip curled in disgust as he read the inflated price that the farmer was obliged to charge for his produce. It was a bone in both Protestant and Catholic throats that they had to pay a tithe on their own produce to support the Anglican Church, established by the English to be the official Church of Ireland. The working people were bitterly resentful of a system that put them to double the expense, for they had to support their own clergy as well.

There existed a whole segment of society made up of Irishmen, both Protestant and Catholic, who found repugnant the very idea of signing an oath of allegiance to a country that had taken the roof from over their heads, snatched the bread from their mouths and sucked the very life's blood out of their bodies.

And so, some people worked outside the law, as did Siobhan, whom Donald paid under the table. The jobless were legion and ended up in the back alleys of the cities, living under appalling conditions, as many as seven to a small room, and subsisting on what they could beg, borrow or steal. It was to such an alley that Seamus gravitated on his arrival in Dunbury to teach the children of the poor.

As for Donald, he played it both ways. He played the loyalty game in the open as a draper employed by the English-owned Davenport Bleaching House, but played the patriot game behind the scenes. He felt justified in helping to break the system he considered grossly unfair to all Irishmen and believed it to be his patriotic duty to fund any organization dedicated to Irish rule and the removal of the oppressors.

His employment as a draper afforded him the perfect opportunity to fulfill that duty. From autumn to spring, Mr. Graham, the Davenport manager, would periodically supply Donald with a purse of money with which to purchase webs of linen cloth from weavers in the outlying regions of the county.

Donald used a double bookkeeping system with which to cheat his employer. He bought the raw linen from the rural weavers at below market price, paid them from the Davenport purse and marked the purchase price in his personal ledger. In the Davenport ledger, he processed the same transactions, but inflated the purchase price paid to the weavers. He kept a little back for runaway money in the event that his scheme was discovered, and funneled the difference into the coffers of whatever Irish revolutionary movement he was sympathetic to at the time. They came and went like the seasons. When one was ferreted out and shut down, another sprung up to take its place.

Donald had no way of knowing if the weavers were coerced by the movement concerned to sell to himself at lower prices, or whether it was voluntary, and he didn't feel that it was his concern. He only knew he had no shortage of weavers patronizing his stall.

Freedom didn't come cheap, he believed.

                    *   *   *

That evening as Donald entered the park, he spotted Seamus, bundled up against the cold and pacing up and down. The cold December moon lit up the snow that lay in patches on the grass and turned the limbs of the trees into shadowy spectres. With their breath fogging in the night air, the two men strolled the perimeter of the park. The clatter of horse's hooves echoed down High Street, as a lone carriage creaked its way along the cobbles.

"I need to take you into my confidence," Donald said to Seamus, "but I scarcely know where to start."

"The beginning seems as likely a place as any."

"Well, then," Donald said, "it all started from the time that mother and I moved to Dunbury. By the time you were reached with the tragic news and arrived here yourself, as you well know I had secured employment at the Davenport Bleaching House. What you were not aware of, was that I was embroiled in something bigger than I had ever known before."

Seamus said nothing, only shoved his hands deep in his pockets and whistled noiselessly through his teeth.

"I had met some people," Donald continued, "who were involved in trying to boot out the English, and the fact of the matter is, within a short while, I found myself caught up in a scheme to siphon money out of the Davenport coffers to fund their cause."

Seamus grunted. "I suspected something was going on."

"—and yet, you said nothing."

"Would it have made any difference if I had?"

"I don't suppose," Donald allowed.

"Well, then." Seamus stopped walking. "Does Reanna know any of this?"

"She doesn't. Not that I haven't tried to tell her, but she turns queer on me if I so much as try to talk serious to her, she's that delicate, you know."

Seamus leveled his gaze at Donald. "Why are you telling me this, for you're surely not looking for my blessing?"

"Hardly, for I know what I'm doing is against your principles. However, I do need to ask you a favor."

"I'll do what I'm able."

"When I had only myself to think about, my misdeeds seemed worth the risk, but now, with a family to consider—" His voice broke. "I've been worried sick about the consequences to my family when they come for me, Seamus."

Seamus opened his mouth to speak. Donald placed a hand on his arm. "I need Reanna and Erris away and safe, before that day arrives. I'm asking you as my dearest friend, to take them back to Ballymullian and safety at the first sign of danger."

"You know that I will, for they're as dear to me as my own." Seamus walked away shaking his head, then turned and faced his friend. "You do have a strange sense of safety, Donald."

Donald caught up to him. "Whatever do you mean? Why wouldn't they be safe in Ballymullian?"

Seamus looked at him in disbelief. "Do you mean to say after almost two years of marriage, the woman's told you nothing?"

Donald's voice hardened. "What is there to tell?"

Seamus raised his hands. "I'll say no more."

Donald, gray eyes blazing, spat out. "It's past the time for delicacy. You appear to know a damn sight more about my own wife than I do." He stepped back. "I mean to find out what is going on, and if she won't tell me, then you'll have to."

Seamus rasped his hand over the stubble on his cheek. "Well, it seems there was some dirty business with her employer at Crofton House, a lecherous sot by the name of Lord Dalton. She ran into him in a dark room." He shook his shaggy head. "He fouled her in unspeakable ways, I'm afraid. That's why she ran up here to Siobhan."

Donald's voice shook. "I'll kill the rotter."

"Well, that's the thing of it, Donald," Seamus said softly, "Reanna thinks she may have done it, her ownself."

Seamus's shocking revelation tore Donald apart. He raised his hand to Seamus in dismissal. "I have to go home and see about this." He turned on his heel and stomped out of the park.

His thoughts were in turmoil as he strode towards home. His wife, the mother of his beloved child may have killed someone? His heart thudded into his stomach as the unthinkable crossed his mind, and he frantically counted up the months in his head. Was Erris his child or did she lie about that too?

He arrived home to a sleeping household. Only the loud ticking of the clock in the hallway broke the silence. He shrugged out of his coat and hung it on the hallrack. A dim glow from the far end of the flat cast shadows on the wall, and drew him like a beacon to the kitchen. On the table, sat a covered dish. He lifted the lid. It was his supper and it was cold. He left it there.

He picked up a note from the table, unfolded it and read. *Donald, I've gone to bed early with a headache. Please don't disturb me. Love, Reanna.*

Bloody hell," he murmured exasperated, running a hand through his hair. He crumpled up the note and threw it on the fire. Mumbling, he lit a candle and tiptoed up the stairs and into Erris's room. She lay sprawled on her back, dark curls framing her chubby face, cheeks rosy with sleep. He wanted to pick her up and never let her go, but he didn't want to risk having her wake up and demand his attention. He had business with her mother to attend to. Instead, he tucked the bedclothes around her and walked down the hall to confront Reanna.

She lay on her side, faced away from him. Her slight frame, outlined by the coverlet, rose and fell with each measured breath. He placed the candle on the wash table, undressed quickly, watching in vain for a break in her breathing to signify interrupted sleep.

He blew out the candle and crawled in beside his sleeping wife. He wanted to shake her awake and confront her with his discovery of her secret, but knew he would be wiser to wait until morning when he'd calmed down enough to talk rationally. He tossed and turned in the bed. Unanswered questions tormented him. Why did he have to wait almost two years to learn anything about her past and then have it told to him by someone else? Why did she not trust him enough? What did she think he would do?

In all probability, exactly what you are doing now, he rebuked himself. He lay on his back and stared out the window into the black night. The wind whipped the tree branches into a frenzy and they scraped the glass as though trying to gain entry.

Donald turned over in bed. If she had killed the man, that would eliminate Ballymullian as a haven for his family if his embezzlement was found out. Where else could he send them, if not Ballymullian?

His mind went around and around, getting nowhere, until exhaustion took over and he fell into a disturbed sleep that opened the door to his nightmare.

     *   *   *

In the dream, he was fourteen years old again, barely conscious, clinging to the doorframe for support. An English soldier, musket in hand, stood at the foot of his parent's bed, shouting at his father. With his mother's screams echoing in his ears, Donald tried to leap on the soldier and knock him to the ground, but try as he might, his feet were frozen to the floor. Then in slow motion, the musket blast threw his father back against the head of the bed and then forward onto his mother's lap, splattering her white bed gown with his blood.

It was at this point that the dream ended. In the sixteen years since his father's murder, it had never varied. Always in times of strain it came back to haunt him. He lay on his back in a cold sweat, heart pounding in the wake of the horror he'd relived once more, and feeling more alone than he'd ever felt in his life.

Reanna's soft voice startled him. "Is it the nightmare again, Donald?"

The loving concern in her voice was almost more than he could bear. His voice trembled. "It is, but I'll be fine in a few minutes."

"Why won't you tell me about it, love?"

"Are you certain you want to hear it?"

In answer, she held his trembling body close to her own. In a ragged voice, he began to relate his nightmare to her. When he reached the part where he was unable to prevent his father's murder, he broke down into sobs.

Reanna's limbs began to shake. She sat up in bed and covered her ears. "Please don't cry, Donald." Her voice quavered. "You're my rock. If you break, I don't know what I'll do."

Reanna's tortured outburst, coupled with her shaking limbs, shocked Donald back to the present. He choked back his tears and rolled away from her. He was torn between anger at her for not allowing him to express his grief, and shame for having broken down in front of her in the first place, a mistake he determined not to repeat in the future. He lay looking through the rime-covered window into the dark night, unable to go back to sleep.

After a while, he roused himself, lit a candle and stumbled down the stairs and into the breakfast room. He bent down and extracted a key from a ledge underneath the chiffonier and opened the drawer. Three ledgers and a tin box full of money mocked him from their hiding place, and he cursed the day he ever got mixed up into this intrigue in the first place. Then the vision of his father's murder swam into view and his justification renewed itself. He closed and locked the drawer and replaced the key in its hiding place.

He roamed throughout the flat, rekindled the fire in the parlor and pulled up a chair. He sat in front of the flickering flames, and wondered what was going to happen to them all. After a time, his grief and anger gave way to pity for the child Reanna had been when he'd first picked her up on the road; how terrified she'd been of that British soldier in the market square. It's no wonder she's a little queer with the terrible thing she's been through, he reasoned.

In the end, he was grateful that he'd pulled Reanna's secret out of Seamus. Finally, a break in the mystery that was Reanna, he said to himself. Perhaps when she realized that her secret was out, she might be more open to hearing about his own hidden life. He trudged dispiritedly back upstairs.

*   *   *

Reanna lay curled up in bed in abject misery, listening to Donald's footsteps recede down the stairs. She wanted to cut her tongue out for having pulled away from him when he was in so much torment, but as he related his nightmare, her own past rose up to disable her. Her scalp prickled in warning, her insides began to quake with a terrible fury. She knew what was coming. Very quickly, her shoulders would seize up, her jaw lock, and her limbs would go into spasms.

She'd hugged Donald's body to her own in an attempt to maintain control of her body. She'd tried. God in Heaven, she'd tried so hard. But it didn't work. She'd had to pull away from him before the spasms became a full-blown attack. For if he saw how flawed she was, she would surely lose him.

She heard a new sound from downstairs, like the chiffonier drawer scraping open. She always wondered what dark secret Donald kept in there, but curiosity always lost to her fear of confrontation. Truth be told, if she started questioning him, it let the door open for him to start questioning her. She might be forced to tell him about her past and she couldn't let that happen. Most days she could pretend that her past had been a bad dream, but some nights, as she was dropping off to sleep, the reality of it would drop over her head like a thick blanket and she feared she would smother from the memory of it.

She calmed herself down and in a short while, she heard Donald's footsteps coming up the stairs. She swiped at the tears in her eyes and pretended to be asleep.

                    *   *   *

Donald snuffed out the candle, slipped underneath the covers and pressed his body close to Reanna's back. He raised himself on one elbow, lifted the fragrant hair from her neck and pressed his lips against her warm skin. An overwhelming surge of love melted his heart for his troubled wife. She really had come a long way since they'd met.

"Well done, Reanna," he whispered. Her breathing continued, measured as ever, but he suspected she was feigning sleep. He rolled over onto his back. For the longest time, he lay there, head cradled in his hands, putting off the inevitable, not knowing how to broach the subject of her past, but determined to get it out in the open before the night was over. Finally he could stand it no longer. He sat up and jostled her awake.

"What is it, Donald?" she said, her voice heavy with sleep. She sat up rubbing her eyes awake. "Whatever is wrong?"

"I want you to tell me about Lord Dalton," he said. It took all his control not to spit the man's name out.

Reanna leapt out of bed and stood there shaking, mouth agape in shock.

Donald reached out for her hand. "Don't upset yourself, Reanna," he said. "You don't have to pretend anymore. Seamus told me everything." He drew her back to bed.

She sat, knees to chest, covers drawn up to her chin. "What…what did he tell you?" she asked in a barely audible voice.

"He told me about Lord Dalton and the reason you left Mayo."

She dropped her head onto her knees and rocked back and forth. He gathered her into his arms. She sobbed until she couldn't catch her breath.

Donald lifted her head and brushed her hair back from her tortured face. "Why did you not tell me yourself? Why did I have to hear such a thing from Seamus?"

She shook her head. "I was that ashamed, Donald."

He wiped the tears from her face. "The shame is not yours, cara."

She grabbed his hands and brought them to her lips. "You're so good, Donald, but it is my shame, for I hid the fact that I didn't know whose child I…"

"—and do you know now?"

She shook her head slowly. "Not for certain."

"Well, she has my hair, complete with cowlick, so I don't think there's any doubt that she has me for a father."

"—and a murderer for a mother."

"Shhh, love," he whispered, "stop crying, for I don't really think you could have killed the bastard in any case, you know."

"I didn't?" she asked, trembling.

He snuggled her head into his shoulder and stroked her hair. "I can't say for certain, love, but I think the English authorities would have hunted you down by now if you'd killed one of their own."

A look of hope crossed her face. "Do you truly think so?"

"I do," he said and kissed her tenderly on the lips. She returned his kiss with an abandonment she'd never shown him before. Donald wondered if her desire was born of gratitude, and decided he didn't care if it was. He gathered her to him, his blood surging with a passion he'd never known. His ardor seemed to fuel her own. She raised his nightshirt and ran her hands feverishly over his body.

He groaned with pleasure, eased her over onto her back and lifted her nightdress over her hips. Eagerly, she raised herself to meet him. They loved each other until exhaustion took over. Then, limbs entwined, they slept. The last thing Donald remembered before sleep took over, was that he still hadn't told Reanna about his double life.

Chapter 4

▼

Ulster, September 1794

Donald walked the familiar route to the Davenport Bleaching House as he'd done almost daily since he was a lad of fourteen. As he approached the outskirts of town, the cobbles of High Street gave way to dusty Yarrow Road, with its ever-increasing jumble of cabins and patchwork fields which fed the growing population of Dunbury. As he did most mornings, Donald tipped his hat to a familiar face in the neighboring field. The farmer, harvesting autumn wheat, laid aside his scythe and returned the greeting.

Amidst the changing seasons and landscape, the one thing that had remained constant in his life, aside from his family and Siobhan, was his lifelong friendship with Seamus, and he thanked God for it. But now, the very thing that pulled them together in the first place was threatening to tear them apart.

*   *   *

His feet moved forward on the dusty road, while his mind fell back to a snowy evening three years ago. He and Seamus had attended a debate demanding Irish reform and had both come away highly impressed with the sane rhetoric of Theodore Wolfe Tone, a Protestant barrister from Dublin. As one of the founders of the newly formed Society of United Irishmen, (SUI), Tone had spoken out against the religious tyranny of English rule against Irish Catholics. Donald's simmering rage against the English was fueled by Tone's impassioned plea for Irish control over her own destiny and religious equality for all. Before they left the hall, both Donald and Seamus had secured membership in the SUI.

On the walk home, Donald made a decision. "I'm considering switching my contributions to the SUI," he'd said to Seamus. "They seem more in a position to change things than the hot-heads I'm involved with now. From them, I've seen only retaliation, no changes to speak of."

Even Seamus had appeared enthusiastic. "You're finally seeing the light. The English will always have more and bigger guns than we do. To fight against that is folly." He'd smacked his fist into his open palm for emphasis. "Education and reform. That's the answer."

And so it had been the answer for both men at that time, but after three years of inflamed speeches, Wolfe Tone and the other SUI leaders had been arrested and the movement forced underground, where it appeared bent on revolution. This turn of events had caused Donald to escalate his fund raising. Seamus, on the other hand, was talking about pulling out of the movement altogether. Their opposing decisions had become a bone of contention between the two friends. It seemed that every meeting between them recently had ended in an argument. In recent weeks, known and suspected SUI members were being systematically arrested by the authorities and Donald feared that it was just a matter of time before they came looking for him.

                *   *   *

Donald's mind was no clearer by the time he arrived at work. He entered the Davenport gates, and walked down the long road, that sliced between a patchwork of linen sheets, in varying degrees of whiteness, that were spread out on the grass along either side.

Barefoot workmen, pants rolled up, legs and feet red with the cold, were already at work, wetting down the sheets and moving them about in the final bleaching process. The rising sun warmed the air and began to dissipate the mist that still blanketed the dammed up river.

Within weeks, the sun's warm bleaching rays would be replaced by winter rains and the bleaching process would be finished for another year, to resume again with the coming of spring and the sun's return.

Donald heard a warning whistle and moved to the side of the road. He was overtaken by a horse drawn wagon, driven by an old man. It creaked past him and made its way towards the whitewashed two-story bleaching house at the foot of the road, and made the right turn towards the yawning double doors of the shipping and receiving area.

Donald reached the end of the road and turned left onto a small bridge that spanned a fast moving creek and led to the processing rooms downstairs. Deep in thought, still trapped in a situation from which he saw no escape, he folded his arms on the wooden railing and watched mesmerized by the scene below, until he became the churning water, caught up in the great water wheels and forced inside the mill.

He was the linen, fed into large vats of water, beaten with paddles and tumbled about to lift out impurities and dirt, laid on a table and soaped up for a final wash. Then dumped into a huge vat of boiling water and sulfuric acid to achieve the desired purity.

He shook himself free of his morbid thoughts and hurried across the bridge. He eased himself down the steep path towards the back of the mill. Here, in the early morning, everything was in shadow. Trees blocked whatever sunlight the building didn't shade. The wide doors remained open to release the fumes and steam from the operation inside and to take advantage of whatever daylight was available.

Donald walked to the other end of the building and up a steep tree-lined path and came around into the sunlight again. He stood aside as workmen loaded the wagon with crates of bleached linen, destined for a finishing house in London. The old horse, nose in a feedbag, waited patiently alongside him. Donald absently read the yellowed sign posted on the outside wall, as he patted the horse's side.

RULES AND REGULATIONS
of the
DAVENPORT BLEACHING HOUSE

1. Work to commence at 6:30 a.m. and cease at 6:30 p.m. Monday through Saturday.
2. At 6:30 a.m. everyone is to be at their respective stations and ready to begin work.
3. Tardiness will not be tolerated. One late of five minutes will be charged one penny. One late of fifteen minutes will result in a one shilling fine. Three lates of fifteen minutes duration within a six month period will result in instant dismissal.
4. Any outside person wishing to speak with an employee must first get permission from the mill manager.
5. Any mistakes made by workers causing loss to Davenport will be charged out of that person's wages.
6. Talking, scuffling or boisterous conduct will not be tolerated during working hours.
7. No alcoholic beverages will be allowed on or near the premises.
8. Any person taking a leave of absence from Davenport without express permission will be summarily dismissed.
9. The above rules will be strictly enforced and violation of same will result in instant dismissal.

        *   *   *

At six thirty that evening, Donald left work and began the two-mile walk home. He threaded himself between the other pedestrians on High Street. A crowd of men milled around in front of the Dunbury Times Register. Donald's scalp prickled with premonition as he crossed the street and pushed his way through the crowd to the window to read the newspaper. The words on the page leapt up at him.

'Wolfe Tone exiles himself to America to avoid charge of treason.'

It's over, Donald said to himself. He walked blindly, his mind in turmoil. He turned the corner, more convinced than ever that time was getting short for them all. He walked over to a lamppost, fished a slip of paper out of his pocket, held it against the post and penciled a hasty note to Seamus. *Please meet me at the Tin Whistle at once. Donald.'*

He stopped a street urchin with eyes wiser than his years. "Do you know Biggens Alley?"

The boy allowed that he did.

"Do you know the schoolmaster, Seamus O'Dowd?"

"Yes, I do, and I know right where he lives."

Donald gave him the message and a coin for his trouble. The boy sped off skipping down the street.

Donald crossed the street, walked hurriedly down towards the door of the Tin Whistle tavern. He swung open the door and stood inside for a moment while his eyes accustomed themselves to the dim interior, then he walked over to the bar. He withdrew a coin from his pocket, picked up two tankards of ale and weaved through the maze of occupied tables to an empty one that sat against the back wall of the tavern. The crowded room felt stuffy. Donald loosened the collar of his shirt, undid the buttons on the front of his frock coat and sat down to wait for Seamus. He tapped his fingers nervously on the table. His eyes darted towards the door every few minutes.

Within a short time, the door opened and Seamus appeared, looking concerned. His eyes scanned the crowded room. Donald gave him the high sign from the back of the room and Seamus made his way towards him.

"I was in the midst of teaching a class," he said, frowning. He pulled out a chair and sat down across the table. "What is it?"

Donald lowered his voice. "Have you been to the window of the Times Register."

"I have."

"Things are heating up to the boiling point, I'm afraid."

Seamus sat up straight in his chair. "Indeed they are and that's why I'm out of it."

Donald, all thoughts of Ballymullian driven from his head, whispered fiercely, "what are you talking about, you're out of it?"

"Precisely what I said," Seamus replied. "When Wolfe Tone was leading the debates in the open and there was a chance for change, I supported it. With him out of the picture, and the SUI forced underground, I don't hold out too much hope for change from now on. All the talk I hear now is about revolution. That's not why I joined the SUI."

Donald locked eyes with Seamus. "You're a dreamer if you ever thought there was a hope for peaceful changes. You know as well as I do that the English live to crush us under their heels. It's like some sick game they've played for centuries. They watch us build ourselves up, then kick us down again."

Seamus slapped his hand on the table. "I'm done with it."

"I don't believe what I'm hearing. The English killed both our fathers, as I remember. Do you feel nothing?" he whispered hoarsely.

Seamus's face paled in anger. "I'll not even honor that question with an answer, but I'll say this. Regardless, of what's gone before, killing is not the answer, or do I have to remind you that it's been going on for hundreds of years without a solution?"

Donald raised his head. "At least we die fighting."

"But we still die and nothing changes," Seamus spat back.

"If we don't fight, we are teaching our children to cave in to tyranny."

"And if we do fight—what? It just goes on for hundreds more years." He took a deep breath. "Do you see an end to it any time soon?"

Donald glared his answer.

The two men sat, each in his own thoughts, drinking his ale.

Seamus finally broke the silence. "Who do you suppose is going to teach our children if we're dead? Do you not see, we need to be alive to teach them about our ways? For that we need to find solutions other than killing."

"Such as what, rolling over and playing dead?"

Seamus glared at him. "I said it before and I'll say it again. Education; beating the English at their own game. Using our wits instead of guns."

"Teaching our children to expect anything different from the English than they see right now is just giving them false hopes," Donald spat. "After all the degradation they've heaped upon us for centuries, do you ever imagine a circumstance where they'd be thick-headed enough to pack up and go home, leaving Ireland like a festering wound, living this close to their shores?" He gripped the rim of the table, his face twisted.

"She's cruel and vicious, Seamus, but she's not stupid."

Seamus's face turned to stone. He slammed his tankard down and pushed himself away from the table. "It's not a schoolmaster's place to fill children full of hate," he said and stomped angrily out of the tavern.

Donald sat at the small table, still furious, but mortally ashamed that he had let his rage get the better of his common sense. He sat stunned at the realization that Seamus's and his lifelong friendship had crumbled, perhaps beyond repair.

Chapter 5

▼

Ulster, September 1796

Reanna opened the hinged lid of the sewing basket beside her chair and rummaged through it until she found a length of red ribbon. In a basket of linen remnants, rejected from the bleaching house, she retrieved a hand-stitched navy blue collar and settled back into her chair by the window. Siobhan, her hands still bearing traces of blue dye, placed the last pin in the hem of Erris's dress. She sighed in relief and sat back on her heels.

"You're turning into a fine big girl, Erris."

The child's serious face broke out in a smile. "I know it. I'm almost ten. Soon I'll be as tall as mam."

Siobhan groaned and rubbed her back. She held her hand out to Reanna. "Give me a hand up, will you love?" Reanna was at her side in an instant. She raised her cousin to her feet and led her to a chair on the other side of the sewing table. "Are you in pain?" she asked, a worried look on her face.

"Don't worry yourself, Reanna. I'm more than fine." She crossed her fingers for luck. "So far, that is." She touched her stomach and a smile creased her broad face. "God willing, I'll have a healthy baby come Easter."

Reanna clapped her hands. "Oh, Siobhan, isn't that grand. I can scarcely wait to tell Donald."

Siobhan's face sobered. "I wanted to tell you about it sooner, but with things as they are between Donald and Seamus—"

Reanna held up a hand and turned to Erris who stood still as a mouse, ears at attention.

"Go and make some tea for Auntie Siobhan, lovey, there's a good girl."

Disappointment crowded the child's face. She heaved a sigh. "Will you help me off with this dress first, then?" she asked, fingers akimbo. "The pins are sticking my legs."

Reanna raised the dress over her child's head and helped her back on with her clothes. She sent her on her way and turned to Siobhan.

"What do Seamus and Donald's foolishness have to do with us? It's not made any difference in two years, why should it now?"

"Because Seamus is talking about moving to Mayo."

"Mayo?" Reanna sat down heavily in the chair beside Siobhan. Her voice trembled. " I see."

"The thing of it is that before this bad blood came between them, Seamus made a promise to Donald to look after you and Erris." Siobhan lowered her voice "—in the event of a particular situation."

Reanna's eyes shot towards the kitchen and caught a glimpse of Erris, hovering near the door. "Erris," she called out, "the tea, dear—" and heard the rustle of Erris's skirts as she scooted back to get the tea. Reanna whispered, "That. Yes, there's been no talk from Donald in that vein, lately. I suspect it's because of the season. I'm always relieved when he's off the road and spending his days at the bleaching house."

Siobhan whispered, "But, if we move to Mayo and the situation comes to a head for Donald, we won't be here when you need us."

Reanna waved a hand at her. "We can look after ourselves. In any case, I don't think they'll ever find out." She pursed her lips. "He's been doing it for years, you know." She rose from the chair, poked at the fire in the grate, and turned back to Siobhan. "What made Seamus decide on Mayo at this particular time?"

Siobhan clasped her hands together between her knees. "It seems the ignorant have banded together, calling themselves a lodge, and are making it their business to get every Catholic out of Ulster if they have to kill them to do it."

Reanna whispered, urgently. "Then go, Siobhan. Seamus is right. You'll be safer out and away from it, altogether."

Siobhan picked up Reanna's hand and tears filled her eyes. "I can't desert you again, cushla."

Reanna patted Siobhan's stomach. "You need to think of your family's safety now."

Siobhan turned away and wiped at her eyes as Erris walked carefully into the room, balancing a tea tray in both hands.

"I made enough for all, and some of those jam biscuits you made, mam." She placed the tray carefully on the sewing table, pulled her stool up to it and sat down. She folded her hands primly on her knees and waited for the conversation to begin again.

*   *   *

Later that evening Donald sat down at the supper table with his usual feeling of isolation. Reanna and Erris chatted their way through dinner, while he sat like a great lump surrounded by his own silence. Ever since the evening two years ago when Seamus ended their friendship by stomping out of the Tin Whistle, Donald had felt like an outsider. Anything concerning Seamus was not mentioned in his presence. Truth be told, he would like to have had it back the way it was. He missed his old friend.

"Donald. I'm talking to you."

"What is it, Reanna?" he said crossly, not really caring one bit what it was. It wouldn't involve him anyway.

"I have some good news and bad news to tell you. Siobhan is expecting a child again after all these years. Isn't that grand?"

"Not so grand to think of bringing a child up in Biggens Alley," Donald countered, crossly.

Reanna's face crumbled in sorrow. "Well, that's the bad part, Donald. They are talking about going back to Mayo."

His fork stopped midway to his mouth. "Are things that much better in Ballymullian?"

Her voice quavered as she poured a stream of tea into his cup. "No, but I suppose if you have enough money, anywhere is fine."

Donald was surprised at his feeling of loss at the news. Ever since the night two years ago, when Seamus had ended their friendship by stomping out of the bar, Donald had waited for the right time to patch things up with Seamus. The right time never came and now he was afraid it was too late.

Reanna buried her face in her apron. "I don't want them to go, Donald. I'll miss them terribly, and not to see the baby and all." She wiped her eyes on her apron.

*   *   *

Erris jumped up and ran to her mother's side. She stroked the bowed head and looked miserably over at her father.

Donald pushed himself away from the table and stood up. "Erris, be a good girl and take Pegeen upstairs."

Erris made a face, picked up her doll and left the room.

Donald sat in silence for a moment, and then turned toward the door. "Are you out there, Erris?"

I'm going, Da." When he heard her footsteps receding, he raised his wife to her feet and took her in his arms.

"You and Erris could always pack up and go with them you know."

"I won't leave you, Donald. We'll stay here together and face whatever comes."

He took her by her two arms. "Seamus has promised me that when things got dangerous, he would take you both to Ballymullian. If they are leaving, it has to be now. There is no one else I can rely on and I won't be here to look after you and Erris."

"Where will you be? Won't you be coming with us?"

"You must know I can't do that."

"Whyever not?"

He sighed impatiently. "Because it would raise suspicions if I up and left, without a by your leave."

"I don't want to go back there without you, Donald. Were still not certain that I'm in the clear. Is there nowhere else we'd be safe?"

"Not in the north there isn't that I'm aware of. In any case, I couldn't have you and Erris going off to stay in a strange place by yourselves." He shook his head. "No, you'll have to go with them." He sat down heavily in the chair, wondering how in the name of God he was going to make it up with Seamus now without it seeming as though he were using him for his own gain.

*   *   *

The next morning, Donald left for work. He closed the door of the flat behind him and stood for a moment in the damp chill of the stoop. The street cobbles glistened from rain that had fallen during the night and the lone lamppost on the corner wore a halo of fog. He shivered, turned up his collar and stepped into the street. He blew a kiss to Erris, who stood in the glow from the window, Pegeen clutched in her arms.

His neighbour, Joseph Casey hailed him from the open door of the next flat. He'd just lifted a crude sign from his door and motioned Donald to join him. He walked up the stoop and Joseph, purple with rage, all but threw the paper to him. Donald read the misspelled words:

Joe Casy, Mary Casy, Eilen Casy, Brain Casy, you hav twenty-for hours to sel your things, leve these loggings and go to Connut or yu wil go to hel.

"I checked," Joseph said, his voice thick with anger. "There is three more flats is papered on this block alone. They'll take my home over my dead body. Just let them try. We'll be waitin' for them."

*   *

Ever since the fight between the Catholic Defenders and Protestant Peep o' Day Boys in County Armagh the year before, the Protestant victors had made it their mission to eliminate every Catholic from Ulster. To this end, they had been aggressively posting the threatening notices on Catholic doors in the dead of night, and burning to the ground the houses of those who didn't heed the warning to leave the county. In spite of the fact that there was a nine o'clock curfew and armed patrols to enforce it, the perpetrators were not being arrested for breaking curfew and the local government was turning a blind eye to the papering.

*   *

Donald breathed in the smells of the sea and fallen autumn leaves as he rounded the corner onto High Street. His footsteps echoed on the cobbles. Joseph Casey's dilemma was too close to home. Maybe he'd better not wait any longer to talk to Seamus. He rubbed a hand over his eyes. He was getting a blazing headache.

Forty minutes later, he arrived at work. He walked through the wide doors of the shipping area and glanced in the mill manager's office. Old Mr. Graham sat at his desk, head nodding towards his folded arms that lay across his chest. Donald sidestepped two men, who were measuring and marking the finished linen cloth for shipping. He walked through the receiving area to the small office he shared with Sandy Wiggins, the untidy little man who was overseer of bleaching operations. Sandy's unoccupied desk sat in front of a window where he had a bird's eye view of the bleaching operation downstairs.

Donald pinched the bridge of his nose and shook his head. The clatter and the sharp smell of sulphuric acid only increased his discomfort. He removed his hat and hung it on a hook beside the window and sat down at his desk. He pulled a stack of work towards him and began to invoice the finished cloth for shipping to England.

He couldn't seem to concentrate on anything this morning. His worries kept interfering with his work. He pushed himself away from his desk in dismay and stood up. With hands clasped behind his back, he stared unseeing out the front window at the men moving the large webs of linen around on the grass below.

A voice at his shoulder almost made him leap out of his skin. "Morning, Donald."

He turned in alarm and tried to still his pounding heart. "Morning Sandy, I didn't hear you come in."

The little man sat at his desk, "It's a restless one you are this morning, Donald. Most days you're glued to that desk."

"Too much breakfast, Sandy," Donald replied with a conspiratorial wink, rubbing his stomach. He clasped his hands in front of him and stretched to make it look good, then went back to his desk.

As the day wore on, his apprehension worsened at the thought of having to approach Seamus for a favor after all these months of mutual silence. He decided putting it off wouldn't make it any easier. He would just do it.

Just before quitting time, he looked up to see old Mr. Graham, limp wearily into the office, leaning on his cane. His face was white with strain. Donald pulled up a chair for him and the old man sank down into it.

"Donald," he said in a shaky voice, "I've had some disturbing news from England. I received a letter today, informing me that they want me to retire and they are sending over a new manager to take my place."

Donald feared that his bowels would let go. "But why?" he managed to ask.

"The gist of it is that they think I'm too old to run the operation efficiently."

Donald sat frozen to his chair, his throat dry. He kept his face expressionless.

Graham went on, "They said that this bleaching house continues to lose money, while other bleaching houses they own in Ulster fare better."

Donald folded his shaking hands underneath his arms and forced himself to sit still and hear the old man out.

"They question why we buy our linen from outlying markets at higher prices, instead of at market price in Dunbury like everyone else." He threw up his hands in exasperation. "I've gone through this with them time and again. In times past, I've told them that we use dependable and loyal weavers that we have dealt with for years and that is the way we have always done it."

Donald's heard his own repeated excuses to his manager's queries come back to haunt him. Guilt twisted the knife deeper into his stomach for the years he had deceived the old man.

The mill manager hung his head, discouraged; "I guess those aren't good enough reasons anymore." Then he rallied himself, slapped his knee and reached for his stick. "In any case, that's the way it is and there's nothing I can do about it."

Part of Donald knew he must act normally and the other part wanted to cut and run. The old man's voice cut through his panic.

"The new manager and the company auditor will arrive tomorrow. They want to see all the ledgers and invoices for the past five years. If you would be so kind Donald, would you scare your records up for me and drop them off at my office on your way out tonight?" He rose from the chair and tottered towards the door.

Donald choked out a reply, "Would tomorrow be acceptable? You see, I have some finishing up here to do with the recent ones and some of the older ledgers are at home in a box."

"Certainly Donald, that would be fine." Mr. Graham turned around and waggled a hand at him. "Tomorrow then."

Donald got up out of his seat, walked stiffly over to the window that overlooked the bleach room and watched Sandy scurry around downstairs like a beetle with two legs missing. He had planned for this moment in his mind many times over the years and now when he needed to think rationally, he was overtaken by panic. An examination of the ledgers would show the same names appearing over and over again. An auditor might assume that these weavers were being paid above market price as a bonus to friendship. If that auditor took his suspicions to the authorities, a ready-made list of patriots would be brought in for questioning.

He could not let that happen. The burden was his. He would have to destroy all his ledgers, warn the others, get his family to safety and make arrangements for his own escape. He took out a handkerchief and wiped his forehead. For now he would just have to stay calm and finish out the day as usual.

*   *   *

At six-thirty, the noise downstairs lessened as the workers began to shut down for the night. Sandy bid Donald goodnight. Alone in the office, Donald picked up all incriminating evidence, hid it on his person and left as the clock struck seven. The lantern cast eerie shadows on the walls as he descended the narrow staircase and entered into the smothering darkness of the receiving room. The hair stood up on the back of his neck as his footsteps echoed hollowly on the dusty planks. He hurried toward the door, blew out the lantern, placed it on a shelf, locked up and walked out of the building into the cold, night air.

*   *   *

Reanna had just taken a round loaf of hot fruit bread from the griddle when she heard the front door open. Donald rushed into the kitchen looking as though he had seen a ghost. She ran over to him and grabbed him by the arm.

"For the love of God, Donald," Reanna cried, "what has happened?"

"The worst, I'm afraid," he answered distractedly as he pulled ledgers out from underneath his coat and laid them on the table.

He turned a chalk white face to her and took her hands in his own. She looked away, panic fluttering in her breast, as she fought for control.

He turned her face toward his own. "Don't look away Reanna. Listen to me. We have to leave here this minute." He pushed a ledger into her hands. "Here," he said, "rip the pages up into small bits and feed them to the fire. Don't ask me any questions, just do as I ask."

He picked up a kitchen knife and proceeded to hack the ledger covers into burnable pieces. He poked them into the flames till they caught fire, then scattered the charred embers around the grate.

Erris stood frozen, eyes wide in the light of the blazing fire. "Mam, what's happening?"

Reanna, on seeing the fright on her daughter's face, dropped the ledger and reached out a hand. She gathered her daughter in front of herself, and felt the beat of her child's heart through her own crossed arms.

Donald turned to her from his place in front of the fire. "Reanna, did you not tell Erris about County Mayo?"

"No. I was going to, but I didn't think it would be this soon."

"Hell's bells." Donald swore underneath his breath. He turned around and put another ledger into Reanna's hands. "Rip these up—and hurry."

He knelt in front of Erris. "I have to go away for a while, ansa. You and your mother are to go to Mayo with Seamus and Siobhan."

He turned to Reanna, "Did you and Siobhan discuss what we talked about at breakfast?"

"Yes, we did," she answered defensively. "You know we talk about everything. She said that we'd be more than welcome to come with them when they leave."

"—and when is that?" Donald inquired impatiently.

"Within the week. Probably a few days."

"Then you and Erris will have to stay with them until they do. You'll be safe there. I'm leaving in the morning."

"Where?"

"It's better if you don't know." He turned to his child. "Erris, I want you to run upstairs and gather up your things. Dress yourself in as many clothes as you can comfortably wear. The weather is turning cold and you'll need them. Put your cloak on top of everything else and then come downstairs—and hurry."

He followed her into the hall and whispered hoarsely at her as she scurried up the stairs. "You'll be walking for the better part of a week, so don't bring any more than you can carry."

He hurried back into the kitchen and turned to Reanna, who had collapsed into a chair.

"You go and do the same. Get your household money and bring all the food you can fit in your market basket as well."

Reanna sprang into action and flew down the hall. Donald extracted a small key from his vest pocket, unlocked the drawer of the chiffonier, opened the tin box and stuffed notes into every pocket in his clothes. He strode down the hall towards the front door.

"Hurry," he called urgently up the stairs. "We need to get there before nine o'clock curfew. I don't relish walking into that alley in the daytime, much less at night."

Reanna ran into Erris's room, grabbed her by the hand and they flew down the stairs to the door, where Donald waited with his hat on his head and a wild look in his eyes.

They left the flat behind them and walked down the street into the chilly night. When they reached High Street, Erris gave a cry, pulled her hand out of her mother's and ran back towards the flat. Donald dropped the overloaded market basket to the ground and sped after her. He picked the sobbing child up bodily and carried her back to where Reanna waited with her arms outstretched.

"I forgot Pegeen, Mam. She's still on my bed. I have to go back for her."

"We'll get you another doll," Donald said firmly. "We've no time to go back."

Down High Street they went in the dark. As they passed the Tin Whistle pub, the door opened and light spilled out two men who weaved their way down the street, singing at the top of their lungs. The pub door closed and it was dark again.

It must be getting close to curfew, Reanna thought. The streets were emptying themselves of people. Even the beggars had thinned out. Reanna, with a weeping Erris in tow, thought her lungs would burst, trying to keep up with Donald's pace.

They left High Street and turned onto Buffen Street. Mother of God, she thought, is this what it's come to? Being dragged along a dark street like a sack of meal. Is this your protector who will love you and nurture you back to sanity? Is this the man you put your trust in, to end up here?

The narrow street was empty now, except for a dark figure slouched against a tenement wall. Reanna saw him straighten up and hold out his beggar's hand as they approached. Reanna's thumb automatically moved in fright to her finger to turn her gold and ruby ring face down in her palm. Her thumb touched a naked finger and her heart froze in her chest.

"Oh my God, Donald, my wedding ring! It's in the pocket of my apron. We have to go back."

"Are you mad?" he hissed. "Where do you plan on spending the night?"

The fast approaching curfew was the last thing on Reanna's mind. Her ring was the only thing left of her secure life and now it was gone. She began to cry silently as Donald pulled her along.

       *   *   *

A thundershower dumped rain on them as they turned into Biggens alley. Erris tightened her grip on her mother's hand. "Is this where Aunt Siobhan and Uncle Seamus live, Mam?" she asked in a frightened voice.

Reanna, still in despair over the loss of her ring, hadn't thought to prepare Erris for the shock of the alley. She'd never let her come here before. Things were happening too fast.

"Yes, but it'll be fine, love. Don't you worry. We'll be there soon, and it's only for a few days."

       *   *   *

A few moments later, they trooped up to the landing and rapped on the rough door. Seamus opened the door. His face expressed shock at the sight of his visitors. He looked from one to the other. "What in the name of God?"

"May we come in?" Donald asked in a noncommittal voice.

"Do." He opened the door wide to admit them.

The two men stood in uncomfortable silence. Seamus closed the door and looked expectantly at Donald.

Donald took a deep breath and spoke. "I'm asking you to take my family to Ballymullian with you. Will you do it?"

"We will indeed," Seamus agreed, "but what's happening?"

"My books are going to be audited tomorrow," Donald replied stiffly.

Seamus motioned to Donald to join him on the floor. "In that case, maybe we'd better leave as soon as curfew is lifted in the morning."

"That would be grand, Seamus. I'd be eternally grateful."

At that pronouncement, Erris burst into fresh tears. Siobhan brought her over to the hearth. "Shhh, shhh, ansa, ten year old girls don't cry like babies."

"It's Pegeen, I forgot her at home," the heartbroken child sobbed.

"There will be other dolls, you'll see." Siobhan poked the fire and settled the crying child on the floor near the hearth. She sat down beside her and picked up a book of Gulliver's Travels. "You cozy up with your Mam, and I'll read you to sleep. Your Da and Uncle Seamus have grown-up things to discuss."

The two men settled themselves on the floor, their backs against the wall, arms crossed over their knees.

Seamus turned to his old friend. "And you Donald—where will you go?"

Donald gazed sadly at his family by the hearth. "I've already made arrangements for my safe passage out of here. I leave early in the morning."

"Will you be spending the night with us, then?"

"I'd be ever so grateful, Seamus."

"No need."

The two men sat in silence. Donald placed his hand on his friend's arm. "I'm heartily sorry for the bad blood that's come between us, Seamus. I never meant for it to happen at all, and certainly not ever for this long."

Seamus patted his friend's hand awkwardly and then rubbed his hand over his own face. "It's water under the bridge." Then he coughed. To cover his own emotions, he tried for a little levity, "It's a cursed shame to have to leave all of this, you know."

"Why are you leaving it, Seamus?"

Seamus turned sad eyes to Donald. "I'm sick to death of fighting a losing battle."

At his words, Siobhan, who'd been reading softly to a sleepy Erris, handed the book to Reanna and came over and sat beside her husband.

"I've given almost thirty years of my life to this cause and I'm tired."
Seamus stuck out his chin. "We've lived here with next to nothing
because I hoped I could make a difference in these children's lives." He
lowered his head to his folded arms. "I fear it's been a fool's dream."

Siobhan placed her hand tenderly on her husband's head. "You're
nobody's fool, Seamus."

He picked up her hand, patted it absently and turned to Donald. "We
didn't have anything here and that was fine, we didn't need much. But
now it's different. By the Grace of God, Siobhan is in the family way
again, probably for the last time. I want to be able to live to see my child
grow up. I don't see that happening here."

                    *   *   *

Hours later, Reanna, unable to sleep, lay on her back on the bare
floor. Angry words carried themselves in through the open window and
mewling babies cried out their discontent behind closed doors. She
feared for her husband's safety; he was leaving in the morning, she knew
not where or how long it would be before his return, if ever. The flood-
gates of her mind opened and all her hidden pain gushed out. She felt
her life here was over. The thoughts of returning to Ballymullian tortured her. She knew just how Fergus and Ma would react to the news
that she had married a Protestant. Marriage to a bloody Protestant is no
marriage at all, Fergus would snort. Meeting her precious child would
just add more fuel to his bigoted fire. Another bastard Protestant, he
would say—just what the world needs.

She turned over onto her stomach, stuffed her hand in her mouth
and sobbed as though her heart would break. She felt Erris stir beside
her. She rose and knelt beside her family. Erris curled up tight in a ball,
Donald twitching restlessly. Her hands trembled as she touched his
shoulder to waken him. Donald raised himself on his elbow and gently
stroked her hair.

"What is it, Reanna? Are you all right?"

"I'm just so frightened to go back there, Donald," she cried, "I can't live like that again."

He lifted up his frock coat that he was using as a pillow and out tumbled the bundles of pound notes. He held them out to her. "I was going to give you this in the morning. It's for your and Erris's future, Reanna. You don't have to live like you did before. You said yourself that if you have money, you can live anywhere."

She clutched at his two arms. "You're talking like you're not coming back," she cried.

"Don't be foolish," he said, "You and Reanna are my life. " I told you, I'll be back when it's safe." He folded her in his arms and kissed her goodnight. "Try and get some rest now, love."

*   *   *

Some time later, Erris opened her eyes and looked over at the outline of her parents lying beside her on the floor, remembering what brought them to this awful place.

Last night, disturbing sounds had wakened her. She sat up. Her mother lay face down, head in her arms, her body shuddering with sobs. Tears of sympathy had run down her face. It was just too terrible. She thought her mother was probably crying because her ring was gone. She would sneak back to the flat, fetch Pegeen and Mam's ring and be back before anyone woke up.

She tiptoed over to the window. It was still dark out. It still must be the middle of the night, she reasoned. Her heart thumped in fear and her resolve faded. She turned back to the room and looked around at her grim surroundings. She wanted her own comfortable room back. Her chest ached for Pegeen and her eyes filled with tears. She'd had her since her fifth birthday. Her Mam had said the doll had reminded her of Erris and so she should have it. Her Mam had even helped her choose

Pegeen's name. She had a china head with eyes that opened and closed, and she wore a lace trimmed linen bonnet that covered her dark curls that were made of real hair. The matching dress was ivory colored and had lace panels in the skirt. It covered her soft cloth body and flowed down to her shoes. She had china hands too, with indents where the nails would be. She was the grandest thing Erris had ever owned in her life and she meant to get her back. She'd be in big trouble with Da for going back to the flat, but when she came back with Mam's ring, he couldn't be too mad at her, could he?

She thought about how she would present the ring to Mam. She hugged herself in excitement as she pictured herself slipping the ring on her Mam's finger and then waking her up for the surprise. She'd better hurry before someone awakened and stopped her.

She picked up her navy blue cape that she had used as a coverlet and tiptoed across the room. She skirted the loose board that stuck up, opened the door, went out and silently closed it behind her.

*   *   *

She tiptoed down the stairs, holding her breath and trying not to touch anything. She slipped out of the shabby tenement and pulled the ill-fitting door closed behind her. It had rained during the night and across the alley, a beggar lay curled up in a tenement doorway, much like the one she had just left. Her courage deserted her. She re-entered the tenement and stood in the fetid darkness just inside the door. Thoughts spun around in her head. Last night when Aunt Siobhan was reading Gulliver's Travels, she had told her that it was about how a lot of little people could subdue a giant if there were enough of them, they were smart and had a passion to do it.

Erris didn't understand it. All she knew was that the O'Dowds lived in one room in a cramped, musty, evil smelling tenement. They had neither light nor air except for a small window at the far end of their attic room. They didn't have a chair to sit on, nor a bed to sleep in. They ate what little they had sitting cross-legged on the middle of the floor. From the conditions of the other rooms in the tenement, seen through the open doors in the hallway, Aunt Siobhan and Uncle Seamus were among the lucky ones. Siobhan had told her that some of the people who lived here were crammed in as many as seven to a room. Plus, she had heard what went on last night when they thought she was sleeping. She didn't believe that book for one second. It was not a good thing to be Irish, Protestant or Catholic. She would be something else.

She opened the door again and stood hesitantly on the stoop. She looked to the right and then to the left of her. It was still dark out and the tenements loomed menacingly on either side of her.

She stepped off the stoop and into the dirt of Biggens Alley. She zig-zagged around the papers and trash that rolled towards her in the ever-present wind. A rat scurried across her path. She fled out of the alley and up Buffen Street. She headed up High Street in the dark, keeping an eye out for patrols and taking care to stay close to the buildings. When she reached the park, she scooted across the paths and into the back alley that ran between High Street and Henry Street. When she emerged from the alley at *St. Andrews Church* on Keeley Street she heard voices coming around the corner from High Street.

She crouched behind a hedge and peeked fearfully from her hiding place. A gang of toughs with torches came down Keeley Street toward her. She held her breath as they crossed the street in front of her and headed toward Henry Street. They turned the corner. Heart pounding, she jumped up from behind the hedge and ran across the street after them.

They passed the Campbell flat and stopped at the Casey's flat next door, faces aglow in the reflected flames of their torches. Erris watched as one of the toughs stood back into the street and aimed a mighty throw at the Casey's roof. The torch landed in a cloud of sparks and caught the roof on fire. Someone else threw a rock into the front window and threw a lighted torch after it. Flames leapt up from the billowing lace curtains. Mr. Casey and his friends stormed out the front door, followed by the rest of the Casey family. Both sides got into a terrible row, with truncheons and sticks flying. One of the toughs ran up to the door and threw a blazing torch down the hall. Within minutes, the whole place was ablaze.

Erris saw her chance. While everyone was occupied, she stealthily opened the front door of the Campbell flat next-door and crept inside. She felt her way to the kitchen and lit a candle. She stood in the middle of the room trying to remember where her Mam had said that she'd put her ring. Her apron pocket, that's what she'd said. She ran over to the peg by the hearth, got the ring and shoved it into her own pocket. Then, shielding the candle's flame, she hurried up the stairs to her bedroom. It was so bright from outside she didn't need the candle. She blew it out.

Pegeen, arms and legs askew, lay on Erris's bed, just where she'd put her so she wouldn't forget to bring her along. She picked Pegeen up just as a loud crash sounded from her parent's sleeping room. She jumped in fright and ran out into the hall and into a wall of smoke. She watched in terror as flames ate up her parents' bed. She made her way to the stairs. Flames licked up the wall of the narrow stairwell. She ran back to her bedroom, struggled the window open. She stood there crying and choking on the thick smoke as the men below, forming a bucket brigade, threw pails of water into the Campbell flat in a vain attempt to stem the advancing fire. People down below yelled at her to jump, but she stood rooted to the spot, mouth agape, howling in fear, Pegeen clutched to her breast.

*	*	*

It was still dark when something jolted Reanna out of a fitful sleep. Panic bore into her stomach like a burning fist. Something was terribly wrong. She jerked to a sitting position. Donald lay curled up next to her.

Erris was not in the room. Reanna sat there shaking, fist to her mouth. Merciful God, has that stubborn child gone back to the flat after her doll? And she knew that she had. She turned to wake Donald, and stopped with her hand poised in mid-air. I can't let him go after her, she thought anxiously. If a patrol picks him up, he'll be put in prison.

She wrung her hands in despair. "God help us all," she whispered and she knew that it was going to be up to her. She snatched up her cloak and turned toward the door. She tripped over a loose board in the floor and pitched forward into the door, waking up the whole household. Donald jumped to his feet and ran over to her. He picked her up off the floor. "Where do you think you're going at this hour?"

Reanna tried to keep the panic out of her voice. "I'm certain our foolish child has gone back to the flat. She's put herself in jeopardy for that cursed doll. I rue the day we ever got it for her." She put her hands up to her face and began to weep.

Donald's voice shook. "Don't worry yourself, love. I'll go fetch her." He headed for the door.

Seamus leapt to his feet. "I'm going with you."

Reanna and Siobhan joined them as they hurried out the door. Seamus turned around to Siobhan. "Please, will you stay? Donald and I will bring her back safely."

Siobhan's eyes narrowed in anger at his suggestion. "I'll have none of it. If you're going, we're going with you."

Seamus shrugged his shoulders in defeat. When Siobhan made up her mind to do something, no amount of arguing would change it.

*   *   *

A few minutes later, all four of them rushed down the stairs and in the fetid darkness of the alley. Dark gray clouds, heavy with rain, rolled across the sky, helped along by a stiff wind. Thunder grumbled in the distance. Reanna put up the hood of her long black cloak. Siobhan held her shawl closed against the wind. As they turned from Buffen Street onto High Street, Donald spotted two soldiers walking towards them in the distance. He ran through the park, followed by the others and into the back alley that ran behind the buildings on High Street and Henry Street. They sped safely past the Armory and after two blocks had almost reached Keeley Street. As they hurried in the pitch black of the alley, the back door of the Tin Whistle tavern creaked open. They flattened themselves against the side of the building, scarcely daring to breathe.

An old woman, framed in the dim light from inside the pub, aimed a pail of slops at a large garbage container in the dooryard. It missed its mark and splattered onto the cobbles. Rats scurried up to it from all sides of the alley and began to feast on the rotted food.

Seamus heard a sharp intake of breath from Siobhan. He put one arm across her body and a hand over her mouth to quiet her. The little man went back inside and closed the door. The alley was once more smothered in darkness.

Siobhan slapped Seamus' hand away from her mouth. "Damn it, Seamus," she whispered hoarsely, "a bloody great rat ran over my foot. I wasn't going to scream. Have you no faith in me at all?" She walked away in a temper toward Keeley Street with Seamus following after her.

She hadn't gone the length of a tenement when a harsh voice shouted, "Halt, who goes there?"

Reanna and Donald turned tail and fled back up the alley and around the corner to Henry Street.

Siobhan stood rooted to the spot in front of Seamus. In her path, stood a British soldier, his musket aimed at her heart. When Seamus tried to pull Siobhan behind him, the soldier pulled the trigger. Siobhan, eyes wide in shock, fell to her knees, and then pitched forward onto the ground like a stone. Seamus let go with an inhuman cry, jumped onto the soldier's chest and knocked him to the ground. The musket skittered across the cobbles. The two men rolled around in the dirt, grunting and fighting for their lives. The soldier pulled a knife out of its sheath and took a wild stab with it, aiming for Seamus' back, but struck him a glancing blow on the thigh instead. With his remaining strength, Seamus rolled over on top of him. Blind with desperation, he put his hands around the soldier's throat and squeezed with all his might. When he felt no more resistance under him, he rolled off, and was sick to his stomach. He drew a deep breath, pulled himself to his knees and crawled over to Siobhan.

She lay on her stomach, head turned to the side. Her voice trembled. "The baby…Oh, God, Seamus…I fell that hard on my stomach."

Seamus knelt beside her, with trembling arms he gathered her to him. "Thank God," he sobbed, "you're alive. I thought he'd killed you." Then he whispered urgently, "We have to get to safety, love. Are you able to walk? I'd carry you—but my leg—it's hurt."

She rose to her knees and Seamus helped her to her feet. As they started out of the alley, Siobhan doubled over in pain.

"Mother of God," Seamus choked and lifted her into his arms. "I'll get you to a doctor," he promised. "The baby will be fine." He fled out of the alley with his wife in his arms, his own wound forgotten.

*   *   *

As Reanna and Donald ran across High street the sound of a musket shot stopped them in their tracks. Their frenzied eyes locked on to each other. Reanna opened her mouth to scream.

Donald shook her till her teeth rattled. "Stop it, Reanna. There's nothing to be done. We have to find Erris." He took her hand and they ran blindly up Keeley Street, not seeing any patrols, but not caring either. Fear for their daughter's safety increased when they saw black smoke rising into the early morning sky from the direction of Henry Street.

As they sped down Keeley, a horse drawn fire wagon with bells clanging, charged up behind them. Firemen stood on the side of the wagon. A megaphone blared at them to clear the road. They jumped aside and the horses clattered past them and turned the corner onto Henry Street.

They ran after the fire wagon and saw flames, fanned by the stiff wind, shooting into the air from the Casey's tenement and watched a wall of flames make its way across the roof to their own flat. Water slicked the cobbles in front of both tenements, as the fire brigade and neighbors relayed buckets of water, trying vainly to contain the fire, while bits of soot rained down from above and thick smoke choked the breath out of them. Tongues of flame licked out of the tops of the tenement windows and established new pockets of fire on the roof. Smoke billowed out the front door of the Casey's flat, turning the limestone wall black in its wake.

Reanna spotted Erris, standing in front of her bedroom window on the second level, clutching Pegeen to her breast, her small figure outlined by the flames that licked the wall behind her. Donald ran towards the front door of the flat. A policeman grabbed him by his two arms. "You can't go in there," he shouted, "Are you mad?"

Donald struggled to free himself. "Let me go, you bastard out of hell," he yelled, tears streaming out of his eyes. "That's my child in there." He kicked the legs out from under the policeman and ran through the door into the burning tenement, shouting. "Hang on, Erris! I'm coming to get you!"

Firemen, arms outstretched, gathered below the window, shouting for her to jump, but she stood frozen in fear, Pegeen clutched to her chest.

Reanna ran to the biggest fireman at the window. "She'll never jump. Please," she cried, "get her out."

A fireman hoisted himself onto the shoulders of another and after what seemed like forever to Reanna, a tower of men reached the terrified child and lowered her safely to the ground.

Reanna grabbed Erris into her arms and burst into tears of relief. She led her away from the flaming tenement and off to the side of the crowd. "Stay here, Erris and don't move," she cried frantically. "I have to go after your Da." She ran as close to the burning building as the scalding heat would allow.

"Donald—oh God, Donald—" She clasped her hands in prayer. "Jesus, Mary and Joseph, please let him come out."

A thundering creak of falling timber drowned out further words. Reanna watched in horror as the roof of the tenement caved in on itself.

Her mind and every inch of her body screamed with denial of that which she knew to be true. Donald was not coming out. A wail started at the base of her brain, scalded her throat as it passed through, and what issued from her mouth was a howl of intense pain, the likes of which she had never felt in her life.

A soot-covered fireman put his arm across his face to ward off the intense heat and walked as close as he could get to the door of the flat. He turned around and walked back, shaking his head. "He's a goner," he said, "nobody could live through that. The whole roof has caved in."

He turned to the crowd, "Where is that woman and the child that he belongs to?"

His words cut through the fog in Reanna's mind, and her instinct for survival spurred her to action. To admit who she was, would be to deny Erris a mother as well as a father, for surely she would be taken into custody and punished for Donald's crimes. She ran over to Erris, took her by the hand, and they melted into the crowd.

When they reached Keeley Street, Erris turned her soot stained face up to Reanna. With a strangled cry, she threw herself into her mother's arms. "Mam," she cried, "It's all my fault." Her chest heaved with sobs. " Da is dead and it's my fault."

Reanna tried to comfort the child, but her voice shook. "No, no, it isn't, Erris." She shook so badly she was unable to stand, and sat down in the street. She pulled Erris into her arms and rocked her, oblivious to the stares of the people running in the early morning light, toward the tower of smoke.

On High Street, it was business as usual, but to Reanna, it appeared as a dream world. She walked numbly, clutching Erris, urging her along towards Biggens Alley and the O'Dowd flat.

Her mind tried to make sense of it all. That shot they heard when she and Donald ran out of the alley…Were Siobhan and Seamus gone as well? How was she going to break it to the child? Rage welled up inside her and she railed against a cruel fate that would let this happen.

They trudged down High Street past the peddlers who were setting their wares out on the street. How is it that everything looks the same? It's not got any business looking the same. Donald's gone, and this poor child thinks she is the cause of it all. Those maids over there giggling, she thought, and she felt an almost uncontrollable urge to run over and pummel them till they lay bleeding at her feet. How dare they laugh. Don't they know what has just happened here. Have they no respect for the dead? As her brain finally admitted to the reality of Donald's death, she began to shake from head to foot. Fear for their future and rage for his bad judgment consumed her. She railed at him in her mind, like she never had when he was alive. What were you thinking? Why did you let yourself get involved with those people? You had good employment. You had a family to take care of. Why didn't you think of us first? What is going to happen to us now? Tears of rage ran down her cheeks.

Erris reached up and brushed Reanna's tears away with a sooty hand. "Please don't cry, Mam," she pleaded. She fished in the pocket of her apron and held up a gold band with its inset of rubies. "See, Mam, I got your ring back." She slipped it onto her mother's finger.

Reanna's rage melted into relief that her beloved child had been spared. She hugged Erris as though she would never let her go. "It wouldn't have meant a thing to me, if I'd lost you for it, cara."

*   *   *

Reanna, with a sinking heart and holding on to Erris for dear life, opened the door of the O'Dowd flat and stumbled in. She looked at Siobhan and Seamus as though she were seeing ghosts. She ran over to her cousin and threw herself in Siobhan's arms. "You're alive. Thank God. I thought I'd lost you both as well," she sobbed.

Seamus attempted to rise where he sat, back against the wall, leg bandaged. His face registered her words. "What do you mean? Where is Donald, Reanna?"

Reanna's voice broke. "There was a fire, Seamus. Erris was inside. He went in after her. The roof fell in on him. He's gone, Seamus." A fresh wave of grief hit her and she collapsed in a heap on the floor. Sobs shook her body. Erris dropped to the floor beside her mother, mouth agape in misery, as they put their arms around each other for comfort. Siobhan and Seamus struggled over to them.

Reanna pounded on the floor with her fists. "It's not right. Damn you, Donald." In the next breath, she crooned, "I'm sorry, my love, you did what you felt was best. I just can't bear it that you're gone."

Erris put her arms around her Mother and in a frantic voice said, "I'm here, Mam. I'll never leave you. It'll work out, you'll see. I'll help."

Seamus and Siobhan, tears running down their faces, looked helplessly at one other and putting aside their own hurts, put their arms around both Reanna and Erris and rocked them till they fell into an exhausted sleep.

*   *   *

After a while, Reanna opened her eyes and thought it had all been a bad dream, until she smelled the smoke that permeated their clothing. Then the reality of her loss hit her like a fist in the stomach. She lay with hands clasped together on her bosom like a dead woman. Wave after wave of bereavement washed over her. Yesterday her life had begun so normally, and then it had unraveled with sickening finality. Event after nightmarish event flashed through her mind. Then from somewhere deep inside she began to feel a strength that would not let her give in to self-pity. She had to be the strong one now. She sent a prayer for help, heavenward.

She turned over and gazed at Erris, curled up on the floor, her sleep interrupted by shuddering sobs, red face marred with tear tracks. She reached out, smoothed the hair off her child's face and made her a silent promise. We will get through this together and I will take care of you myself. No one will ever hurt you, she whispered fiercely. The question about how this would be accomplished she would deal with later, but one decision she would make now. She would not pick up with her family again. She would not subject herself or her child to that way of life. That was the past and it was finished. She would make a good life for herself and Erris.

She sat on her heels and reached for Donald's frock coat. She brought it to her face and breathed his scent. She removed the bundles of notes and emptied them into her lap, spilled the coins out of Donald's small purse and added them to the pile. There was plenty of money to assure their security. She wouldn't have to return to the poverty she left. That's what had started it all, she told herself—the poverty. She would get a job in town and a nice place to live. We'll be fine, she told herself.

She looked out the window at the brightening sky. She picked up her cloak, picked open a seam in the lining and fed in the pound notes that Donald had brought from their flat. She took a linen handkerchief out of her sleeve, emptied half the coins in it, placed it in her bosom and slid the coin-filled purse into the pocket of her cloak.

She eased Pegeen from Erris's hands, lifted the voluminous skirt and opened a seam in the doll's waist. She slid her wedding ring well into the cloth body and stitched it back up. She fluffed out the skirt and gently replaced the doll in her child's arms. She had no doubt that her ring would be safe.

She sat beside Erris and stroked her hair till she wakened. "We're going to have to leave soon, love." She showed her where she had secreted the money, and warned her never to let Pegeen out of her sight again. "When we get to Ballymullian," she promised, "we'll find a nice flat, just as nice as we had here. Things will work out, you'll see."

"Will I get to go to the country to visit my grandparents?"

Reanna held back a denial. "We'll see, won't we?" They wouldn't borrow trouble with that one. That was past and the past could take care of itself. They had the future to think about now. To thwart any further questions about grandparents, Reanna arose and said to Erris, "Gather up your things, lovey."

She tiptoed quietly over to the hearth, where Seamus and Siobhan slept spoon fashion. Beside them lay their worldly goods. Siobhan had gathered up their few belongings in a square of cloth and strung it over a pole. Seamus had strapped his pen and paper together with the last of Donald's books.

Reanna gently shook her cousin's shoulder. "Siobhan," she whispered, "it's time."

Siobhan patted the hand on her shoulder. "I'm awake," she answered and sat up. Seamus opened his eyes, ran a scraped hand over his grizzled face and struggled to his feet. He helped Siobhan to her feet. "How are you this morning, love?"

"I'll be fine. The rest did wonders, you know," she answered bravely. "And yourself?"

Before he could answer, Reanna noticed his bandaged leg for the first time. "Your leg, Seamus. What has happened to it?"

He stood up and tested his leg. "It got cut. We can go into it later, Reanna, we have a long ways to go."

"Are you sure you're up to it, Seamus?" Siobhan asked worriedly.

"It's not like we have much choice in the matter, is it?" At the look on his wife's face, he softened his words. "I can walk on it, don't you concern yourself."

Seamus looked at Erris and Reanna's shod feet. "In the interest of saving shoe leather," he suggested, "you might want to tie your laces together and carry your shoes around your necks."

Reanna declined, thinking to herself, we may have to walk with the herd, but we don't have to look like them. "Thanks, but no, Seamus. We'll be more comfortable with them on for now." She picked up Donald's black frock coat. "Would you have any use for this, Seamus?"

He accepted with thanks. It was too small for his rangy frame, but he put it on anyway. "Now I look like a proper schoolmaster," he teased. He picked his teaching supplies up by the strap and struck a pose.

Siobhan shook her head. "I don't believe you feel too badly about leaving at all, Seamus." She pulled a faded tan shift on over the nondescript one she was wearing so she wouldn't have to carry it.

"If the truth be known, I feel that anything has to be better than living in the likes of this."

"God help us, I hope you're right." She knotted her blue shawl under her bosom.

"What's Ballymullian look like, Mam?" asked Erris.

"It's a town much like this one, near the Rathskill Mountains and Innislow. It's boggy and it rains." She adjusted the collar of Erris's blue cape. "Altogether, I guess Seamus would be right. It's a damn sight better than this alley." Or decidedly worse, she said to herself, depending on the fates and if Lord Dalton was still alive. It had been ten years, after all. A lot could happen in that time. She closed her eyes and his foggy image swam into view. Nausea flooded through her at the memory of the sour smell of his breath as he lay over her, his rough sleeve laying raw her cheek as he held both her arms pinned over her head. She pushed away the memories and breathed warmth into her cupped hands.

What if he is dead? If I confessed to it and told them the circumstances, what would they do to me at this late date, she wondered. The answers she came up with did nothing for her peace of mind. She dismissed the thought. She had a child to raise. How could she confess to a crime that would take her away and leave her child with no parents at all? What Ballymullian held for her, she feared, was a possible indictment for murder, an uncaring family and perhaps, for all she knew, the return of a brutal father to add to the mix.

"Mam, it's time to go."

They all stood at the door waiting for her. Reanna picked up the overloaded market basket, and checked to see that Erris had Pegeen in tow.

"I'm ready."

Seamus slung his books over his shoulder and picked up the stick the doctor had given him. Siobhan set the pole on her shoulder and they all four picked up and left the flat without so much as a backward glance.

Chapter 6

▼

The Road to Mayo, September1796

Seamus filled up a leather skin with water at the tap in the alley before they began their journey.

Siobhan handed a tin cup of water to Reanna. "Drink this, love."

Reanna's head hung low. Torn as she was with conflicting emotions, she couldn't get any words out past the lump in her throat. She berated herself for not having claimed Donald as her husband at the fire and be damned the consequences. Instead she was playing the traitor, leaving town and abandoning his body to the enemy. She reached out and took Erris's hand for comfort as they turned onto High Street. The stale smell of smoke from the fire that still hung thick in the air, only served to add to her misery.

They joined dozens more exiles who, judging from their burdens, had been papered as well. The young and the tough walked four abreast, arms linked, united in their defeat, but undeterred in purpose, prepared to fight another day. Men and boys trudged along, shoulders burdened down under the weight of bog-cutters, over which hung cooking pots and other worldly goods knotted in ragged blankets. Pregnant women hobbled along on swollen feet. Mothers of all ages, babies strapped to the front of them, pulled along bawling children with legs too short to keep up. Skinny youngsters whooped along down the middle of the road, making a game out of it, not knowing where they were headed, but happy to be on their way.

Reanna's ears burned in humiliation to be on display for the privileged, who gawked from their safe places on the side of the road. Some looked on with pity, others with contempt. Head held high, she trudged along, gripping the wooden handle of her stuffed market basket while Erris walked beside her, sharing the burden. Seamus and Siobhan, walked behind them, speaking softly to each other. Reanna mentally patted the pound notes in the lining of her woolen cloak and told herself that this humiliation was only temporary.

However, she still had one more hurdle to clear before they were safely out of Dunbury. By now, she feared, the auditor would have arrived and Donald's absence from work, coupled with his missing ledgers, would be viewed with suspicion. Perhaps, a messenger had already been sent around to their flat to inquire about his absence. He would learn of Donald's death in the fire and discover that no one knew the whereabouts of his family.

Reanna set the heavy basket down on the cobbles and rubbed the red ridges out of her hand. "Switch sides with me, love."

They switched hands and continued down the High Street towards the other end of town. Her worries began to plague her again. What steps, she wondered, might Davenport pursue to insure the return of Donald's missing ledgers? Would they assume that the ledgers went up in flames along with Donald and call it finished? Or, when a search of the storeroom at the bleaching house turned up none of his records from years past, might that not renew suspicions? At that point, might old Graham, be forced to contact the authorities to locate Donald's family and have them returned to Dunbury for interrogation about Donald's business dealings. She felt her face flush with shame for the deception Donald had perpetrated on him.

As they reached the outskirts of town and neared the bleach green, Reanna gave Erris the full burden of the market basket and sent her over to the far side of the road. Then she fell back, said a few words to Siobhan, handed over her black cloak and threw Siobhan's tatty shawl over her own fiery hair. She melted into the crowd and made her way over to where Erris struggled along with her burden. When they passed the gates, Reanna stole a glance across the road and was relieved to see nothing but a man holding the reins of an old horse hitched to a wagonload of bleached linen. He waited patiently for the people on the road to clear a path for him.

Reanna kept watch on Siobhan and Seamus bobbing along in front of them on the other side of the road for another mile or so. When she felt danger was past, she and Erris caught up with them, switched clothing and put distance between themselves and the Davenport Bleaching House.

What had started out as a cool, foggy morning, turned clear, with the bright sun high in the sky. Mile after mile they walked, up and down rolling hills, through little hamlets with whitewashed cabins, past cultivated fields of flax and fenced in bleach greens. By noon, Reanna and Erris had belatedly taken Seamus's advice and removed their shoes from their blistered feet and tied them around their necks.

By midday, their throats were parched and they were on the lookout for somewhere to stop and rest for a while. On the other side of a little hamlet, they saw the sun sparkling on a dammed up river by a bleach green. They hopped the fence near a grove of trees and sat down on the bank of the river to refresh themselves. After they drank the cool water out of tin cups, Reanna pulled cheese and the fruit bread she'd made for Donald out of her basket. They ate while soaking their burning feet in the cold water.

"Seamus, your leg needs attention," Siobhan said. "Give it here."

Seamus sat down beside her. Siobhan removed the bandage, and her face blanched at the sight of his leg. She left his side, wandered up and down the ditch by the side of the road for a moment and returned with some green leaves.

Seamus eyed them with suspicion. "What is that?"

"It's plantain. I need to make a poultice for your leg—here." She shoved a handful of leaves at him. "Chew this up." She tore off some of the leaves and did the same. She washed his wound and the bandage in the river, applied the plantain poultice to his leg and wrapped it up again.

Reanna's eyes widened in shock at the extent of his wound. "Will you tell me what happened to your leg, now, Seamus?"

He looked over to where Erris sat with Pegeen on her lap. "Not in front of the child," he whispered. "Later."

They heard a loud, angry voice issuing from the bleach green, and looked up to see a little man heading towards them, waving a big stick.

"Get away out of that," he roared.

They quickly gathered up their belongings, headed back to the road and lost no time looking around to see if they were being pursued.

*   *   *

Late in the afternoon, they caught up with the straggly line of exiles. Erris took the hands of two thin little girls who were traveling southwest to Boyle with their widowed mother. Their mother carried an infant in her arms, while two crying boys clung like monkeys to her shabby shift. The widow told Erris of a prophecy that assured Catholics that safety lie beyond the Shannon River, where they would prosper. To Erris, it sounded more like a trick to get them to leave Ulster, but she kept her thoughts to herself.

*   *   *

Seamus looked behind him to make certain Erris was well out of earshot, then over and whispered into Siobhan's ear, "I'm going to tell Reanna what happened in the alley."

Siobhan gave him a poke in the ribs. "Do you not suppose she has enough secrets of her own to keep without burdening her with ours?"

"It might be a small comfort to her to know she is not the only one on the run," he said and hailed Reanna.

His voice broke as he related the previous night's event in the alley.

"I didn't mean for him to die, but I was beside myself," he said, as if in a trance. "And at that point, with a knife staring me in the face, it was either him or me." Siobhan put her arm through his and laid her head on his shoulder as they walked.

"After I did the deed," he continued, "I took Siobhan to a doctor I'd heard of, who, thanks be to God, lived nearby. He examined her and said she just had the wind knocked out of her. I was that frightened. I thought I'd lost her." He patted Siobhan on the arm and then fell silent. "He bandaged up my leg. We stayed there till curfew was lifted and then made our way home."

Reanna struggled on alone, carrying her market basket and limping along on blistered feet. Seamus's confession weighed heavy on her mind. Even though the English had murdered both their fathers, Seamus's aversion to killing had led him on a different path from Donald and had even been the cause of the breakup of their life-long friendship. After all this, to be forced into killing anyway. A terrible thing altogether to have happened. Reanna felt the tears gathering in the corners of her eyes and brought her handkerchief up to her face. The overpowering stench of smoke from it awoke the memory of her own loss and brought her to her knees. She covered her face with her hands and her body shook with sobs. Siobhan ran to her side and gathered her into her arms.

"What's going to happen to all of us, Siobhan?"

"We'll do fine, cara, we just have to stick together."

"I'm so frightened of what might await me in Mayo."

Siobhan took Reanna's hands away from her face and smoothed her cousin's hair back from her hot forehead. She led her over to the side of the road, lowered her to the ground and sat down beside her.

At the sight of her mother's plight, Erris dropped the children's hand and broke into a run. Seamus waved her off. Erris walked ahead, a child on each side of her, but kept looking back to check on Reanna.

Seamus eased himself down beside the two women. "Do you not think if you had murdered Lord Dalton, the authorities would have been at your door by morning checking on your whereabouts with Fergus and your Ma?"

She shook her head. "They wouldn't have any idea where I'd gone, Seamus. I didn't go home after I left Crofton House."

Siobhan snorted. "And you don't suppose Fergus wouldn't send them high tailing it to Dunbury, knowing you'd come here to me?"

Reanna looked at Siobhan and slowly nodded her head in agreement. Yes, she thought to herself, I think he probably would. There'd been no love lost between the two cousins. Fergus had always been extremely jealous of Reanna's attachment to Siobhan. He'd accused her of giving Reanna ideas above her station.

Reanna wrapped her arms around her knees. As well as all that, without her support, he would be left penniless and forced to go to work or starve. That being the case, out of sheer meanness, he might well tell the authorities where to find her.

"Well, then, if that is the case, perhaps you're right." She got to her feet and extended a hand to Siobhan. "Perhaps his nibs is still among the living after all."

Siobhan snorted. "More's the pity, I say."

Reanna spotted Erris ahead of them on the road. Her shoulders drooped and she had a child's hand clutched in each of hers. Reanna's heart broke at the sight of her child. So young to be so burdened.

"Erris! Come here to me, love."

Erris turned, then spoke to the widow, and ran back to her mother. Reanna dropped her basket and enfolded her child in her arms.

*   *   *

At the end of the day, they washed up by a river, exchanged a couple of potatoes for some turf, cooked some supper and settled down together for the night in a farmer's field.

Reanna lay on her back and rearranged her cloak to avoid having the hidden pound notes poking into her back. With her arms under her head, she stared up at the clear sky. If Lord Dalton was alive, what were the odds of running into him in Ballymullian? Her breath caught in fear. She shook it off. She was tired of being afraid. All things considered, she would just have to be on the lookout for anyone from Crofton House and avoid them at all costs. Her heart began to pound in fright. Stop it, she told herself. The chances of running into Lord Dalton were very slim indeed as long as she got a job that didn't involve trade with Crofton House. Then she remembered the bustling millinery shop where Alex stayed with his aunt, Mae Proulx. Maybe the old woman would hire her on to help out. She could learn to make hats. She could.

She remembered the times that Alex would invite her in for tea and biscuits when they walked home together from Crofton House. She rolled over and lulled herself to sleep with memories of happier times.

*   *   *

The next morning, while Seamus and Siobhan rested, two men caught up to Reanna and Erris on the road. The one with the pox-marked face attached himself to Reanna and pestered her with questions. "The name's Eoin." he said, holding out a grubby paw. His crooked smile revealed equally crooked teeth. "Travelin' alone…a widda woman, er ye?" He eyed her black woolen cloak up and down. "And why'd the likes of ye be footin' it, instead of takin' a carriage?"

Reanna bristled at the boldness of his question, but told herself that it was her own fault. Their good clothing stood out among the shabbiness of their fellow travelers. Her cursed insistence on separating them from the herd had brought unwanted attention to them. And now, she feared, she might have made them a target for thieves. She determined to purchase some second hand clothing from the next ragpicker they came across.

Eoin was not to be ignored. "Where did ye say ye were goin' again?"

Reanna used her old trick and turned his questions around on him. "West." Where are you two coming from, then?"

"Benny and me—he's me brother—we're from up north."

On hearing his name, slab-faced Benny danced in front of her, vacant eyes searching her own. "Benny—that's me," he said, pointing at his chest.

Frightened, she took Erris by the hand and they stepped to the side of the road to wait for Seamus and Siobhan. She watched the brothers out of the corner of her eye as they fell back into the handful of stragglers. A man with a slane broke off from the crowd and hopped a fence into the bog where some men where cutting turf in hopes of exchanging work for enough to buy potatoes to eat when they stopped for the night.

A humiliating thing it was to be driven out of your own country, Reanna fumed. A humiliation made worse by tenant farmers who armed themselves with sticks and stood guard over their potato beds to protect them from being stolen by the hungry exiles. However, she noticed, they stood prepared to sell them to anyone who was lucky enough to have the means to buy them. The destitute had to be satisfied with any green thing they could find growing on the side of the road that they could boil up for their supper when they stopped for the night. The old, the sick and the weak who could not keep up, simply sat down on the side of the road to await their fate, whatever it might be.

Reanna slipped her hand into the pocket of her cloak, picked a coin out of her purse, and handed it to Erris with a few words. The child ran over and climbed up the grassy slope to where the farmer stood. She handed him a coin and he filled her apron with potatoes. She ran back to the widow and children with the gift.

*   *   *

As darkness fell, they turned off the road and made their way towards a river that one of the exiles had spoken of as being far enough out of the way not to be noticed. They sank gratefully to the ground.

After they had eaten, Seamus sat by the fire and began to read aloud from Robinson Crusoe. Men, women and children gathered round, sitting a respectful distance away. Tired spirits revived and the miserable present was put aside for the moment by the magic of a human voice spinning a tale of intrigue.

Reanna sat exhausted, apart from the others, her back against a tree. She covered herself over with her cloak. She looked for Erris and found her lying on her stomach, fists under her chin, engrossed in the tale Seamus told. She stealthily removed a note from the lining of her coat and slipped it between her breasts. When she looked up, she saw Benny, the simpleton, mouth open and a vacant grin on his face, standing in front of her.

"God in heaven," she breathed. Then anger took over. "Be off with you," she snapped at him. "Lurking around in the dark like a mouldy cat." He turned and stumbled off into the night.

Reanna thanked God that it wasn't Eoin, and hoped that Benny was too simple to remember what he saw. For safekeeping, she put her shoes onto her cracked and sore feet, and called Erris over to do the same.

"Erris," she whispered, "put your arms through the slits in your cloak before you lie down to sleep. Then, wrap yourself in it. Be sure to hang onto Pegeen with both your hands. I'm going to sleep now."

After Erris went back to the fire, Reanna laid her cloak on the ground, and rolled up in it. She closed her eyes and listened to the rhythm of Seamus' voice and the strains of far away music. Finally, utter exhaustion took their toll on her. Sometime later, she woke up chilled to the bone, face buried in her arms. The music had stopped, Seamus's voice stilled. She heard only the night sounds of frogs and crickets. She reached for her cloak to cover herself. It wasn't there. She was lying on the damp ground. She jumped to her knees and whimpering, scrabbled around on the ground, fingers groping in the dark. Her cloak. It had to be here. She reached up to her bosom and touched the pound note that was still held there securely.

"Erris," she called hysterically, "wake up."

Erris sat up, rubbing her eyes.

"Do you have Pegeen?"

"I do. In my cloak."

"Get up," she cried, "I can't find my cloak. Help me look."

The hubbub wakened Seamus and Siobhan.

When Reanna told them about the missing cloak, Siobhan shook Reanna by the shoulders. "Calm down, it's only a garment. You'll get another one."

Reanna sat back on her heels and rocked in anguish. "You don't understand," Reanna cried. "Every penny I own in the world was in the lining of that cloak." She choked out the whole story.

"Merciful God. Did anyone know you had money?"

"Benny," she said. She jumped up and peered among the bodies stretched out on the grass.

"Don't bother looking for him," Seamus admonished. "If he's stolen your cloak, it wasn't to keep himself warm. He and his brother are probably miles away by now."

Reanna dropped down underneath the tree, fuming at cruel fate and railing at her own stupidity for not following her own advice about securing her cloak. Her tears spilled over and streamed down her face.

*　　　　　*　　　　　*

As soon as it grew light enough to see her hand in front of her, she resumed her search to no avail. Dejected, she stumbled back to where the others still slept and rummaged in her market basket for something to eat for their breakfast. She sliced up the last of the fruit bread she'd made on her last day in Dunbury and woke the others.

Before the day began for most people, Reanna had located a rag-picker who had a bag of second hand clothing brought over from Scotland. She bought some ill-fitting shifts for Erris and herself and reluctantly rolled their good clothing up and tied it in a belt.

*   *   *

Late in the afternoon, they approached the town of Armagh, the stronghold of the Orange Lodge. Seamus stopped to read a notice on a rough wooden building. It informed all, that a curfew was in effect, no one was to be on the streets after dark and no lights were to be seen. Seamus called them all together, including the widow and her children.

"There has been some trouble here recently," he told them. "Bigoted feelings are running high. Reanna, Erris, Siobhan and I will each take one child. Erris, you take my other hand. We need to stay together. No matter what happens," he told them, "don't let go of the children's hands. Just look straight ahead and keep moving.

They walked into the town. Soldiers with muskets patrolled the streets. Many elderly, and those exiles with children, including Seamus and his little group, sped up to be well ahead of the rowdies in their own ranks, in the event that trouble spilled over again.

Seamus spotted a gang of local toughs up ahead, lining the street to make sure that none of the exiles stayed. They began hurling insults at them as they passed. One of the exiles pulled a green ribbon out of his pocket and displayed it on his hat. The street erupted in violence as both sides went at it with fists and sticks. Seamus herded his group to the side of the road and they hid under a wagon. Militiamen fired their muskets into the crowd and broke up the melee. The exiled rowdies were herded away to prison; from there, all knew that they would be rounded up and put to work on prison ships, perhaps never to return to Ireland.

*   *   *

The sun had set by the time they cleared the Ulster border. After a long day on the road, the dispirited refugees broke into small groups. They lay silently in a field until a young man pulled out a flute and began to play a lively tune. An old man playing a fiddle and someone beating time on a bohdran soon joined him. People, who had dragged their beaten bodies for many miles, flocked to the exhilarating sounds and were renewed.

The rowdies who escaped with their lives from Armagh, sat apart in a field, surrounded only by the darkness and plotted a terrible vengeance on those who would dare to evict them from their own land.

Erris sat with her chin on her knees, a thoughtful look on her face. "Mam, why were those men fighting and hurting each other this afternoon."

Reanna looked over at Seamus for an answer. He raised his eyebrows back at her and inclined his head toward Erris.

Reanna's brow furrowed in concentration. "They hate each other, I guess."

"Why is it?"

Reanna looked pleadingly at Seamus.

He said softly, "It started hundreds of years ago, ansa, long before any of us were around. The English invaded Ireland. They did some terrible wicked things to us, the least of which was trying to shove their Protestant religion down our Catholic throats."

A puzzled look crossed the child's face. "But we're Protestant, Mam."

Reanna's fingers began to pleat the shabby shift she wore. "Yes, we are."

Siobhan interjected, "But your Mam used to be Catholic before she married your Da."

Reanna shot Siobhan a look that clearly said, I'll handle it.

"Your Da and I had to tell a lie to be able to marry. You see it's against the law for Protestants and Catholics to marry each other."

Seamus opened a book and looked over at Erris. "Do you know who Jonathan Swift is, ansa?"

"Yes," she replied, "he wrote Gulliver's Travels."

"He also wrote this." Seamus flipped over some pages and read; '*We have just enough religion to make us hate, but not enough to make us love.*'

Chapter 7

------------------------▼------------------------

County Mayo, October 1796

Reanna walked with a sinking heart down Crofton road towards Ballymullian. Each step that brought her closer to the past weakened her resolve to deal with it. It crumbled along with her former life in Dunbury as Mrs. Donald Campbell. This identity was now rolled up in a navy blue dress that Reanna carried underneath her arm. Her old identity, Ronny O'Neal rose to the surface, fearful and unsure, dressed in the ill fitting clothes much the same as she'd worn as a child growing up here. Then, she remembered the promise she had made to her ten-year-old daughter on the terrible day of Donald's death. *I will take care of you forever… no one will ever hurt you.*

A protective fierceness for her child surged into Reanna's chest and overcame her own fears for the future. She would not subject her child to Fergus' cruel tongue and her mother's slatternly behavior. In Dunbury, on the few occasions Erris was allowed to pull up a chair for tea and gossip with the grown-ups, they had regaled her with funny stories about Siobhan's parents, but had put off any of the child's questions about Reanna's family. She would simply continue to do so.

The countryside began to take on a familiar look. Until now, Reanna had never realized how different from Dunbury it was. Inland, a fuchsia and rhododendron lined road had led them over softly rolling hills and through fields of green. As they drew closer to the ocean, windswept trees, gray rock and green bog replaced it. She breathed the sharp smell of the sea deeply into her lungs.

The road ahead curved around an outcropping of rock, where an unexpected profusion of autumn wildflowers, in brilliant shades of yellow and pink, sprouted from the crannies. They stood beside the road and watched as Erris, in her secondhand clothing, scrambled up the side of the rocks in her bare feet and plucked a bouquet of flowers that she divided and presented to Siobhan and her mother.

Erris plucked at her skirt. "Is this where you used to work, Mam?"

Reanna's breath caught in her throat as she realized where they were. The gold lettered sign **CROFTON HOUSE** jumped out at her from the black wrought iron gates that enclosed the property. Thanks to Seamus's tutoring, she now understood the lettering on the gate. Nothing had changed, that she could tell, except this late in the season, all of the summer flowers were gone. A bank of purple asters and pink fuchsia lined the drive that curved around in front of the two-story limestone mansion. Green hedges edged the wide stone steps and red geraniums spilled from large granite pots that fronted the stone pillars at the entrance doors. The stone gargoyles still kept watch from each corner of the sloping rooftop.

Erris's voice was insistent. "Mam, is this where you worked?"

"Yes, it is, lovey." She took Erris's hand and hurried her past the closed gates.

She shivered in the chilly air, pulled her thin shawl closer around her and smothered her anger as she remembered the terrible shape her own beautiful, warm cloak had been in when last she saw it.

*   *   *

Two days after its disappearance, Reanna, dressed now in rag picker's clothing, recognized her cloak's soft black folds from the back. She ran up and accosted its wearer, a wild haired woman, red of face with a mean eye, who walked bold as brass, flanked by two bow-legged lads. Reanna's cloak was ragged and filthy, the red lining half-torn out and hanging in shreds.

She'd planted herself angrily in front of the woman. "That's my cloak you are wearing. Where did you get it?"

The woman pushed Reanna with a grimy hand. "Be off with ye, or I'll kick yer arse. I found it in a bog with the insides ripped out, so it's mine."

The woman's voice had a ring of truth to it. It confirmed Reanna's suspicion that Benny's dullness had indeed been an act. He and his brother no doubt worked the roads, preying on the unfortunate. At this point Reanna wouldn't have taken her cloak back at any price, so she had turned and walked away, ears burning in defeat and humiliation.

      *   *   *

Here I am, she fumed, walking the road to Ballymullian, penniless once more. And she wallowed in wicked thoughts of revenge against the brothers who had stolen her secure future.

As they reached the outskirts of town, clear skies gave way to roiling banks of storm clouds. A stiff wind blew in from the Atlantic to Innislow Bay. Reanna watched the sturdy curraghs as they made their way home through the churning water. Water that at low tide would become a turbid mud flat, with only a deep channel down the middle of it. She felt again, the mud sucking at her bare feet as she walked into the water to dig for clams and mussels. The truth of it was, if she didn't find her food and cook it, she didn't eat, except for the scraps from the dinner table at Crofton House when no one was looking.

A short while later, they walked down steep, cobbled Hill Street with its limestone tenements and shops on either side, into the thriving town of Ballymullian. Her heart pounded in fear as she passed the barracks building that took up the better part of the block. The English standard on a flagpole, snapped in the brisk wind. It had been ten years since she'd had walked these streets on her way to work at Crofton House.

I never thought I'd be back here again, she thought, and certainly not under these conditions, alone and with a child to raise. She looked over at Siobhan, who was wearing a grin that threatened to split her face, while Reanna herself, walked as though she was on the way to the gallows. She could never understand Siobhan's attachment to this place, given the conditions in which she lived, at best not much better than Reanna's, but for the fact that Siobhan's family cared for each other, whereas in the O'Neal family, it was everyone for himself.

Reanna tried to look at her surroundings through Siobhan's eyes. The town might have a certain charm, she told herself, as she watched people going about their business, in and out of the shops that lined the narrow street. It didn't work. It held too many hateful memories, especially concerning Crofton House.

They walked along together to the Market Square. It was abuzz with activity. Reanna's eyes scanned the milling crowd. Two horse traders closed a sale with a hearty slap to each other's hands, while the poor squatted by the side of the road, with their meager offerings, the sale of which would have to feed them until next market day. Those who have and those who don't she thought bitterly. Some things never change. The scene before her strengthened her resolve to be once more among the haves at any cost. I left here ten years ago as a wretched Catholic, but I'll not come back here to live as one again, she vowed.

They walked towards the wooden bridge that spanned the creek and led to the coast road.

"Do you even have a place to lay your heads when you get there, Seamus?" asked Reanna.

He ran a hand over his face. "Supposedly. I'm to look up a Bandy McFee person. His name was given to me by an acquaintance in Dunbury. He said that he lived somewhere around the foot of Sleive Rathmill. As it was told to me, he will help get me settled. By the grace of God, I hope to be able to teach and write enough letters for rent and a few potatoes."

Reanna had to bite her tongue not to blurt out that there was no pay for teaching poor Catholics here either. You'll be lucky to feed yourselves, she thought. As for the writing of letters, miserable old Father Meehan had those pennies sewed up tight.

Erris took Siobhan's hand. "Will I be able to come out and visit you?"

On seeing the closed look on Reanna's face, Siobhan replied, "You'll have to ask your mother, cara."

"Love," Reanna answered, fending her off, for she had no intention of letting Erris loose in the country by herself and she certainly had no intention of returning there herself, "none of us knows even where we are going to lay our heads tonight. Let's handle first things first."

*   *   *

They reached the little wooden bridge over the creek and hugged their good-byes.

"Until next market day," said Siobhan. "Why don't we meet here in the afternoon?"

"That's a fine idea." Reanna reached into her market basket and shared what food they had left. "Here…take some of this with you."

Reanna and Erris watched Seamus and Siobhan walk over the bridge to the coast road. Now that Reanna had determined to stay in town and not venture out into the country, she was anxious to seek out Alex's aunt, Mae Proulx. They walked back to Shop Street.

"There it is, Erris," Reanna said, pointing across the street to a little millinery shop, sandwiched between the bakery and the shoemaker shop.

The words were barely out of her mouth when she caught sight of a familiar figure weaving down the street towards them. It was her brother Fergus. Her jaw dropped in disbelief. In her ten-year absence, he had grown to look the spit of their father, a cowardly braggart who took out all his frustrations on his family. Her stomach turned sick at the look of him. She grabbed Erris by the arm and ran across the street into the doorway of the millinery shop. The hand lettered sign in the window read LA MODISTE and underneath in smaller letters, Miss Mae Proulx Proprietor. Through the glass in the door, she saw an old woman, sewing by the light of a candle. She sat in a high back chair, and her feet hung short of the floor. Her oversize head of gray curls bobbed slightly. No comb had ever tamed Mae's wiry locks. Her dainty hands carefully stitched lace onto the brim of a green felt hat.

Reanna dropped her bundle and smoothed her shift with her hands, ashamed to be caught looking so tatty; then she remembered that Mae wouldn't remember her any other way. Reanna picked up her bundle, took a deep breath and pushed open the door. Erris followed, carrying the market basket.

At the tinkle of the bell that hung on a cord from the door, the little spinster's black eyes flicked away from her task. She looked up at her visitors through spectacles that magnified her eyes, giving her the appearance of an inquisitive owl.

"May I help you?" she asked in a sweet voice.

Reanna walked closer. "Miss Proulx," her voice cracked. "It's me, Reanna. Do you remember me?"

The old woman blinked her eyes and shook her shaggy head. She leaned forward in her chair.

"You do look familiar, but…"

Reanna ran her fingers nervously through her hair and smoothed her shift with her hands. "I used to work with your nephew Alex at Crofton House ten years ago."

The old woman's expression didn't change. Reanna was panic-stricken. She has to recognize me, she thought, it's my only chance...I've nowhere else to go. Tears of desperation crowded into her throat. She swallowed hard.

"Remember...sometimes I'd have tea with you and Alex?" she finished lamely.

A smile of recognition lit up the old woman's face. "God in Heaven," she breathed.

She laid aside her work and clapped her hands in delight "Of course you did...Reanna, now I remember." She squirmed off the chair.

Reanna was shocked to see her pick up a cane and totter towards them. Her legs had always been badly bowed, but Reanna had never seen her use a cane. Miss Proulx hung the cane over her arm and took Reanna's two hands in her own.

"We wondered what became of you. Poor Alex never stopped searching for you. For some reason, he was ready to run off up north to look for you when we got word that his poor father had died." She shook her shaggy head in sorrow. "Then of course he had to go back to France."

"I'm sorry to hear that," Reanna whispered distractedly.

"Never mind that now, it was a long time ago." The old woman squeezed Reanna's hands. "Where did you drop from after all this time?"

The question took Reanna by surprise. What was I thinking, she scolded herself, not to have a story ready? "I ran away and got married," she stuttered, making it up as she went along, "with a salesman from Sligo. We had a daughter, Erris." Reanna felt Erris's eyes boring into the back of her head at this boldfaced lie. She pushed her daughter in front of her by way of introduction and to get her child's accusing eyes off her.

"No mistaking this one." The old woman reached a hand up to Erris and brushed a stray tendril of dark hair behind her ear. "Eyes as blue as the skies, just like her mother's."

Mae took Reanna's hand in hers and led her over to a bench. She cleared a bolt of green felt off it and laid it on a wooden shelf near the door. "Sit, sit, and I'll fetch some tea."

When Mae disappeared behind the faded curtain, Erris fixed Reanna with a distressed look and whispered, "Mam, why did you lie?"

Reanna shook her head, put a finger to her lips and mouthed, "no questions." To escape her child's probing eyes, she walked over and peered out the small window in the door. She saw Fergus and his loutish friends lounging in front of the pub across the street. She turned back to Erris, who sat on the bench, legs swinging, a disturbed look on her face. Reanna sat beside her, smoothed the black hair away from her daughter's high forehead. She enfolded Erris's hand in her own and held it quietly while she looked around at the dingy walls. Cobwebs hung undisturbed from the corners and underneath the wooden shelves. In the old days, those shelves had held an array of jewel-toned hats in all stages of fabrication, bolts of multi-colored felts, pristine lace, vibrant netting and bags of iridescent peacock feathers. She remembered the tickle of a peacock feather held against her face as she stood in front of the mirror in the small shop, dreaming of the day when she would wear a hat as grand.

Now, a rust colored hat, its wide brim adorned with a greenish feather and a large amber hat pin, sat in lonely splendor on a hat stand on the bare shelf across the room from where they sat. Naked hat stands lay tumbled in disarray in a wooden box on the dusty slate floor.

The old woman's voice from behind the curtain interrupted her reverie. "Reanna, will you give me a hand back here?"

Reanna jumped up from the bench and parted the curtain that separated the back room. She stood still a moment till her eyes accustomed themselves to the change. In the diffused light from a hearth fire on the right wall, she saw a stairwell on the opposite side of the small room and supposed that it led upstairs to Mae's quarters.

The grand sight of the fire and the warm milky smells from the tray, made Reanna weak in the knees. Blinking back her tears of desperation, she picked up the tray from the little table in front of the fire. It held a fat brown teapot, china cups, and a plate of thinly sliced buttered bread and a pot of jam. She followed Mae into the shop and placed the tray on the dusty display counter. She pretended not to notice that there was nothing on display here. Fear gnawed at her stomach as she looked around the shabby millinery shop; she concluded that the old woman was probably doing barely enough business to support herself, and not very well at that. She and Erris moved the bench over beside the old woman's chair.

The little spinster poured milk into the dainty cups, added the steaming amber liquid and passed a plate of brown bread to Erris.

"Help yourself to jam, love," she offered as she seated herself once again in her chair. She turned her big black eyes on Reanna, "So, tell me, where is your good man then? Are you moving back to Ballymullian?"

Reanna's hand trembled and she replaced her cup on the bench beside her. "I'm a recent widow," she began in a shaky voice. Upon hearing the pronouncement from her own lips, her self-control deserted her. Tears ran unbidden down her cheeks as her desperate plight manifested itself. "I have to find work to support us," she choked out. The words came out of her in a flood. "I was hoping you could teach me millinery...I learn really fast...I just need enough to feed us...I can cook and I'll clean. Erris is a big help. I'll earn our keep. I promise, you won't be sorry."

Mae looked at her with pity and answered in a pained voice. "Reanna, Reanna, I wish I could...if there was any way to accept your offer, I would my dear." She hung her head, "but sadly, I can't."

Reanna tried to hold back her tears, but they continued unabated. She fumbled for a handkerchief, realized she didn't have one and wiped her eyes on her shift. She made one last plea. "I'll work for no pay, just let us stay here on the floor, out of the cold. Six months, it's all I ask. If, after that time, I'm not bringing in money I'll leave, but I promise you, I'll work very hard to see that it doesn't happen."

The old woman had tears in her eyes now. "Reanna," she whispered, "you're breaking my heart, dear. Even loving your offer as I do, I'm afraid I couldn't even afford to buy the materials to work with. I'm barely making the rent. Business hasn't been very good, you see." She lifted a dispirited hand. "Guess I'm getting too old and too slow."

At the finality of those words, Reanna hung her head in despair, too crushed even to cry.

Erris tugged at her mother's sleeve. "Pegeen, Mam," she whispered. "Your wedding ring." She dug in the market bag, retrieved Pegeen and placed the doll gently in her mother's lap.

With a happy cry, Reanna lifted the doll's skirts, fished the gold band out of its body and held it up in triumph.

*   *   *

It was late afternoon by the time Seamus and Siobhan headed down the heavily populated coast road. Sleive Rathmill, high enough to catch the clouds, rose up in the distance to the left of them and the wind ruffled the gray water of Innislow Bay on their right. Seamus leaned heavily on a stick that he'd had to fashion out of a hickory branch. Siobhan's plantain poultices kept down the infection, but what he chiefly needed to do was rest his leg. However, he'd insisted on continuing on their way.

Siobhan, herself, would have welcomed a sit by the road for a day or two, for she feared her pregnancy was not going well. Ever since the incident in the alley, when she fell on her stomach, she'd suffered cramps in her stomach and back. She worried that something might be wrong with the baby, but she'd kept her fears to herself.

She felt weak and hungry all the time, but she wouldn't say a word to Seamus; bad enough he'd had to kill because of her, he didn't need to hear her whining about not having enough to eat. She hadn't dared say anything to Reanna either. She'd have insisted on staying put till Siobhan was better, and the poor wee thing needed to put Dunbury far behind her as quickly as possible. No, Siobhan told herself, I did the right thing. When we get settled in and get rested up. I'll be just fine. She sighed and rubbed her back.

*   *   *

As the sun dipped below the horizon, they reached the mountain. The wind that had threatened to blow Siobhan's shawl off her back, eased off and the clouds rolled in from the North Atlantic. Siobhan pointed to a steep trail that wandered up to the mountain's rocky height. "At the top is where Father Meehan holds Mass outdoors of a Sunday. It'll be grand not to have to attend Mass in Biggens Alley."

"Grander still if I'm able to make the climb."

Around the base of the mountain, hundreds of thrown-together shacks huddled together, chimneys leaking skinny threads of turf smoke. The wind picked up the smoke, trapping it against the side of the mountain where it hovered in an acrid cloud over the rooftops. Hundreds more cabins of all descriptions, strung themselves out as far as the eye could see along each side of the coast road, looking as though they had been strewn there by an untidy giant. Seamus and Siobhan turned onto a side road that wandered through the congested landscape and eventually turned off onto one of the trails that zigzagged through the area. They stopped at a cabin made of stones, with a sod roof, out of which emitted a feeble plume of smoke. The decrepit door was constructed in two parts. The bottom half was closed to keep out a dung covered pig that snuffled around the outside yard. The upper part admitted a shaft of light into the dim recesses of the cabin. Outside in the fetid air, an angular woman sat at a spinning wheel. She dipped her fingers into a little cup of water and nimbly worked the fiber down a stem of flax; her bare foot moving up and down on the treadle as she spun the fiber into linen yarn.

"Pardon me missus," Seamus inquired, "could you be telling me where it is I might find a man by the name of Bandy McFee?"

She stopped her work and her broad nose twitched like a rabbit as she peered up at him. "Bandy McFee is it?" she snorted, voice thick with contempt. "And what would you be wantin' with the likes of him?"

The O'Dowds looked at each other in consternation. Who was this Bandy and what were they getting themselves into?

Siobhan answered quickly, "We just need to know where he lives. We have a message for the family."

The woman's face softened up considerably. "Aah, that would be his old mother then. She's a dear old soul, so she is." She shook her head. "I don't know how it is she puts up with that Bandy one, bad cess to him."

When they had wrung the directions out of her, and were out of earshot, Siobhan asked, "What do you think of this turn of events, Mister O'Dowd?"

"Bedeviled if I know," he answered. "I suppose we'll find out soon enough."

"Good day to yez." Turning to locate the source of the greeting, they saw smoke coming out of the top of a grassy knoll. When they got closer, they saw that a hole had been dug into the side of the hill. An old man sat in its shelter, his abode scarcely big enough to spread his arms, but he and his turf fire were out of the weather.

The wind died down and an overpowering stench of pig manure took over, mixed with the sour smell of poverty. In front of a nearby hut made out of stones stuck together with clay, a runt of a man sat with his back against the wall. He looked at them with a squiffy eye that held a suspicion usually reserved for the taxman. They had found Bandy McFee.

*   *   *

They introduced themselves, and Bandy led the way into his hut. Their eyes gradually accustomed themselves to the dimness. His old mother hobbled around fixing Siobhan some tea and eventually settled down with her in a corner. Seamus sat himself down on the earthen floor, legs splayed out in front of him. Bandy sat himself down on the only seat in the place, a three legged stool, and with a wink at Seamus, reached a hand into a scabby dresser that sat against the wall. He produced a bottle of poteen. He tipped it to his lips, had himself a snort of the homemade brew, wiped his mouth with the back of his hand and passed the bottle to Seamus.

Now there's a man who's good to himself, thought Seamus, he on a seat and his old mother squatting on the cold ground.

"So," began Bandy, "Mickey tells me ye had a little set to in an alley up there in Dunbury and yer needin' a place to hide out."

Seamus's face paled. Now, why in hell's name did that idiot Mickey think he had to blather my business to the likes of this one.

"First of all," Seamus said, bluffing, "I made no mention of hiding out."

Puffed up with his own self-importance, Bandy went on as though he hadn't heard a word. "Well, you come to the right place. We take care of our own around here."

"Second of all," Seamus interrupted, " I haven't been involved in the movement for almost two years. I'm coming here to start a new life with my family."

Bandy's voice was deadly quiet. "Once you're in, you're in."

A chilling thought sent a shiver down Seamus's spine. Maybe it was not going to be as easy getting out of it as it was getting in. He would have to tread very carefully, he felt.

He said in a measured voice, "I'm hoping to be able to teach here."

"Well, I don't think you're going to find conditions here any better for teachin' Catholics than they were in Ulster," Bandy snorted.

Siobhan's answer to a question about her pregnancy was cut off in mid-sentence by the old lady, who was listening with half an ear to both conversations. She piped up from the corner, "Now, that's not quite the truth of it, son. Don't I attend Mass on the mountain, myself? There's never any fuss at all, at all. I think a teacher will be a welcome sight around here."

"Aah, me arse," Bandy said disparagingly, "you know a lot for somebody never goes out of the house, old woman." He turned back to Seamus with a wink of his good eye. "Pay no attention to her. It's the same as it's always been. The poor starve while what food there is, is shipped over to England to be sold."

Siobhan spoke up from the corner. "I heard that in one of the towns around here, Westport, I think it was, Lord somebody or other was welcoming flax spinners from Ulster and setting them up with wheels in their cabins."

Bandy dismissed her remark with a wave of a skinny hand. "Aah, well, forget that," he said. "They'll give 'em all to the Protestants. Besides," he added, turning his head so as to look directly at Siobhan out of his good eye, "takin' that kind of charity might be considered by some to be sleepin' with the enemy." He turned back and fish-eyed Seamus.

"No indeed. That would never do," he asked quietly, "would it?"

No one spoke.

"Anyhow," Bandy continued, "you'll be needin' some place to stay." He sat back on his stool. "A close, personal friend of mine…Hennessy, by name, owns a cabin down the road from here. He only comes by every so often, and I have the run of the place while he's gone. You can stay there."

He turned to his mother. "Old woman, why don't you take Seamus's wife outside and show her the hen?"

The old woman gave Siobhan a toothless grin and said confidentially, "We don't have a hen. He's just trying to get rid of us."

When the two women left the hut, Bandy rubbed his hands together. "Now to business," he said. "The SUI is alive in Mayo, but they're not movin' fast enough for some of us around here, so me and some of the lads…"

Seamus held up his hand. "I don't want to hear anything about it. I've given to the cause in one way or another near all my life, and I'm done with it. My wife is going to have a child and I intend to stay alive to raise it in the best way I can, and so I told Mickey in Dunbury and I'm telling you here, I'm out."

"That's what I'm after tellin ye. We're fed up of it, too." He whispered confidentially, "So, some of us have banded together with some people who aren't content to wait till the world ends to get our country back."

Seamus rose to his feet with difficulty. "Like I said, I'm out of it."

Bandy pulled on his nose with a 'we'll see about that' expression on his face and replied as though he had heard not a word that Seamus had spoken. "Well, I'll get you right on over to the cabin, rent free," he paused, "for tonight anyway, and tomorrow I'll introduce you to some of the lads."

*   *   *

Siobhan held onto the back of Seamus's coat in the pitch dark, as he followed the bent figure of Bandy down the rutted path to Hennessy's cabin. Laughter and harsh words drifted out of open doors as they passed, babies cried, children argued. Out of the dark, a reedy voice sang a baleful tune.

Bandy creaked open the door and they walked into the cold dark room. It smelled of stale turf embers and dirty feet. Bandy fumbled around for a candle, lit it and replaced it in a wooden sconce on the wall.

"I'll be around in the morning," he said and let himself out.

In the diffused light, they saw that the inside of the cabin was a duplicate of the one from which the rabbit-faced woman had given them
directions, with a few exceptions. It contained one room with a beaten
earth floor as well, but the hearth contained a large cooking pot that
hung from an iron hook. In front of the hearth, sat a rough wooden
table that had once been red, with two round stones to sit on and the
match of the stool that Bandy had in his own cabin. To the right of the
hearth, sat a disreputable dresser of sorts, with a shelf that held a few
cups and bowls and a square tin.

Siobhan lifted the top from the tin, dipped a finger in it, tasted it and
exclaimed, "Glory be to God, Seamus," she said. "Look at this…he's not
suffering, whoever he is."

"Look at this your ownself," he crowed.

Behind the door, a cailleach had been let down from the wall and was
already prepared for sleeping. Two brown blankets lay folded on top of it.

Siobhan lay on the bed, sighed long and deep, cushioned her hands
behind her head and grinned up at Seamus. He looked back at her with
a worried frown.

"I wonder who this Hennessy person is, to be so much better off than
the rest of the them."

Siobhan shrugged in reply.

"What's this, then?" She jumped up, removed the candle from a
sconce and attempted to raise the lid of a large metal trunk. It was
strapped around with leather thongs and securely locked.

"Bandy said that Hennessy has the key to it and it's not to be
touched." He chuckled.

"With Bandy given the run of the cabin, it's probably a wise
move…still…"

Soon after, Seamus and Siobhan lay in a bed for the first time, watching the embers from the turf fire, their stomachs full of potatoes and
cabbage that old Mrs. McFee had shoved at Siobhan as they left Bandy's

cabin. Now, stick these under your shift, the old woman had said with a conspiratorial wink.

"Are you awake, Seamus?"

"Just barely. Why?"

"I had an ear open to your conversation with Bandy in the cabin, but what happened after the old woman and I went outside?"

He sighed deeply. "Only more of the same. That's what worries me," Seamus replied and filled her in on what had transpired. "I'm afraid," he concluded, "that Bandy is mixed up with the worst sort of refuse from the SUI."

In a small voice, she whispered, "They sound to me like the same brand of thugs that set fire to Reanna and Donald's tenement."

Seamus shook his head. "I'm afraid they are, only this time they are Catholic."

"Mother of God, what did we get ourselves into here?"

Seamus answered, "I'm not sure yet, but I'm determined to stay out of it altogether. I don't know how I'm going to accomplish that, for I have a sneaking suspicion that if I refuse to get involved, Bandy will whisper a word into the right ear about 'Seamus's little set to in the alley,' and I'll be picked up within the hour."

He went on as if to himself, "and say for the sake of argument, I did get involved, it would just delay the results, until the first time I refused to follow the orders of this gang of thugs. So it's just a matter of time, either way." He heaved a sigh of frustration.

"Christ," he said, "I go through all that shite up there, just to come down here and do it all over again. If I'd known it would be like this, I could have stayed in Dunbury and saved myself the walk."

"Well," Siobhan chuckled, "you've still got your sense of humor, Mister O'Dowd."

"Sometimes, it's either laugh or cry, isn't it?"

As comfortable as Siobhan was, in a warm cabin and lying in a bed for the first time, loyalty to her husband made her offer him an out. "We could go somewhere else."

Seamus patted her hand. "Leaving wouldn't solve anything. We couldn't go far enough away that they couldn't find us if they wanted to."

*   *   *

Next morning, when Seamus came back to the cabin with a bucket of water, he found a disgruntled Bandy waiting for him outside the door.

Seamus brought the water inside to Siobhan. What's his nose out of joint for?"

"He just walked in like he owned the place and I walked him right out again, that's why."

Seamus shook his head and left. He and Bandy walked to the cross-roads where a gang of ruffians that he called 'the lads' was waiting. Seamus could scarcely believe his ears when Bandy introduced him as the person who was going to teach the kids the truth about what was going on here.

He noticed that pockets of people were staring suspiciously at him from a distance and wondered if this gang of thugs intimidated them. Not wanting to be found guilty through association, he left Bandy and the others and walked towards the closest group with an outstretched hand. They turned their backs and dispersed at his approach. He made the decision then to avoid Bandy and his gang in the future as much as possible. He went home and wrote himself a sign, poked a stick through it and installed it at the crossroads. It read, **LEARNING FOR SALE. See Seamus O'Dowd.**

Chapter 8

▼

Ballymullian, March 1797

The winter of 1796 had been the coldest in the memory of the town. Snowdrifts plugged up the streets, and the townspeople ventured outdoors only for the necessities of life. The cold frosted over the inside of the windows, and the keening wind seeped through every crack, diffusing the heat that rose up from the hearth and rendering it virtually useless, unless one stood directly in its path. The icy weather played havoc with Mae's arthritic legs. Siobhan made Mae a pair of warm woolen stockings, which helped keep out the cold, but nothing seemed to help the deep aching in the old woman's limbs. She spent most of the day wrapped up in a red wool blanket in her chair by the fire, stitching by the light of an oil lamp, to take her mind off her pain. Liam, Mae's oldest friend, supplied a bottle of poteen each Thursday, which Reanna fixed for her in a cup of hot tea at bedtime to help her sleep.

Each Thursday, Seamus and Siobhan braved the frigid weather for the four-mile walk into Ballymullian to the market, Seamus carrying his learning sign. Siobhan carried stockings for sale that she knitted with wool unraveled from torn sweaters, supplied by Reanna from a rag picker's bag. After market these cold nights, they headed for Mae's millinery shop. There, along with Liam, they gathered in Reanna and

Erris's flat in the back of the millinery shop for gossip and tea that was liberally laced with Liam's poteen. The more tea was drunk, the louder the laughter got. It tickled Reanna to see Mae's plain face become almost beautiful in its merriment. Afterwards, Mae climbed the stairs to her flat, and Liam made the long trek home to his stable room at Crofton House. Seamus and Siobhan spent the night with Reanna, and while the others slept, the two women talked far into the night.

*   *   *

In February, thunderous amounts of rain-washed away the last dregs of snow, but the hottest fire on the hearth couldn't seem to dispel the dampness. Many nights, Reanna watched as Mae labored up the steep stairs to her flat. By the creaky third step she would have to sit down and rest, before tackling the remainder of the climb. Reanna considered broaching the subject of exchanging quarters, but she didn't have the brass to bring it up.

Finally, as March approached, the warming sun appeared, a welcome respite from the harsh winter. The approach of milder weather brought Mae some relief from her arthritis, and she, herself, suggested the exchange of flats.

*   *   *

Liam, as general handyman as well as head groomsman at Crofton House, offered to build a second bed in the upstairs sleeping room so Reanna and Erris could each have a bed. He arrived early Sunday morning after Mass with his tools and left late that night.

Reanna was delighted with the arrangement, and she and Erris had packed up all their bits and pieces and moved them temporarily into the shop while they made the transition. They cleaned all Mae's belongings, whitewashed the downstairs back room and moved Mae's things out of her upstairs flat into her new quarters. They had to complete the transformation before Monday, so the shop could be opened at the usual time.

Erris had stayed home to help. She had developed into a happy, gangling eleven-year-old, still serious, very bright and the joy of Mae's life. Reanna had given Erris permission to spend most weekends with Siobhan. It was to help Seamus with teaching, so she said, but Reanna suspected she wanted to visit with her new friend, Paedar, who was about her age and the first real friend she'd ever had. Reanna had developed a fondness for him as well and looked forward to his visits. The lad had taken to coming in to town on market day with the O'Dowds and staying for supper at Reanna's.

*   *   *

Sunday afternoon, Reanna stood with her hands on her hips and surveyed the dingy upstairs flat. The great room had plank floors, a hearth and a casement window that overlooked Shop Street. Until today, it had held a good many years of an old woman's treasures. All that remained was an overstuffed chair that Liam had taken from his own room over the stables at Crofton House. Late last autumn, he'd pulled it all the way into town on a borrowed two-wheeled cart for his friend, when her bones could no more tolerate her straight hard-backed chair.

Reanna wrinkled her nose at the fusty air and opened the windows. All week, the warm sun had drifted in and out from between the clouds, but today a soft rain fell. She rolled up her sleeves, and broom in hand, attacked the cobwebs in the corners of the room; then, she put Erris to work, washing the window inside and out.

Liam's merry blue eyes and smiling face popped up from the landing. "I come to move that chair downstairs," he said. He eased it awkwardly over to the stairwell and bumped it down the stairs.

Reanna swept the turf ashes from the hearth with a straw broom, poking around the fire in the grate, and swept the two rooms clean.

"Reanna," Mae's reedy voice called from the bottom of the stairs, "would you come down here when you have a minute? I've something to show you."

Mae sat by the fire in her comfortable chair with a box in her lap. A wide smile creased her face. "Look what I came across in some papers." She held out a letter to Reanna. "It was the first word I received from Alex after he left Ballymullian. Would you care to read it?"

Reanna's heart fluttered in her chest. "I believe I would…yes." She took the folded letter from Mae's outstretched hand and hurried up the stairs. She brought it over to the window, and sat down on the floor. Her hands trembled as she opened the letter and looked at the date. He'd written it three years after Reanna had run away.

December, 1788
Paris, France

Chère Tante Mae:
I hope this letter finds you in the same good health that you enjoyed when I left Ballymullian. I apologize for taking so long to send you a letter, but so much has happened since I came back. Good and bad.

First of all, I must know, did Reanna ever return? If so, I'd like to clear up the mystery. Would you ask her to dictate a letter to you so I can put my mind to rest about what really happened that night? I keep going over it in my mind, wondering if I missed something.

I remember on the day Reanna disappeared, she had me read a letter from her cousin, Siobhan in Dunbury. Reanna spoke often of joining her in the future, but I can't believe that she would run off without telling me. This is where I reach an impasse. People don't just disappear into thin air. The puzzle remains.

And now to my news. First of all, let me say that I have no permanent address where you can write to me, but you can write to The French

Directory, Paris, France, in care of General Emile Forget, Languages Section, General Staff. He is a friend of Liam's and is my mentor. He will know where I am and will forward the letter to me.

Let me try to bring you up to date. Where shall I start? As you know, when we got word in Ballymullian that Papa had died and I had to go home, I thought my life was over and that I would have to spend the rest of my days working in the tailor shop with Pierre. When I confessed my fears to Liam, he said that tailoring would be a waste of my talent for languages, and he gave me a letter to bring to General Forget. Now that I look back on that situation, I can't imagine how it was that Liam knew the General, but at the time I felt too sorrowful about Papa to question it. His kind letter made me feel worse, because as much as I despised the idea of working under my brother in the shop, my loyalties lay with my family and I could not choose otherwise.

When I left Ballymullian, I made my way to Westport, and worked my passage back to France on a cattle boat, an experience I hope never to repeat.

Much to my surprise, I arrived home to discover that I was to be an uncle. Pierre had married himself a wife named Simone and she was enceinte. They were living in the apartment above the shop. I asked Pierre if he needed me to stay and work with him in the shop. He replied that no, he did the tailoring, Simone did the mending, and that was all that was needed. I was so greatly relieved that I signed over my half of the business to him in gratitude.

The next day, I delivered Liam's letter to General Forget. Within a week, I was in uniform, mucking out stables and grooming the officer's horses. Except for the officers' presence, I might have thought I was back at Crofton House or on that cattle boat. After six months, to my great relief, I became enrolled in language school outside of Paris, where I study to this day, happily becoming fluent in Italian and German.

You would be delighted to see Pierre now, Tante Mae. He is a happy man and I enjoy his presence as I never did when Papa was alive. He's blossomed through the goodness of Simone's love. They have an adorable little girl, Emilie, who is two years of age, and Pierre is foolish about her. She has dark eyes, like you and Maman. However, I see them only when I travel to Paris, which is not as often as I would like.

Give my best regards to Liam. I look forward to hearing from you with news of Reanna. Stay well and I will try to keep in touch with you more often.

Your loving nephew,
Alexandre Tuillere

Reanna rested her head against the wall. Memories washed over her. That last morning they were together, twelve years ago, his arms around her, his mouth firm against her own. His eyes…She jumped up, feeling muddled. This was no way for a respectable widow to feel, she told herself. She pushed the window open, captured some drops of rain in her cupped hands, ran them over her flushed face, dried her face and hands on her apron and brought the letter back downstairs to Mae.

"It was a grand read, thank you Mae," Reanna said and handed the letter back to her.

"I have more here somewhere," Mae said, digging in the box.

"I really must get back upstairs, Mae. We need to get the whitewash done while we can catch the light." She softened her refusal. "Besides which, I'd like to sit down and read them when I have the time to enjoy them." She turned to go, then turned back again.

"Where is Alex now, then?"

"I don't know," Mae said worriedly, "the last letter I received from him was two years ago. I am beginning to wonder if he is safe."

"I'm sure he is, Mae. As his next of kin, you'd surely have heard from the French Army if anything was wrong." Reanna headed for the stairs. "Enough woolgathering."

She hummed contentedly to herself as she brushed the whitewash back and forth over the dingy walls, her mind skipping around in six directions at once.

"Mam," Erris called from across the room.

Reanna looked over enquiringly at her daughter who squatted on the floor, brushing whitewash over the bottom half of the wall.

"What is it?" she answered absently.

"Why did you lie to Aunt Mae about our Da?" Erris croaked in a half whisper.

Reanna felt her heart skip a beat. She put a finger up to her mouth with a "wssht", dropped her brush into the bucket, hurried over to Erris and sat down in front of her.

"It's a long story." Her fingers pleated her shift nervously, and then gently asked, "What do you remember of the last days in Dunbury?"

"I remember when Da came home and grabbed the tin box from the chiffonier and we had to leave," Erris said, her eyes looking very big in her face.

"Do you know why we had to leave, then?"

"I do. It was because Da stole money from his work."

Reanna's throat was so dry she thought she would choke. "Why would you say such a thing, Erris?"

Erris's voice broke, "I heard you and Da talking that night when we slept on Seamus and Siobhan's floor. You thought I was sleeping, but I wasn't." She swiped at the tears in her eyes.

Reanna felt tears gathering in her own throat. She took her child in her arms and stroked her hair. "Shhh, ansa," she whispered. "I never wanted you to know about that. I wanted you to have good memories of your Da."

In a muffled voice, Erris answered. " I do have good memories. He was my Da and he loved me."

Reanna asked hesitantly, "What else did you hear?"

"I heard the bad thing that happened to you and what you did to that awful man."

Reanna began to cry softly. "Erris," she said, "you must never tell anyone about any of this. Your Da's crime is why I had to tell Mae we were from Sligo." She took Erris's arms in her two hands and spoke in a measured voice. "No one must ever know we're from Dunbury."

"But we don't even have the money anymore, Benny stole it."

"It makes no difference, does it? The fact of the matter is, a crime has been committed, and no one has been punished for it yet. If the authorities find us, the punishment will be mine."

She heard the third step creak and placed a finger up to her lips.

*   *   *

Liam crept back down the stairs and spilled these new developments directly into Mae's ear.

*   *   *

Monday morning, Reanna and Mae stood together, grinning at the newly renovated shop, paid for from the proceeds from Reanna's gold and ruby wedding ring. Liam had built shelves onto the wall that separated the shop from Mae's new living quarters.

Reanna had replaced the shabby curtain with a length of linen damask. She and Erris gave the whole of the downstairs a coat of whitewash, and scrubbed the black slate floor until it shone. The supplies that Reanna had ordered had arrived and now the freshly painted display counter held rolls of red, topaz and cobalt blue ribbons set out on creamy lace, and a tall vase held brightly colored peacock feathers and a variety of amber and jade hat pins. Bolts of netting, jewel-toned velvet and felt filled the shelves. The hat stands stood proudly once again, showing off their latest creations.

Mae's hats were works of art, sedate in design, with each stitch precisely executed. What Reanna lacked in craftsmanship, she made up in style. Her head was full of ideas, and once she learned the basics of hat making, she was able to make reasonable copies of the fashions she remembered seeing in Dunbury.

Reanna walked over to the hat stands and removed her latest creation, a claret colored velvet hat with an upswept brim. With the exception that her own hat had been emerald green with a peacock feather on the brim, it was a duplicate of one she had admired in Dunbury, the first time she had walked out with Donald. He had bought it without her knowledge and given it to her as a wedding gift. It was her favorite, and she knew it had cost him a pretty penny.

She walked over to the looking glass, smoothed the bodice of her navy blue dress, positioned the hat behind her fashionable upswept hairdo, and secured it with a hatpin. She pinched her cheeks and bit her lips to add more color. With eyes bright in happiness, she twirled away from the looking glass. "What do you think of this, Mae?"

Mae looked reflective. "The style looks lovely on you Reanna. It sets off the fire in your hair."

"I'm going to make a green one next, with a peacock feather on the brim."

"Where do you get your ideas?"

Reanna's face flushed with shame for taking undeserved credit for the designs. She dropped her eyes and made a production out of removing the hat and replacing it on the stand. She stood for a moment in reflection, with her back to Mae, sick of the deception she felt forced to live. She had felt a load lift from her back on discovering that Erris knew of Donald's crime, and had been waiting for an opportunity to tell Mae the truth about her past. It's as good a time as any, she decided and turned around to do so, when the tinkle of the doorbell announced the first customer of the day.

For the first time since last October when she began her apprentice-ship, the doorbell had caught Reanna off guard. To ward off meeting anyone from her past, she'd made a practice of sitting at her work in the shop with a good view of the door. At the first sight of anyone, she excused herself and slipped into the back room until they left. However, with the onset of winter and Mae's trouble with her legs, the little spin-ster had been spending more and more time sewing in her comfortable chair in front of the fire, leaving Reanna to attend to customers.

With her heart in her throat, Reanna spun around. A pouter pigeon of a woman swept through the door. She wore a fashionable gray coat and a pair of tiny spectacles perched on her beak-like nose. She was fol-lowed by a little dumpling of a woman, who barely stopped chattering long enough to take a breath.

"Look over here, Irene," she said in a stage whisper as if those around her were deaf.

"Didn't I tell you these hats were every bit as nice as the ones you see in Dunbury?" She bounced from hat to hat. "Isn't this lovely!" she exclaimed, her pudding face beaming as she held up the hat that Reanna had tried on for Mae.

The older woman looked at the hat with disdain. "Of course it is, Finola. As it happens, it's almost an exact duplicate of one I have at home…one that I bought in Dunbury last year."

The blood drained from Reanna's face and she'd have sold her soul to be anywhere but in this room. Mae noticed the panic on Reanna's face and stepped forward to smooth the waters. Reanna feared her friend was about to defend her honor and was not about to allow Mae to lie for her. Reanna put a restraining hand on the old woman's arm and stepped forward. She lifted one of Mae's latest creations off its stand and with a bright smile on her face, walked over and placed herself between both women. She presented the hat to the pouter pigeon as though it were gold. "This is one of the finest hats we have in the shop, madam."

Reanna placed the hat against the gray sleeve. "Look how beautifully the plum tones complement your coat."

The woman plucked the hat from Reanna's hands and checked the workmanship thoroughly. She removed the hatpins from her plain gray hat, and set it on the counter. "It won't hurt to try it on," she said grudgingly, "but I have quite enough hats at home."

"I promise you, not like this one," Reanna countered. "It truly is one of a kind. May I?" she asked, removing the hat from the woman's hands and placing it on the severe pompadour. She arranged the veil in a cloud around the upswept brim, and held the mirror up to her customer's face.

"The effect is quite charming, madam," breathed Reanna, amazed at the truth of what she was saying. The softness of the veil and a little color had made a remarkable improvement in the woman's appearance.

"Yes, I quite agree," the woman said breathlessly, as though she could hardly believe it herself. "I believe I'll take it with me."

*   *   *

When the door closed behind the two women, Reanna turned to Mae, who said nothing, but searched Reanna's eyes with her own. Reanna lifted her hands and then dropped them to her sides. "I don't know where to begin, Mae."

"How about where we left off…when you left Ballymullian?" Mae led the way into the back of the shop. Reanna followed, feeling like a convicted criminal.

Mae hung her cane over her arm and silently poured milk and tea into their cups. She placed Reanna's tea in front of her and joined her at the small table.

Reanna looked downcast. "Now that I've broken your trust, will you even believe the truth when you hear it?"

"I've had no reason to consider you a liar in the past Reanna, and so it must be a very serious matter for you to put yourself in this position."

"Oh, it is Mae, and I wonder if in my whole life, I will ever feel safe again." She took a deep breath. "First of all, Sligo was a lie. I ran away to Dunbury, where I met and married a Presbyterian draper named Donald Campbell. We had Reanna, and for ten years I thought I was safe, and then he died and my life fell apart again." She put her head down on the table and sobs racked her body.

Mae pulled a fresh handkerchief out of her sleeve and reached across the table and placed it in Reanna's hand. "What was the terrible thing that made you run away in the first place, then?"

Reanna raised her head, "I was working late at Crofton House, cleaning up after Lord and Lady Dalton's anniversary party," she said woodenly. "Lord Dalton had been drinking. I went into Lady Margaret's room. He caught me unawares and threw me down. I tried to get away, but he was too strong for me. I couldn't stop him." She fumbled a handkerchief out of her sleeve and held it against her streaming eyes. "I grabbed a candlestick and I kept hitting him and hitting him." She put her face in her hands, ashamed to look at Mae. "I was that ashamed and frightened at what I'd done, I ran to Dunbury to Siobhan."

Mae made the sign of the cross on her bosom and stroked Reanna's hair. "Jesus, Mary and Joseph," she said, "what a terrible thing to have happened to a child such as yourself." She sat lost in thought for a moment. "Although it makes sense now, because Alex went back there looking for you when you didn't show up that night, you know. He said when he got there, all the lights were out in the house, so he walked around to the stable yard, and saw a light coming from the scullery window. He tapped on the glass and Maire let him in the back door. She told him that you'd come roaring down the servant's staircase and out the back door two hours before. She said she didn't know why and seemed reluctant to say any more."

"She must have suspected what happened," Reanna sobbed, "for it was herself told me to be on the lookout for the wretched sot."

"Well, it was all kept very hush-hush," Mae said. "The next day, Alex told me that Harriet, the housekeeper, called everyone together in the library and told them that you'd run off, and anyone caught gossiping about your disappearance would be dismissed without pay; then she put one of the housemaids to work checking that nothing was missing out of Lady Margaret's room."

"Reanna's voice wavered, "For ten years I've wondered if I killed him. I was afraid to contact anyone down here, so I still don't know if he's dead or alive." She wiped her tears on the balled up handkerchief.

"Well, set your mind to rest on that score, child, you didn't kill him. He must have gotten up and walked away, more's the pity. He did die, though…on a hunt three years ago. His horse threw him and he broke his neck."

Mae's words of reprieve left Reanna weak with relief. "Probably riding drunk."

The tinkle of the doorbell announced the arrival of a visitor at the shop door. Mae struggled to her feet and patted Reanna on the shoulder. "Someday, you can tell me the rest if you like, my dear. Stay here and compose yourself. I'll take care of things for awhile." She tottered out of the room into the front of the shop. Reanna put her head down on the table and wept tears of relief.

Chapter 9

―――――▼―――――

Rathskill Mountain, April 1797

At mid morning, Seamus finished teaching his lesson and raised his cramped body from its position under the hawthorn tree. He shivered. Spring had not yet dissipated the dampness from the ground. He felt chilled through as he trod the road back to the cabin to check on Siobhan. She had to stay in bed oftener than she wanted to these days and was not suffering idleness gladly. He poked his head into the warm cabin and went over to where his wife lay on her back, belly bulging under the brown blanket. He lifted up a corner and examined the blue-knotted veins that zigzagged down the length of her swollen legs and ankles.

"How are the legs today, my girl?" he asked cheerfully, as he rolled up a second blanket and positioned it under her knees to ease her back. He dipped a tin cup into the bucket of water and brought it to her to drink.

She struggled to a sitting position and held her hand out for the water. "I'm not able to stay upright for any longer than bits at a time." She sank down on the bed with a sigh. "I'm feeling that discouraged, Seamus. God forgive me for saying so, but I'll be that relieved when it's over and done with."

He walked over to the hearth and rasped his cold hands together over the turf fire. "It will be well worth it, you'll see."

She said to his back, "When I heard the door open, I thought it was that cursed Bandy, back again."

"And what did he want this time?"

"Not a thing, as far as I could tell. Where is yer man, Missus?" she mimicked. "As if you were not to be seen sitting in the field among your pupils." She struggled to a sitting position again and swung her feet over the side of the bed. "I tell you, Seamus, he's going to feel the sharp edge of my tongue one of these days."

Seamus stood with his back to the hearth, toasting his bum in the heat of the fire.

"Well, try not to let the man's ignorance upset you, Siobhan," he teased. "You wouldn't wish our child to be born with your wicked temper, would you?"

"You'll not make light of it," she snapped, not to be cheated out of her righteous indignation. "This morning I was trying to rest my poor legs, and in he struts, with never a by your leave, as though he lives here. I won't have him trotting in here any time he feels the urge. Do we not pay rent that we need to be haunted by that little bagger?"

"God knows it's little enough rent to pay for the comfort we live in," he soothed, trying to appease the outburst he could feel building up in her voice.

"That isn't the point of it, is it?" she replied crossly.

He smothered the angry retort that surged to his lips, for he knew Siobhan was not herself these days, but the memory of those who had died needlessly this past winter, still weighed heavy on his heart. He remembered that just a few short months before, snow and sleet in record amounts, accompanied by freezing winds, piled the snow up in drifts against the Rathskill Mountain. The unseasonable cold killed thousands, huddled in their makeshift huts, without heat or enough food. Seamus and Siobhan had discovered their share of frozen bodies on their daily rounds as they and their neighbors checked on the less fortunate. He remembered Siobhan's tortured face, as she carried the stiff, small body of a child out of a frigid hut and placed it tenderly beside the other bodies in a cart. He saw again in his mind, the steady procession of carts squeaking over the snow, filled with the naked bodies of the dead. Carts pulled by people barely alive themselves, who appeared as wraiths in the fog filled morning. Bare feet and hands wrapped in rags, eyes visible through whatever could be found to cover their heads. Bodies clothed in whatever could be rescued from those they put in the wagons. Every night, he and Siobhan had counted their blessings and given thanks on their knees for the roof over their heads and now this, whining from one of the fortunate!

He shook himself loose from the sad memories of the past winter, but still upset with her, felt he just had to have his say. "The point is, my girl, you need to count your blessings."

Siobhan put her hands over her face and her body shook, "Aah, God, Seamus, I don't mean to sound ungrateful, for I know you do the best you're able, but when that little bagger walks in unannounced like that, I feel as if he's warning us not to get too comfortable, reminding us that we live here by his grace; and if we don't toe the line, he could snatch it right out from underneath us." She reached her arms out to him.

He walked over and sat on the bed beside her. He patted her hair clumsily, his emotions in turmoil. He would deal with Bandy's bullying tactics at their next meeting. He would not have his wife upset this way.

"I'm that frightened to be so helpless, Seamus." She clutched at his arms. "I have such bad dreams about us out in the weather when I deliver our child."

"It won't happen, Siobhan. I'll speak to him. I promise you this, you'll be in your warm cabin and I'll be beside you." He kissed her on the cheek and said wearily, "Rest now, I have to get back to my pupils."

Seamus closed the door after himself and with book in hand, limped painfully down the road toward the open field where he was to give his afternoon class. The stab wound in his thigh had healed over, but left a deep scar on his leg, and when the damp, cold weather settled in as it had this past winter, his leg ached horribly. But the scar on his soul, received in the alley, and the ache from that encounter, never left him.

As he slogged down the road, his thoughts returned to Siobhan's tirade and her anger at Bandy. He had rarely seen her so upset. He balled up his fists. "You crossed the line this time, you little weasel," he muttered, "I may have to put up with you for now, but I'll not have you use your bullying tactics on my wife."

Anguish gripped his heart. He had hoped by now to be out from under Bandy's thumb, but it was not to be. Up to this point, he'd been paid very little by his pupils; a few potatoes, some cabbages and carrots, a couple of coins and the promise of more. From the rest, he received a multitude of thanks. The potatoes kept starvation away from the door, but any coin went to Bandy for the rent of Hennessy's cabin. He had nothing put aside in the event that Hennessy returned and wanted to move back into his own cabin. It was a great worry and disappointment to him altogether.

Seamus nodded a greeting to his pupils, sat himself down with his back against the hawthorn tree and opened his book. He looked up and saw Bandy and some of the lads making a seat for themselves in the crowd. Bandy scuttled up to the front row, shoved one of the children aside and plunked himself down dead center, as if he were the king himself. He gave Seamus a wave of his hand indicating that he could begin the lesson and sat back with his arms folded, waiting to be entertained.

Seamus's cheeks burned in anger at the brass of him. " You little shite," he muttered to himself, "if it's a lesson you came for, it's a lesson you'll have."

He closed the book, raised himself to his full height and looked out at the field of faces, men and women as well as children.

"I want to talk about oppression," he began, "and then I want to talk about poverty." Bandy's face split open in a grin of approval. He nodded his head at Seamus.

Seamus gave him a thunderous scowl and went on. "I want to talk about poverty of mind and poverty of spirit."

He raised his voice. "For hundreds of years Ireland has been squirming beneath the English boot. The first question arises: do we want to raise ourselves out of the slime of tyranny and have our country back into our own hands? If the answer is yes, and it is, the second question arises: how can we do it? To answer that, we have to look at what we've done in the past. We've retaliated against tyranny with the same kind of violence that has been used against us. Are we any better off? No, we are not. Will we ever be better off, using violence? I don't believe we will."

The eyes of the audience began to slide around the crowd, locating Bandy and his thugs, in anticipation of their reaction to Seamus's words. Bandy sat under a thundercloud. His thugs eyed each other and awaited Bandy's instructions. Seamus began to pace back and forth, propelled by memories of his own encounter with violence in the alley in Dunbury.

"If we kill, are captured and punished, a life and a mind that could have been used for benefit to ourselves and others is cut short. If we kill and make our escape and have to spend the rest of our lives looking over our shoulders for our pursuers, we still lose our lives and minds, for we can't give fully to the future if we are forced daily to confront our deeds of the past." He paused, "England will always have bigger and better guns than we do. Retaliation is not the way we are going to get our country back, I don't believe."

Bandy struggled to his feet, finger in the air. Seamus pointed at him and roared, "You will sit down and be still until I have finished."

The runty man dropped back down like a stone, mouth agape in disbelief. His lads sniggered behind their hands at his discomfort.

Seamus went on, "I believe we are going to have to change our methods. I believe," he said calmly, "that we must educate ourselves, and use our wits instead of guns. We need to study the enemy, learn his ways, and figure out which of his methods worked for him in the past and which didn't, learn from his mistakes and use his own methods to fight him. In the process, we find out how our own minds work. We find out who the Irish are, not what we've been told we are for hundreds of years, by someone who has only contempt for us."

He held his hands up in supplication. "I believe speaking the Irish tongue in our homes is a grand way to maintain our heritage, but the fact is, to free our land, we must learn to speak English."

The crowd began to shift in place. Murmurs of anger began to gain volume at the nerve of this Ulsterman telling them to replace the mother tongue with the hated English language.

"Be still," he roared, "I will have my say." He glared out at his audience as though daring anyone to interrupt again.

With arms folded, they sullenly returned his gaze.

Seamus slapped a finger in his palm. "First, we need to speak English so we understand what the enemy says when he talks about us, for what he says about us tells us something about himself."

"Second," he said, "we need to learn to read, for as long as we can read, we can't be denied an education. It's easy to control the ignorant, for they don't know any different. Do you suppose it would be easy to control someone who is onto your game and is wary of your every move? I don't suppose." He enunciated every word, slapping his hand into his palm for emphasis, "Until we can read, we are dependent on the opinions of others." He hesitated. "If someone reads to us, they are choosing for us what we will know. If we learn to read, we begin to think for ourselves." Some in the audience listened attentively, some leaned back on their hands and waited. Bandy and his thugs sat with lips compressed.

"Third, we must learn to write English, for it's by writing that we learn to express our ideas and to communicate them to others who need to hear what we have to say. Writing also gives us freedom of expression." He paused to let his words sink in and then went on. "For example, if someone writes a letter for us, we choose our words carefully, for fear of judgment or reprisal. But, if we write it ourselves, we pour our hearts out freely onto the page, knowing that the only eyes that will see it are the eyes of the one it's intended for." He saw tears in the eyes of some of the grown-ups.

"Fourth," he said, "we must learn arithmetic, for it tells us where we've been, shows us where we are, and helps us decide where we are going." He looked out at the sea of faces and saw puzzlement at his words. "Why do we need to know any of this? Because it is this logic that separates us from the animals the English would have us believe we are."

He bent over and picked up a stone. "For the sake of argument, this is a coin. I know how I got it, for it was myself picked it up off the ground. I know that I have it, for I see it in my hand, and it sure as the devil tells me something about the future. It tells me I need to obtain more of them to pay my rent. It prods me to plan for my future and gets me to thinking of ways to get ahead, d' you see?" He held the stone up for emphasis and added with a wry smile, "We also need to learn arithmetic to know if we are being cheated." He dropped the stone at his feet.

"Now, I just want to say a few words on poverty of spirit. If we are not able to read, we lose the opportunity to be inspired by the teachings of others, from the Bible to the great minds of literature. To read allows us to travel beyond our shores, to stretch our imaginations, to discover new solutions for our problems. God knows poverty of the flesh is sad indeed, but poverty of spirit is the saddest of all. It hides in the darkness and mimics only what it sees." He tucked his book underneath his arm. "If we are not able to write, we are not able to put down on paper the full expression of our souls. We may hold the most wonderful of thoughts in our heads, but if we haven't the knowledge to commit them to paper, they die with us and are gone forever, for each of us is given a voice that no one else speaks." He held his book up in the air.

"There are those among us who knuckle under and will starve when there is food to be had and freeze to death in their huts while others have heat. There are those among us who will pick up the pike and die at the hand of the Englishman. But the best of us will educate ourselves, find our own voice and use it for change." His eyes looked into the tearful faces of the crowd before him. "And when the roar of millions of Irish people, Catholic and Protestant united together, are raised in a single voice, the world will have to listen."

His lesson concluded, he turned and limped out of the field. Bandy, followed by his lads, got to his feet and ran after Seamus, intercepting him at the road.

"What in the hell do you think you're doin' feeding that pap to them?" He spit on the ground. "That for your education. You know and I know that the truth of the matter is the only way we'll ever have our country back is to take it."

Bandy's lads began to nod their heads in agreement.

Seamus let fly at him, "I know no such thing. I will teach as I see fit. If you don't approve of my classes, then stay the hell away from them." He shook his finger in the little man's face, "and while you're at it, stay the hell away from my wife and home as well."

Bandy looked around at his thugs, who were having a giggle at his expense. He hopped up and down in anger. Spittle flew out of his mouth. "You'll be sorry." He shook a dirty finger at Seamus. "You don't know who you're tanglin' with. When we get through with you, you'll wish you'd died in that alley in Dunbury"

Seamus twisted his hand in the little man's clothes and pulled him up to his face. "Quit off, you little runt, or I'll root your arse into the middle of next week." He dropped him sprawling in the dirt and walked off under a thundercloud.

A voice hailed him from behind. He stopped and looked around. It was Liam in a two wheeled jaunting cart pulled by a long bodied sorrel horse. He pulled up beside Seamus, helped him up onto the seat beside him, and clicked his tongue at the brown and white horse. The cart jerked to life and the horse clopped slowly down the dirt road.

Liam looked sideways at Seamus's angry face. "I had some business to do for Crofton House out this way, and Reanna asked me to drop this parcel off to Siobhan while I was about it."

The two men rode along in silence. Finally, Liam spoke, "I heard your lesson," he said quietly, "and your words with Bandy."

"Unfortunately, those words with Bandy may have cost us a place to live."

"Bandy is the least of your worries, Seamus."

"What do you mean, Liam?"

"I'm talking about you and Siobhan living in Hennessy's cabin."

"We pay Bandy good money for the rent of that cabin," Seamus said defensively.

"Well then, Bandy may be in more trouble than you are. From what I hear, no one is allowed in that cabin in Hennessy's absence except Bandy, and him only to get provisions in when Hennessy is due. And furthermore, when he is here, the only ones to enter or leave are Bandy and his thugs."

"What are you saying?" Seamus asked wearily.

"I'm saying these people are not just scrappers, they are anarchists hiding under the banner of the SUI and you'd do well to be out and away of it."

"I wish to God I was able to be. You see, by now I'd hoped to have a few coins put aside from teaching and writing letters," Seamus said, "but it hasn't worked out that way. Teaching feeds us, and there's been no letter writing to speak of."

Liam scratched his head, "Well, you know, the priest has always written letters for the poor unfortunates that can't write. But, until you rid yourself of Bandy and the likes of him, don't expect people to be flocking to your door for any reason, especially when the door you're standing behind belongs to Hennessy."

They rode along in silence along the rutted road, the horse's tail switching flies away from his back.

"Who is this man, Hennessy?"

"From what little I know of the man, he's not someone to be fooled with. In any case, if Bandy is renting Hennessy's cabin to you without his knowledge, and pocketing the rent money, he is flirting with his miserable life. On the other hand, if Hennessy is aware that you're living in his cabin, you may be in deeper water than you want to be. He'll not let you live there out of the goodness of his heart. He'll be around to collect his pound of flesh one of these days."

"When did we become our own enemies, Liam?"

Liam shrugged. "When the SUI lost control of itself, I guess, and people either left the movement, or did like Hennessy and this lot, paid the movement lip service, but made up their own rules."

"If the SUI knows who they are, why do they not get rid of them?"

"I don't think they are as organized as they could be anymore, or maybe they have their own reasons. There are a few isolated pockets of SUI with strong ideals that still exist around the country. A word to the wise," he whispered in Seamus's ear, "Wolfe Tone himself is said to be in Paris, trying to get the Frenchies to aid us in a revolution."

Seamus's eyes widened in wonder. "You seem to be pretty well informed for a groomsman, Liam."

"In these times, it pays to keep your eyes and ears open and your mouth closed." He added, "I don't miss much."

"God help us all," breathed Seamus.

Chapter 10

▼

Ballymullian, April 1797

Reanna looked forward to Sundays and a short respite from the hectic week. When the bell at the Anglican Church pealed seven, she'd poked up the fire and dished up the porridge. After breakfast, she helped Mae with her ablutions and settled her in her chair with the beribboned box she'd requested. Reanna had tidied up Mae's flat as well as her own and looked forward to a quiet hour to herself before she prepared lunch for herself and Mae.

Reanna pushed open the window of her upstairs flat and looked down onto the quiet street. On Sundays, Shop Street virtually shut itself down except for the comings and goings of the people who lived there and an occasional horse and carriage that clopped by on its way to somewhere else. Now there was only Erris who turned and blew a kiss at her mother before starting out on the four-mile walk to the mountain to help Seamus teach. This April day had started out soft and bright, but now dark clouds loomed overhead. Thunder rumbled and echoed in the distance. Reanna hoped Erris made it to Siobhan's before the rains came. On black days such as this one promised to be, Seamus usually crowded as many pupils as could be held in the small cabin, and taught the lesson indoors. Poor Siobhan, Reanna thought, already as big as the cabin she lives in. All she needs in the world is to be jammed in with twenty more bodies.

Reanna gave the red and white patchwork quilts a shake out the window, then lifted both back into the room and made up the beds.

She sat in front of the fire, two letters from Alex in her hands. They'd been burning a hole in her pocket ever since Mae had given them to her a few days ago. She'd made herself wait until she could sit down quietly by herself to read them. All the more enjoyable for the waiting.

She unfolded the first one, smoothed it flat on her lap and read the seven-year-old letter written two years after he'd written the first one.

February 1790
Paris, France
Chère Tante Mae:
I was so happy to receive your letter when I got back from America. I'm sorry to hear that you've still had no news of Reanna. I guess we'll never know what happened to her. Tell Liam that I still keep the peacock feather from Crofton House that he enclosed with your letter. I've missed his good humor. I'm happy to report that I no longer have to clean up after the animals, be it peacock, horse or cattle.

Two years ago, I gained the rank of Lieutenant and was assigned to the General Staff as an interpreter. I had the opportunity to travel to America where I met a man by the name of Thomas Paine and an Irishman by the name of Wolfe Tone, who by the by, is in exile from Ireland.

When I left France, I knew the country was in a state of unrest, but by the time I returned the next year, we were in the midst of a full-scale revolution. A mob had stormed the Bastille, ousted King Louis XVI and installed a new government. Since then, all has been in upheaval. Governments come and go like courtesans through the palace doors. Everywhere, there is violence. The last time I returned to Paris, entire blocks of the city had been torched and burned to the ground.

I'm concerned for Pierre and his little family. He puts on a brave face, but I know he is worried for their safety. Simone is so good for him, and Emilie, who is four years of age, grows sweeter every day. However, I don't get to see them any oftener than I did before, which you know by now is not often. I am out of the country for months at a time on assignment, mostly out of the line of fire, and for that I am grateful.

In haste, I remain, your loving nephew,
Alexandre Tuillere

Reanna put her head back against the back of the chair and smiled. She remembered the incident of the peacock feather. When Alex worked in the stables at Crofton House, it was his responsibility to keep the jaunting cart cleaned, polished and ready to go, in the event that Lady Dalton decided to use it for other than her regular Sunday drives. However, she also owned a peacock, of whose feathers she was inordinately fond. She used them to freshen up her hats, and also had them sharpened for the writing quills she displayed prominently in a brass holder on her desk. The peacock had chosen the jaunting cart for its own private toilet, usually right after Alex had finished polishing it and many times in between. After many futile grabs at his tormentor, the day came when, to his own amazement, Alex made contact with a sizable handful of tail feathers, which left the peacock looking decidedly gap-tailed and Alex frightened out of his wits in expected recrimination. Reanna chuckled and picked up the second letter. It was three years old.

December 1793
Paris, France

Chère Tante Mae:
I'm writing to you from a hospital where I am recovering from burns to my back, received in Germany this year as our troops were retreating. I'm afraid I am the bearer of sad news. I arrived back in Paris a few weeks ago

in the midst of rioting. I made haste to the tailor shop to find the whole block in flames and the shop burned to the ground. My dear Pierre and his family had burned to death in their beds. I shed tears again as I think about it. You and I are all that's left of our family now.

Our country is gripped by a reign of terror. It is in so much upheaval, I wonder if it can ever survive itself. I hear numbers of forty thousand people being killed in the riots in Paris alone. The governments change as rapidly as one changes clothes. As one government takes power, another is there to challenge it. Will we ever live through it, I wonder? King Louis XV1 and Marie Antoinette were executed this year along with a lot of other prominent people, whose names probably aren't familiar to you. Close to where I'm billeted is a square that is set up with a guillotine. Public executions are held daily. People gather around to watch as the severed heads fall into baskets. I can't believe what is happening to us and our country. I am so despondent. At times, I regret ever having left Ballymullian. Except for the last few years with Pierre and his family, I look back on that year with you, Liam and Reanna as among the happiest of my life.

Take care, ma Chère Tante Mae. I think of you often.
Your loving nephew,
Alexandre Tuillere.

The letter dropped to the floor as Reanna covered her face with her hands and wept. Poor Alex, to lose Pierre after all the years it had taken to become friends as well as brothers. She and Erris knew only too well the heartbreak of that loss. She took a handkerchief out of her sleeve and wiped her eyes.

*   *   *

She remembered the first time Alex had mentioned his family to her. Thanks to Fergus, Reanna had shown up with a red welt across her cheek when she came to pick up Alex for work. He'd listened in horror to her tales of life with Ma and Fergus, sympathized with Reanna's loneliness for Siobhan and listened to her dream of reuniting with her cousin someday.

Reanna had asked him about his own family. He told her that when he was seven years of age and his brother Pierre was eleven, their mother, who was his Aunt Mae's only sister, died of consumption. Alex's eyes had filled with tears as he confessed that his father seemed to turn to stone after her death. He insisted that Pierre and I learn tailoring, for he said that someday he would be dead and gone and we would inherit the business.

Reanna had taken his hand then, for the very first time. His words came out in a rush after that, as though he'd had them locked inside himself too long. "We lived above the tailor shop in a small flat," he'd told her. "Some days we didn't leave the building except to shop for dinner. I told Papa I didn't want to be a tailor and spend my life up and down between two floors, but he didn't listen. He never did." Alex's voice had turned bitter then. "I watched Pierre turn into a fussy fart just like Papa, both of them sitting stooped over, backs to the window." He remembered the heaped up counter of smelly clothing that needed repairing, and Papa and Pierre with pins sticking out from between their lips, fingers busy stitching and mending. "I watched the business swallow them both up." Alex's yellow eyes had widened then. "Pierre didn't even notice girls and he was almost twenty years of age. I didn't want to spend the rest of my life with my back to the world. I spoke to Papa about my desire to leave, hoping to gain his approval. He strictly forbade it. That's when I decided to leave without his approval. I left him a note and left on a cargo ship headed for Ireland and Aunt Mae."

Reanna felt again the warmth that had grown between them. It was confidences such as these that had cemented the bond between them in the year that followed.

*   *   *

The sound of a child's voice drew Reanna back to the present. She flew to the window and opened the latch. She saw Erris, speeding towards home, bare feet flying, shoes flapping around her neck. "Mam!" she cried.

"What is it, Erris?"

"Mam, come quick! It's Aunt Siobhan. The baby is coming. She needs you."

Reanna hesitated only a moment. So far, she had avoided going back to the place that held such bad memories for her, but she had to put her own feelings aside. Siobhan needed her. She threw her shawl over her shoulders and hurried down the stairs into the dim room. She tiptoed over to where Mae was dozing, her box of assorted memories in her lap. Her skin had an unhealthy gray pallor, Reanna noticed, but when she'd questioned her earlier, Mae had dismissed the inquiry with a wave of her hand and refused to discuss it again. But lately, she spent most of the daylight hours wrapped up in front of the fire, leaving Reanna to run the shop.

Reanna dipped a fresh glass of water from the pail and set it on the table within easy reach.

She kissed the old woman on her forehead and shook her gently. "Mae."

Mae stirred and opened her eyes. "What is it?"

"I have to go to Siobhan now. The baby is coming, but I'll be home as soon as I can. Will you be all right by yourself?"

The little spinster smiled weakly and waved her away. "I'll be fine, Reanna. You run along and take care of Siobhan. Liam will be over right after Mass."

"Have him fix you a bite to eat," Reanna called back and closed the door behind her.

Erris took her mother's arm and they hurried down the street. They hadn't gotten past the bakery next door, when Erris's voice interrupted her flight. "Mam, your shoes," she said, pointing down at Reanna's shod feet.

Reanna frowned her displeasure, but bent down and removed her shoes. She refused to tie them around her neck, but held them underneath her shawl instead. They hurried down Shop Street as the Anglican Church bells pealed twelve o'clock. Lightning flashed, followed closely by a clap of thunder. They pulled their shawls over their heads and lifted up their skirts so they could run faster. Reanna tied her shoes around her neck. She needed both hands to keep her shawl from being blown off her back. The sky opened up, and huge drops of rain splattered onto the cobbles and bounced back up against their legs as they ran. By the time they reached the wooden bridge, they were soaked to the skin.

*   *   *

They walked hurriedly along the coast road. There had always been a large population of the poor, but in the ten years she had been gone, Catholic refugees from Ulster had migrated here for safety and thousands more cabins had been thrown up. They were lined up cheek by jowl by the roadside and spread out across the landscape as far as the eye could see. Only the bog remained cabinless, and it looked as though it had been harvested within an inch of its life. As a child, Reanna had stood in the bog and watched as men with slanes had sliced through the marshy green moss into the black bog below. They removed thick slabs of the turf, sliced the slabs into bricks, and arranged them in ricks to dry in the sun. She had imagined that the bog was inhabited by a family of black, slab-faced bog people with green hair. She had given them names and watched the family grow as new patches were cut. Now, she thought, the bog resembled nothing as much as the side of an enormous layered cake checkered deep with cuts.

The storm eased off as Reanna and Erris came within sight of the bay. It was low tide, and the wind rippled the surface of the dark channel that ran down the middle of the bay. Seagulls, who had waited out the storm from the shelter of the rock outcroppings on the beach, screeched their displeasure at the speckled cormorants who flocked to the mud flats along the shore, long necks reaching, hooked beaks voraciously scooping up every edible thing that lay in their paths. Seagulls picked up cockles and clams in their beaks, flew high and dropped them to shatter on the rocks below, where they could be retrieved and pried open with ease.

"Mam," Reanna asked in a small voice, "is Aunt Siobhan going to die?"

"Musha good God, not at all. Erris, why would you ask such a thing?"

"Because when I arrived this morning, I saw Uncle Seamus carrying her out of the field in his arms. He told me to run back to Father Meehan and have him announce that the reading class would be canceled for today."

"You do know Aunt Siobhan's having a baby, don't you?"

Erris put her head down and rolled her eyes at the obvious question. "Yes, Mam, I know that," she said patiently, "but by the time I got to the cabin, Aunt Siobhan was in bed and she was moaning." She added, worriedly, "Uncle Seamus was sitting beside her, patting her hand. I wanted to help, but Uncle Seamus said not to pester her. Aunt Siobhan asked me to run home and get you. So I did."

"Don't worry about Aunt Siobhan, love. She'll be fine in a while. Having a baby takes time and it does take a lot out of you. Once it's born though, Siobhan will forget she ever had pain. That's the thing about childbirth," she explained cheerfully, "it takes a long time to deliver the baby, but once its over you forget all about the pain." She sent a little prayer heavenward. God forgive me for my lies…but it wouldn't do to tell the child horror stories just yet, there being plenty of time for that after she's had a child of her own and can exchange some stories herself.

She looked down the road toward Bonnagh Head. More cabins. They reached the crossroads at the foot of the mountain. Nothing looked as

Reanna remembered, with the addition of so many more cabins and trails leading to them. She let Erris lead the way. When they left the road and started up a path toward the foot of the mountain, she realized that they were headed in the general direction of where she and Siobhan had been raised. She absently drew her shawl forward on her face. She looked forward to seeing the cabin where Siobhan's parents had lived. She didn't recognize it when she did get there. The whitewashed walls were filthy, the sod roof bowed in the middle, a slovenly woman, arms resting on top of the decrepit half door, fastened a beady eye on them, while a skinny pig rooted in what used to be a little patch of garden alongside the door.

Siobhan must have been heart-broken when she saw this, Reanna thought, and felt a twinge of remorse that Siobhan hadn't felt free enough to mention the fact to her. Since their return, Reanna had thwarted any conversation that involved the past or any part of it.

Now that she was here, she was curious to know if the shack she was raised in, still stood, but that could wait until another time. Siobhan needed her. She plucked at her daughter's sleeve. "We'd better hurry, Erris."

Erris led them down a path to a solidly built cabin with a sod roof. Seamus welcomed them in, wrung out their shawls and placed them by the fire to dry.

"She's sleeping now," he said relieved. "I'm glad you came, Reanna."

"I'm awake, Seamus," Siobhan gave Reanna a weak smile from where she lay on her side and attempted to rise.

Reanna knelt by Siobhan's cailleach and eased her back down. "Don't get up," she whispered. She placed her hand on her cousin's forehead. It was hot and damp. "How close are your pains, Siobhan?"

Siobhan moaned and clutched her back as another labor pain gripped her.

Seamus looked over at Reanna and whispered worriedly, "How long is this supposed to take?"

"How long has it been?"

"She was uncomfortable all night," he said, "but she insisted on going to Mass this morning. I had to carry her out of the field, her pain was that intense."

"How close together were the pains?"

He rubbed his chin for a moment, "Lets see…I said the rosary and part of another before the next one hit. Seven decades of the beads I think it was."

"How close are they now?"

"Closer than that. Before you arrived, I wasn't able to get through the rosary before another pain hit."

"I don't know if I'm going to be much help," Reanna answered helplessly. "Erris came quicker than this and I was attended by a midwife." She turned to Seamus. "I think she should have one as well." She put her hand on Seamus's sleeve. "I'll pay," she whispered.

Seamus patted her hand. "There's no need. Paedar's mammy is the midwife, and has offered to look after Siobhan in payment for Paedar's lessons. But this stubborn woman," he gestured towards the bed, "insisted that you get here first."

Siobhan, whose back was already arched in the throes of another contraction, gasped, "Go tell Paedar's mammy it's time, Erris. And take your mam with you."

Reanna and Erris snatched their still damp shawls and hurried out the door. The rain had eased off and the sun shone wetly through what was left of the clouds. They made their way down the mud-slicked trail and turned into a familiar path. Her breath caught in her throat as she recognized the shack as the one she grew up in.

Had Siobhan sent her back here deliberately? Take your mam with you, she had said to Erris. Reanna's face flushed in anger at being duped. Siobhan has no business interfering in my affairs, Reanna thought bitterly. She turned away from the door and pretended to be examining a gorse bush.

Erris rapped on the bottom half of the door and called through the open top. "Missus O'Neal, are you to home?"

A chunk of a woman with thin, mouse colored hair twisted into a knot, poked her moon face out the top of the door. "Oh, it's you, Erris. What is it, dear?"

Erris's eyes were big in her face. "Mrs. O'Neal, Aunt Siobhan is having the baby. Will you come, now?"

"Right away." She turned back inside. "Fergus, it's Siobhan O'Dowd's time. I don't know when I'll be back." She pulled the bottom half of the door closed behind her and pulled a shabby shawl over her head and shoulders.

Before Reanna could make her escape, her brother Fergus's unshaven face appeared in the doorway. He folded his arms on the bottom half of the door. Pale eyes with paler lashes swept over her from head to toe. "So, you're back," he sneered.

His words made her feel as rotten as they always did. She looked down at herself and saw herself as he saw her…barefoot still. Without a word, she turned on her heel and walked swiftly away. When she was out of sight of the cabin, she slowed down till Erris and her Aunt Biddy caught up.

"Mam," Erris asked puzzled, "Does Paedar's father know you?"

Bile crowded Reanna's throat and she felt that she would burst into tears if she said a word. She held up her hand. "Not now."

Finally, Biddy broke the awkward silence. "Siobhan's had a bad time of it, she has, with her poor legs and all." She stopped and twisted a thumb sized branch off a gorse bush, picked off the thorns between her thick nails, stripped off the yellow flowers and the bark, and broke the branch into a six inch length.

When Reanna trusted herself to speak, she said, "Seamus is frantic, she's been in labour all night long and is in a great deal of pain."

Within a few minutes, they arrived at the cabin. Seamus met them at the door. Biddy took off her shawl and walked over to where Siobhan lay on her side, writhing in pain. She eased Siobhan over onto her back into a reclining position and slid a blanket under her knees.

"Here," she said, giving the stick to Siobhan. "Clamp your teeth on this when the pain gets too bad."

Seamus wrung his hands and looked helpless. "What is it I can do?" he asked.

Biddy looked up at him out of guileless eyes. "Look for the biggest rock you can find," she told him, "and carry it exactly forty times around the outside of the cabin."

Seamus looked down at her with a 'do I look that dim' look on his face and said, "I never heard of such a thing, Biddy. Is it supposed to help Siobhan, then?"

The stocky woman made the sign of the cross, then raised up her hand in an oath.

"Pon' me soul to God," she said in an innocent voice. "One time I chanced to be there and seen the truth of it with my very eyes. And on the fortieth turn, as it happens."

Seamus, not entirely convinced, left the cabin to do as he was bid and Biddy bent over the bed and examined Siobhan. She straightened up with a concerned look, patted Siobhan on the shoulder and said, "Don't force it, Siobhan. It'll be a while yet. We'll just have to wait it out."

Siobhan groaned and bit her lip.

Biddy motioned for Reanna to come outside.

"The baby seems to be turned around. It's going to be a hard one, this."

"But Siobhan will be all right, won't she?"

"Hard to tell right now." Biddy shook her head in dismay. "A time before I had this happen."

Reanna's blood ran cold. "…And?"

"Sad to say, we lost the mother. She just ran out of strength before we could get the baby out."

"And the baby?"

She shook her head again. "By the time we got him out, the cord had strangled the poor wee thing." She placed her hand on Reanna's arm and said with false cheer. "But all births are different, you know. She'll more than likely be fine. We'll say some prayers and leave it in God's merciful hands." She took Reanna's hand and patted it. "You go in there and stay with her. I'll talk to Seamus."

For the rest of the day, Reanna stayed on her knees by Siobhan's side, sponging her forehead, giving her sips of water and praying as she never had before in her life. Siobhan, she told her cousin silently, don't you dare die on me, not after what we've been through together.

As Reanna watched her beloved cousin fighting to give birth to her child, she knew that Siobhan had given life to her as well. If it had not been for Siobhan's love and concern for her, Reanna might well have ended up living like Biddy. It was Siobhan who made her feel that she could rise above her circumstances; like Seamus does with his pupils, she realized. She'd always wondered what had drawn Seamus and Siobhan together. Now she knew. It was caring. In her own way, Siobhan was a teacher as well. Seamus was bringing Paedar along as Siobhan had done with Reanna. Perhaps what she'd thought of as interference was really Siobhan's hope for Reanna's reconciliation with her brother. For all Siobhan's good intentions, Reanna realized that Fergus would never have anything but contempt for her. She would put him behind her and reach out instead to Biddy and Paedar.

*   *   *

Later on in the afternoon, Siobhan fell into an exhausted sleep. Reanna sat on a stool in front of the hearth and motioned for Biddy to join her.

"I suppose you're wondering who I am?"

"I am, that. Fergus seemed to know you quite well."

"Has he ever mentioned having a sister named Reanna?"

"He has, but that was a long time ago. She died."

"I didn't die, Biddy, I ran away."

Biddy looked at her as though she was seeing a ghost. She crossed herself three times in quick succession. "Glory be to God," she breathed, "I'm seeing things."

"You're not seeing things," Reanna said, "I'm real." And she asked the question she'd wondered about for eleven years. "Where are Mammy and Daddy?"

Biddy, quite recovered now, replied, "Och, your father…well, he never returned you know, and your poor mother…" She reached over and patted Reanna's hand. "Sad to say, didn't she die of a terrible bad disease she got," she lowered her voice and shielded her mouth with her hand, "from lying in the bog with a lot of poor unfortunates like herself."

Reanna waited for the grief to set in. It didn't. "And Fergus?"

Biddy's blinked her pale eyes. "Och well, the poor man, he tries you know, but he has the curse of the drink on him."

Reanna thought back to when she had seen Fergus, outside the pub, all bravado, rusty hair and freckles, acting the deuce with his loutish friends.

She concluded that Biddy's sympathy was wasted on him. "And do you have other children besides Paedar?"

"We have an older boy, Conor. Well really, he's mine, not Fergus's at all you see." She tried bravely to still the quivering of her chin. "Sad to say, he left home at the age of thirteen and never returned."

"Where did he end up, do you know?"

"He told me he was heading for England to find work. That's the last word I ever heard from him." She lowered her eyes and plucked nervously at her none too clean shift. "He and Fergus didn't get along, at all, at all. The day Conor left, there was the divil to pay. Fergus came home with a snootful and began tormenting the lad. Conor let fly at him and laid him out in the dirt. Then he left." She blinked back the tears that threatened to spill out of her pale eyes and over onto her cheeks. "At home there is just Paedar and wee Dennis. He's eight years of age." She smiled in pride. "Paedar is a good boy, so he is, smart and strong as a bull. He watches out for his brother." She lowered her voice to a whisper. "Dennis is a little simple-minded, you see, and by times, gets on his Da's nerves."

Reanna placed her hand over the other woman's. "Does Fergus treat you well, Biddy?"

Biddy answered thoughtfully, "Well mostly, Fergus does what he wants and the rest of us try to stay out of his way."

Siobhan moaned in her sleep and tossed her head from side to side as her labour pains started again.

Biddy eased her bulk up off the stool with a sigh and whispered to Reanna. "I hope it'll be over soon, for she's losing strength."

      *   *   *

Daylight faded, the night air turned crisp, and a blanket of stars covered the sky. Siobhan, after an intensive labor, gave birth to a baby boy, born feet first. Biddy successfully removed the cord from around the infant's neck as he entered the world. Seamus, who had spent the last harrowing hours saying his beads by the hearth, flew to Siobhan's side when he heard the infant's cries. Tears ran unashamed down his furrowed cheeks as he held his son for the first time.

When Siobhan reached her arms up for her son, he placed the baby in her arms and whispered in her ear, "Thank you, cara, thank you."

Within minutes, mother and the child, whom they named Troy, had fallen into an exhausted sleep and Seamus was on his knees giving thanks.

      *   *   *

Reanna and Erris walked with Paedar and Biddy to the crossroads. Reanna gave Biddy a parting hug and a coin. "I can't thank you enough for what you did for Siobhan, for without you we'd have lost her for certain."

"I couldn't do less for one of my own, could I?" she replied cheerfully. Erris and Paedar, still giddy at the news of their kinship, yelled their good-byes until they lost sight of each other.

Reanna and Erris turned onto the coast road. She felt not badly about her father's continued absence and the death of her mother, but curiously freed somehow. Fergus, by himself posed no attachment or threat. A pitiful drunk, she told herself, no more, no less. Biddy's problem now and she seemed up to the task.

As she walked down the coast road, relishing the cold wind that whipped around her and moved her along, she realized that Fergus's low opinion of her had served to make her more determined to make something of herself. As she felt the chains of the past drop from her shoulders, she grasped Erris's hands and they spun round and round in the middle of the road in a freedom dance.

Chapter 11

▼

Rathskill Mountain, Octber 1797

It was way late in the evening, and still Seamus sat on the stool in front of the turf fire, cradling a restless Troy in his arms, brushing his lips back and forth across the soft brown hair on the top of his baby's head. His precious six-month-old had failed to thrive on his mother's nurse. Biddy's latest suggestion had been to feed him finely mashed potato mixed with a little butter and warm cow's milk. Reanna had brought some butter and milk from home in the afternoon. The potatoes Seamus had dug from their own little patch outside the door and fed it to Troy for the first time…please God it would work.

Seamus felt as though he were adrift in a very small boat indeed, with two passengers whose very lives depended on his every decision. With each passing day, the feeling got stronger that their luck was running out. They had been living in this cabin for over a year, and in all that time, Hennessy had not shown up. Maybe it was time to move on, before he did. Perhaps to Galway.

A ceaseless rain hammered on the stones outside the door. Then, the distressed squealing of a neighbor's pig, sliced through the stillness of the night. Troy jerked awake and stiffened, screaming in fright.

"Leaving your pig outside as a present for thieves," Seamus muttered, "brilliant!"

He stood up and tried to jiggle the baby back to sleep, holding him over his shoulder and rubbing his back. He limped over to where Siobhan lay asleep on the cailleach, brown blanket pulled up to her chin and one arm thrown over her pale face. All the sleep in the world wasn't getting rid of the dark smudges under her eyes. It seemed to him that the life had drained out of her along with the birth of their son. Even the sunniest summer in memory hadn't given Siobhan back her fire. On those warm bright days, he'd taken the stool outside, so she and Troy could benefit from the fresh air and sunshine, but when he'd return at midmorning, she'd be asleep again, with the baby in her arms.

Thanks be to God, her poor legs had cleared up to their own beautiful state after their son's birth. That blessing had allowed her to drag herself to market with him of a Thursday. Not to sell, for she'd not been up to knitting, but instead, to carry on to Reanna's, where he and Paedar joined them after the market closed. At Reanna's she'd come alive, for a while at least, and even had herself a laugh or two with Liam. The long walk seemed to do her good for a few days, then it was back to sleeping. He had tried teasing her to life, but even that had failed to get a rise out of her.

He missed her companionship, especially now, when he had some decisions to make that would affect all of their lives. Siobhan's clear mind had the ability to cut through the fog that surrounded an issue and get to the heart of the matter, but since Troy's birth, two words out of Seamus's mouth about anything that involved thinking and her eyes glazed over.

He sat back down on the stool and placed Troy face up on his own knees, covered him with Siobhan's shawl and watched his sleeping son, tawny eyelashes feathered against his pale cheeks. Life up to now had been hard, but he and Siobhan, pulling together had always gotten through somehow, but now with a helpless child along, the rules were different. One wrong decision could mean the difference of life and death for their son.

After one year, they still had no other prospects other than staying in Hennessy's cabin. He felt himself pressured more and more by his principles. At what point do we compromise our principles for practicality, he wondered. His principles were barely keeping them fed and if Hennessy showed up tomorrow, his family would be out on the side of the road in the cold, with only his principles to keep them warm.

At the sound of heavy footsteps on the path outside, his gaze swung to the door. A moment later, the cabin door swung outward. A tall heavy-set man stood silhouetted in the doorway.

Seamus sat where he was, too overcome with dread to move, certain that his own miserable thoughts had brought the devil himself to their door.

The man's fleshy face reddened in anger at the scene before him. "What's going on here?" He stepped inside and closed the door behind him.

Siobhan, startled out of a sound sleep, sprung to her knees in dismay, hand to her mouth. Troy woke up and began to wail.

Seamus bounced him up and down against his shoulder, trying to soothe him. "Would you lower your voice? You're frightening the baby."

The man strode over to the hearth and towered over Seamus, his pale blue eyes nailing him to the stool. "My name is Hennessy, and this is my cabin. How did you get in here?"

Seamus's heart thudded to his shoes. Every limb on his body shook with the knowledge that his worst fears were about to happen. Without a word, he got to his feet, gave the wailing infant over to Siobhan's waiting arms and returned to Hennessy.

"We are not squatting," Seamus denied, " we've paid good money to Bandy McFee for the privilege of living here."

Hennessy's fleshy face turned scarlet. "Bandy McFee indeed. We'll see about that." He turned on his heel without another word and slammed the door behind him.

Seamus walked over and sat beside a sobbing Siobhan, who rocked back and forth on her knees, trying to settle the fidgety baby. She looked up at Seamus, brown eyes wild with despair. "What in God's name are we to do now?"

He sat beside her, a beaten man, with his head down and his elbows on his knees.

"Whatever it takes," he answered sadly.

*   *   *

In less than half an hour, they heard a parade of footsteps outside on the path. The door opened and Hennessy, clothes dripping with rain, shoved a wild-eyed Bandy into the room and followed him in.

Hennessy glared at Seamus. "Take a good look at what happens to people who try to work both ends against the middle."

Bandy's eyes were already beginning to swell shut; blood ran freely from his shattered nose and one arm swung at a crazy angle.

Hennessy jerked a thumb towards the hearth. Bandy replaced the stool he'd taken from Hennessy's cabin beside its mate in front of the hearth. Hennessy signaled to one of the thugs outside. He entered the cabin, raised his foot and pushed Bandy through the door. When the footsteps receded into the stormy night, Hennessy turned his icy eyes on Seamus. Seamus couldn't bear to lose face in front of Siobhan. With his heart heavy, he pointed outside. "With your kind permission." He walked through the doorway and prayed that Hennessy would follow him without argument. Follow he did.

With his pride in his hand, Seamus closed the door and in a muted voice, appealed to the man, "Have mercy on us, we've no other place to stay."

Hennessy took measure of Seamus for what seemed like eternity, and then asked, "Do you know how to use a musket?"

The day of reckoning had arrived. He recalled Liam's words to him that day in the jaunting cart, 'Hennessy will be around to collect his pound of flesh one day,' he'd said to him, 'I hope you'll be prepared.'

When he didn't answer, Hennessy continued menacingly, "or is strangling your only talent?"

With his secret exposed, all hope of getting away with his principles intact, deserted Seamus. He stood, sick at his stomach, thankful for the rain that ran into his eyes and disguised the tears that tracked down his cheeks, in spite of himself. He made one last stab at retaining some semblance of his ethics. "I know nothing of muskets and I'll do no killing."

"You'll do as I say," Hennessy commanded fiercely. "As it happens, I have plenty willing to satisfy that requirement. What I do need, is someone with intelligence to train our lads to use French muskets."

Liam had said, in the cart that day, 'Wolfe Tone is in Paris trying to drum up French aid for an Irish revolution.'

"I'm after telling you, I know nothing about muskets, French or any other kind."

Hennessy overrode Seamus's objections with a wave of his hand. "It doesn't matter. You'll be trained by a Frenchie."

All things considered, Seamus told himself, he would be getting off easy if all he was required to do was train others to use guns. On the other hand, he chided himself; his guilt would be just as heavy.

Hennessy's voice hardened. "You'll take the oath of loyalty now."

Seamus complied reluctantly. He put his left hand on his heart, raised the other one and swore the illegal oath, knowing full well that it was forbidden under pain of death to swear an oath to anyone or anything but the English Crown.

"Listen closely to me," said Hennessy, "tomorrow, just after midnight, a French frigate carrying French uniforms, muskets and ammunition, will drop anchor near the mouth of the bay. Our men will row out from the quay in curraghs to meet them. After the cargo is transferred onto our boats, they will row inland to Bonnagh Head, where you and the lads will meet them, unload the cargo onto carts and get it safely up the mountains to the camp. Do you understand?" he asked in a hoarse whisper.

"I do," Seamus answered numbly.

"A French soldier will come ashore with supplies. You will take him up the mountain with you for a fortnight to train our lads in the use of the muskets."

"What about my pupils?"

Hennessy passed it off. "Deal with it any way you've a mind to, it's nothing to me." He stabbed a finger into Seamus's chest. "I've taken Bandy off the job altogether. You'll be taking his place. After all his double dealing, I wouldn't trust him with my farts."

Seamus shook his head. "Why would he pull a stunt like that, when he knew you'd be returning here for the drop?"

Hennessy spat the words out, "Because he is stupid as well as greedy. He thought when he gave me the rent money, I would be impressed by his cleverness, and all would be forgiven." He looked down at his raw knuckles. "And then I find out that he spent the better part of the rent money as well."

He turned to go. "I'll be back in an hour. You and your family can stay in the cabin while I'm here, on the floor, or wherever the hell you like, but I'll be sleeping in my own bed until this is over." He took a few steps, and then turned back. "And another thing, I don't want any outsiders knowing I'm here."

"But people can see you with their own two eyes."

"I'm not concerned about the ones around here. Those who don't want to see things, turn their heads the other way, and they don't ask what they don't want to hear."

Hennessy fixed him with his pale eyes. "If anything goes wrong tomorrow night, it's worth your life. On the other hand, if you do a good job, you can stay in my cabin. But," he added, finger to his chest, "I will collect the rent myself."

A dejected Seamus walked back into the cabin that had become his prison. Somehow he had to find the right words to break the news of Hennessy's blackmail scheme to Siobhan, without giving out too many details. He hoped it would snap her out of herself. Her lethargy was a luxury they could no longer afford.

   *   *   *

ABOARD THE *MIRAGE*, OCTOBER 23, 1797

Stars blanketed the autumn sky, as the French frigate *Mirage*, sails whipped by the North Atlantic winds, sped southward past the coast of Donegal, shortly before midnight.

Tomorrow, if all went well, she would rendezvous with Irish patriots near a large island that perched near the mouth of Innislow Bay.

Alex Tuillere stood on the listing deck, amber eyes slitted and dark hair plastered against his head by the wind driven spray. The breeches, stockings and rough shirt he wore, had a close, familiar feel on his spare body. They were almost identical to the ones he'd worn when he had lived here ten years ago. He felt excited as a schoolboy in anticipation of seeing Liam and Tante Mae again. During the year he'd lived in Ballymullian, Liam had become a close friend. The older man had taken him under his wing and secured him work as stable boy at Crofton House. He'd also taught him to speak English, Irish not being allowed within the boundaries of the big house. Liam praised Alex when after only six months he'd picked up enough of the difficult Mayo tongue to hold his own in a conversation.

When he'd received word of Papa's death and was obliged to return to France, Alex had confessed to Liam that he felt his life was over. The thought of spending the rest of his life handling smelly clothes in the tailor shop, grieved him.

Liam's reaction had been swift and emphatic. "It well might," he'd said, "and a waste of your talent for languages." He had sat down at a table in his room above the stables and written a letter, folded it in quarters and handed it to Alex. "Take this with you," he said, "and when you get back to Paris, and get yourself settled, see that you deliver it. This man is a friend of mine and he'll see that your talents are put to good use."

The name on the paper written in Liam's spidery hand was General Emile Forget and the address was the Languages Section, The French Directory, Paris, France.

After ten years of a successful military career, traveling over a good part of the world, here he was, on a ship returning to the place it all started. He shook his memories loose and ran over his instructions again in his mind.

He'd been told of a deep sheltered cove on the island, not readily visible from the jutting rocks that lined the shore of the bay. A flotilla of a dozen curraghs, manned by six men each, was to set out from the quay, and row to where the *Mirage* was anchored. The ship's cargo of uniforms, wadding and muskets, and barrels of lead shot and gunpowder, would be unloaded into the wide bodied-boats. Alex was to put himself into the lead boat, along with Rory, the Irish navigator, returning home after two years in France. Alex was to oversee the transfer of the French weapons into Irish hands at a sheltered spot called Bonnagh Head that lay just inside the bay.

From there he was to meet with a man by the name of Bandy McFee and accompany him along with the cargo to an unnamed spot in the Rathskill Mountains. There he would instruct the Irishman in the use of the weapons and assist him in training his countrymen. After a fortnight, he would have to make his own way to the north of Mayo, where he would be picked up November mid-month by the French frigate *Integrite* on her way home, after having herself completed an arms drop into the north of Mayo.

After the training period in the mountains was over and Alex was on his own, he could think of nothing in the world that would prevent him from stealing a few hours with Tante Mae and Liam before he left Ireland. God only knew when he would get another chance.

Chapter 12

—————▼—————

Rathskill Mountain, October 1797

Hennessy sat alone in the cabin. He raised his head at the sound of footsteps on the path outside, then a soft rap on the door. He opened it. A man stood outside in the cold, dark night, his face in the shadows.

"My name is Liam. I'd like a word with you."

Hennessy swung the door open wide. Recognition lit up his face. "Come in, come in." He stood aside to let his visitor enter. He waved toward one of the stools in front of the fire.

"I've heard mention of you," Hennessy said, impressed.

"But you've never seen me," Liam stated flatly. He walked over to the hearth, pulled the stool away from the glowing hearth, and sat down in the shadow. Hennessy joined him.

"I was on my way to supper in town," he said, "when I ran across something peculiar I thought you should be made aware of." He fixed his gaze on Hennessy. "I was almost run over by an injured man running out of the Hill Street barracks. He made a beeline across the street to Monahan's public house. I recognized him as a man called Bandy McFee."

Hennessy stared at Liam out of hooded eyes. "And why would you think I might be interested in the doings of this particular man?"

Liam's voice hardened. "For the simple reason, within minutes after he left, a uniformed horseman galloped out of the porte cochere of the barracks heading toward Castlebar."

Hennessy said nothing, only stared at his visitor.

Liam gave him back eye for eye. "Besides which, I haven't walked four miles in the cold and the dark for to answer your questions. I came here to warn you that it could be a disastrous night. As you are only too aware, the armory in Castlebar is well supplied with men and arms."

Hennessy nodded. He got up and began pacing up and down the small room, a thunderous scowl on his face, beefy hands clenched into fists. "Damn the man's soul to hell."

"Never mind all that. What do you plan to do about it?"

"First thing I plan to do, is not to waste any more time." He turned to Liam. "Will you walk back to town with me? I'll pick up one of the lads and we can talk on the way."

"I will not. I want none of your lads knowing my face." Liam stood up and walked to the door. "You will take care of it."

"Rest assured that I will."

*   *   *

Liam was already out of sight by the time Hennessy walked out of the cabin a few minutes later. He strode down the rock-strewn path and rapped on the door of a rundown hut. A squat, muscular man answered. Hennessy hauled him outside. "We have business to take care of in town." The two men hurried down the path toward the coast road.

Hennessy spoke angrily. "I've been informed that Bandy was seen coming out of the barracks in town tonight, after which a horse and rider left galloping full tilt towards Castlebar. My informant said that Bandy then went straight across the street to Monahan's public house. It's a certainty that he'll be there till his traitor's money is gone."

The other man's face paled in anger. "What do you want me to do with him?"

"I want you to go in there, pretend to be sympathetic and find out everything he told them at the barracks. We can't afford to have anything go wrong tonight." He reached into his trouser pocket and handed the other man some coins. "Feed him enough whiskey to loosen his tongue, but don't take too long." He pushed his finger into the man's face. "You are to buy only one drink for yourself...and nurse it. You need to have your wits about you."

"Shall I let you know what I find out, then?"

"No," he answered angrily, "I can't take any chances on being recognized. Besides, we can assume he didn't go in there to pass the time of day. I'm going to make arrangements for someone to set fire to the barracks across the street as a diversion. There are only a handful of soldiers in Ballymullian. That ought to keep every last one of them busy for awhile."

The other man nodded.

Hennessy continued, "Sit facing the door. When you see the flames, draw attention to the fire. Then, in the confusion, get that little weasel Bandy out of there and bring him back here by any method you can. See that he never speaks to anyone again."

"Do you want me to bash him and dump him in the creek under the bridge."

"No, that won't do. I don't want him discovered accidentally. I want to set an example of what happens to traitors."

"Any particular way you want it done, then?"

"Use your imagination; just make sure you're not followed, because what you have to do next is critical."

The squat man stopped and turned towards him, looking intently, listening.

Hennessy spoke quietly, but clearly. "When you have done the deed, I want you to hurry back to my cabin, tell Seamus to have the men bypass

Bonnagh Head, for as a certainty, the British surely will be waiting for us there. Then, I want you to run to the quay as fast as your legs can carry you. Tell the boatmen they are not to row the cargo to Bonnagh Head, but instead, row it back to the quay. Seamus and the men will meet them there for the unloading. Don't waste any time. Everything has to be in place before midnight."

The two men parted company at the wooden bridge that led into Ballymullian.

*   *   *

A burly British soldier, disguised as a peasant sat at a corner table in Monahan's. He congratulated himself. This was turning into a splendid evening. His shift had started out tedious enough, counting inventory at the barracks. Then, a little man with a busted face and his arm in a sling scuttled in the door of the barracks, spouting talk of an arms drop and the fact that 'the big Irishman' was in town to oversee it. The captain had sent a rider to Castlebar for reinforcements. He'd been sent to follow the little man when he left the barracks, in hopes of being led to the ringleaders. He hadn't led him far, only across the street to Monahan's where he sat with his face in a bottle of whiskey.

What a feather in his cap if he could get his hands on 'the big Irishman'. He'd been a thorn in the British side for years, operating like a ghost in the night. He never stopped anywhere long enough to leave a footprint, just did his dirt and left. Maybe this would be the night 'the big Irishman's luck would run out.

The soldier scanned the noisy room that smelled of ale, unwashed bodies and stale vomit. His eyes returned to Bandy, slumped over a small table, clutching a half-empty bottle of the best whiskey in the house, mumbling to the empty glass that sat beside it.

The heavy door swung open and a stocky man with a bent nose entered the room. He walked over to the bar, ordered a drink, stood for a moment and then made for the table where Bandy sat. He put his hand on the other man's shoulder and pulled up a chair. Bandy raised his bleary eyes to the newcomer, recognized him and shielded his face. The bent nose man put his arm around Bandy's shoulder and began to talk to him reassuringly in a low voice. Bandy started to cry and poured himself out another glass of whiskey and drank it up. With eyes earnestly searching his companion's face, Bandy babbled through his tears. The other man nodded sympathetically. The soldier strained his ears to overhear their conversation amid the laughter and boisterousness around him, to no avail.

Then, all hell broke loose. Someone standing near the door, yelled, "FIRE!" The soldier looked to the door to see what had caused the excitement. When he looked back at Bandy's table, its occupants were gone and so was the bottle of whiskey.

Shoving his way through the crowd that funneled out the narrow door into the street, the soldier strained to see over people's heads, knocking onlookers left and right in his haste to relocate his prey. People stood mesmerized, faces illuminated from the flames in the dark night as tongues of fire licked at the walls of the wooden barracks. The soldier in pursuit, jumped up to see over the heads of the crowd. He spotted two men, one of whom carried a bottle, scurrying away from the fire. He weaved his way after them, down the empty street, staying half a block behind them for good measure.

*		*		*

By the time Liam arrived back in Ballymullian from seeing Hennessy, he was late for supper at Reanna's. He rang the doorbell. Erris, book in hand, let him in and he followed her back into Mae's room. The old woman removed her spectacles, rubbed her eyes and started to rise from her chair. "I guess I dozed off."

Liam raised a hand in greeting on his way up the stairs. "Don't let me disturb you. I'm late for supper as it is. I'll just go on up. I'll see you on my way out if you're still awake, Mae."

A few moments later, his head appeared at the top of the stairs.

"There you are, Liam," Reanna exclaimed, "I'd begun to think you got lost."

"Not lost, only delayed." He shrugged out of his thin coat. "Am I too late for supper, then?"

"Not at all, not at all," she assured him, "sit yourself down."

"Forgive me for being late." He pulled a chair into the table. "I hope your good supper didn't get cold, for it smells grand." He rubbed his cold hands together in anticipation. "Mutton is it?"

"Mutton it is, and nothing that won't keep, Liam," she smiled, and ladled some mutton, potatoes and cabbage onto his plate, passed him a plate of oaten bread and poured steaming tea into a cup. "I just hope you don't mind that we went ahead and ate without you."

She sat down across from him at the small table. She lowered her voice to a whisper. "Mae would have been asleep had we waited. She's so tired these nights, Liam."

"Now that you make mention of it, I believe I wakened her when I came in."

"I wouldn't be at all surprised." She poured herself a cup of tea. "Erris reads to her for company while she sews in her chair, but lately, her eyes are closed within the hour."

"Well, that doesn't sound too farfetched to me, Reanna." He swiped a piece of bread around the gravy on his plate. "She and I, we're getting on, you know. I, myself, take to my bed as soon as I get the horses settled."

"She hasn't been herself for some time though, Liam." She lowered her voice. "There is something else I think you should know. A few days ago, I had the occasion to tuck her quilt around her while she slept in her chair and I felt a big lump right here," she said, placing her hand on her upper abdomen.

Liam, bread in hand, halted it midway to his mouth. "A lump," he repeated in dismay.

Reanna nodded her head. "The size of a large potato, it was. I asked her about it, and she passed it off as nothing, but I'm that concerned about it, Liam. I asked her if I could have Doctor McCabe come to see her, but she wouldn't hear of it. Will you have a talk with her."

"Yes. I believe I'll go down now and have a few words with her before she falls asleep again." He scraped his chair back from the table and rubbed his stomach. "Grand supper, Reanna. Thank you."

As he rose to leave, the sounds of pounding footsteps and people shouting drew them to the window. Shop Street was filled with people running toward the corner of Hill Street.

Reanna undid the latch and opened the window. "What's happening?"

A woman stopped in mid stride and shouted up to the window. "The Hill Street Barracks…they're on fire."

Liam yanked his coat off the hook, mouthing apologies for his rude departure over a shoulder and shot down the stairs. Reanna heard him yell to the others that the barracks were on fire, then the slam of the shop door.

Erris hurried up the stairs to her mother's side. The child still had bad dreams about the terrible fire in Dunbury that had taken her father away. Reanna put an arm around her daughter's shoulder and led her toward the hearth. "How about I make us all a nice cup of tea and some bread and jam?"

Reanna was pouring out the tea when an ear-shattering explosion shook the building. They ran downstairs to Mae, who was struggling to get out of her bed. They all hurried outside into the clear night and stood talking to neighbors. The sky was lit up and sparks flew everywhere. Soldiers on horseback clattered down the street, scattering people before them. Shouting through megaphones, they ordered everyone back inside.

*　　　　*　　　　*

Some time later, Reanna, an unfinished hat in her lap, fell asleep in her chair by the hearth, lulled to sleep by the sound of the rain. A racket from outside awakened her. She jumped up and ran to the window. Through the drizzling rain, she spied a contingent of soldiers on horseback, clattering down Hill Street towards the coast road.

*   *   *

RATHSKILL MOUNTAIN

Thunder clapped over the bay and lightning split open the sky. The wind keened like a crazy person, and sent waves crashing onto the rocky shore of Innislow Bay. Rain thundered down out of a black sky and beat on everything in its path. It poured itself down the gullies of the mountain, and pounded mercilessly on the wretched cabins that huddled about its base.

"Cursed weather," Seamus mumbled as he and Siobhan hurried into the darkened cabin and closed the door. Hennessy was nowhere to be seen, and there was no sign that he'd ever set foot in the place.

Seamus shivered and pulled his thin jacket tighter around his bony frame. "I wonder where he's got to?" he said, "I can't imagine why he isn't here now, on this of all nights, unless he's out getting someone else to do his dirty work for him."

Siobhan lifted Troy out from underneath her shawl and deposited him on the bed.

"Thanks be to God he's not here. He makes my skin crawl." She shivered, "Eyes like a dead fish."

Seamus limped over to the turf fire and poked at it till the flames licked up from the middle of the pile. He held out his big hands to the warmth. Worrisome thoughts chewed away at him. Would Hennessy let him off the hook after tonight or would the man continue to use his knowledge of Seamus's crime to keep him under his thumb.

Siobhan lay on the bed with her eyes closed, Troy cuddled in her arms.

Seamus whispered, "I have to go now, love. Make sure you're not in that bed when Hennessy returns."

Siobhan made a face and got out of bed, but left Troy where he was and covered him up with a brown blanket.

She opened the door. "Take care, Seamus."

He tried to dispel the concerned look on her face. "And why wouldn't I, with the likes of yourself to return to." He pulled his cap on over his head, jammed his walking stick into the pit of his arm and let himself out the door.

Siobhan crossed herself worriedly. "Safe home," she whispered to his retreating back.

He set off down the path to pick up Paedar. The rocky path was now slick with mud. The rain had settled into a steady downpour. He picked his way along, using his walking stick as a brake. Only the soft snuffling of pigs disturbed the rhythm of the rain. The smell of excrement, both human and porcine, combined with the acrid smell of hundreds of peat fires, burned his eyes and nose. He pulled a balled up rag from his pocket and wiped his eyes.

Paedar stepped out of the shadows and joined him on the road. "Evenin' Seamus," the boy said, using the older man's Christian name for the first time.

"Evenin' Paedar." Seamus's mouth twitched in a grin at the boy's attempt to be grown up, but caution made him repeat the instructions he's given the lad earlier in the day. "You do know Paedar, you're not to be involved in anything other than being my legs and my eyes, don't you?"

"That I do, Seamus," Paedar said, blue eyes serious. "I'm to be the lookout up at the road, and if I see anything, I am to run down to the beach and warn the others."

Seamus ruffled the boy's coarse red hair with his big hand. "You're a good lad, Paedar," he said. "Did you have any trouble getting out?"

"None at all," he said, "Dada had a snootful by suppertime. He's been laid out on the floor since it got dark."

"Is he likely to wake up before you get back home?"

"Naah," he replied, "he's been into the poteen since early afternoon. He won't move till morning. We just leave him where he falls and it's a relief to everyone when he does."

One by one, other men stepped out of the shadows and joined Seamus and Paedar, till there was a growing column of men slogging down the road in single file. A driving rain started up again as they turned onto the coast road, sending a river of muddy water gurgling and swirling down its rutted length. Paedar sloshed through the puddles, well ahead of the others to spot anyone coming towards them from Bonnagh Head. Two of the men fell back to bring up the rear and watch for anyone walking downroad from town.

Seamus hunched his shoulders deeper into himself, wrapped his woolly scarf tighter around his throat and covered his mouth and nose. Even his warm breath couldn't mask the chill that permeated his bones. He clutched the ratty jacket over his chest and recalled their last day in Dunbury when Reanna had asked him if he would have any use for Donald's jacket. Never in a million years would he have imagined he'd be using it on an occasion such as this.

The rain stopped as suddenly as it began, and a thick blanket of fog rolled in from the bay, curled over the road, past the bog and crept up the mountain. Seamus raised his cramped neck out of his collar and shook himself like a wet dog. He gulped in the briny smell of the sea air as though it were his last breath. The cabins thinned out as they got closer to Bonnagh Head.

Paedar came running back down the road towards Seamus, frantically waving his arms. At Seamus's signal, the men scattered into the bog.

Seamus hailed Paedar from the side of the road. "For the love of God, son, what's wrong?"

The boy, retching in horror, grabbed Seamus's sleeve, and pointed up the road. His voice shook. "There's two bodies beside the ditch. One is Bandy...he's had his throat cut and he has his tongue in his hand."

One of the men with Seamus started to rise. "I'll tell the others."

Seamus took hold of his sleeve. "Stay where you are, I'll take care of it." He'd known that something was not right from the moment he and Siobhan had entered the cabin earlier and discovered Hennessy's absence.

The first thing he needed to do was to get the lad out of danger and see that Hennessy was informed of this latest development.

He took the boy by the shoulders. "Paedar, listen to me. I want you to go to my cabin..." Then, he remembered Hennessy's warning to tell no one of his presence. Sending Paedar to warn him could put the boy in mortal danger. Even under these circumstances, he couldn't be sure that he wouldn't harm the boy, given the punishment Bandy had received for renting Hennessy's cabin without his permission. What Bandy had done to get his throat cut didn't bear thinking about.

All at once, the certainty that he could be sending the lad into danger, hit him like a blow to his stomach. "I've changed my mind," he said to the lad. "I want you to go straight back to your home. Tell no one where you've been and say nothing to anyone if they ask."

"But Seamus..." the boy began.

"You'll be in danger here, don't argue with me, lad. Just go on back home."

The boy turned on his heel and walked back down the road, still shaking with the knowledge of what he had just been witness to.

You're in it up to your neck, now, me boy, Seamus told himself. He called the men together in the road.

"The lad has just found the bodies of Bandy and another man just beyond here, by the ditch." A murmur broke out among the men.

"I don't for sure know what this means, but we need to go through with our plans in any case. We have other lives depending on us to do what we came for. But, we'll need to watch our step."

The men nodded and murmured their agreement.

Seamus turned to two of the men. "Go on up ahead and get the bodies out of sight. We'll pick them up on the way back."

Not a whisper was heard for the rest of the walk, only the shuffle of men's feet as they slogged down the muddy road.

*   *   *

As they arrived at Bonnagh Head, Seamus made out in the dense fog, a line of hand held carts that had been pulled off the road and sat partially hidden in the bushes. A group of men waited beside them. Seamus and his group joined them.

One of the men looked over the new arrivals. "Where's Bandy?"

"Bandy's met with an accident," Seamus replied. "I'll be giving you your instructions."

Another opened his mouth to speak. Seamus nipped the question in the bud. He pointed to a bowlegged old man. "What's your name, sir?"

"The name's Dan."

He picked up a lantern and handed it to him. "Take this lantern and stand down by the water's edge. When you hear the boats on the water, start swinging it to guide them in. A Frenchie by the name of Alex Tuillere will be in the lead boat. Send him up here to me." He turned to the others. "The rest of you men will unload the curraghs as they come in, make a chain and pass the crates and barrels up to the road. My leg won't support me on the climb, I'll have to stay up here with the carts and act as a lookout. If you hear a whistle from me, scatter and go back to your homes.

The men, boots sliding on the slick mud, lined up the creaking carts one after another along the road. The others, who were to unload the boats, picked their way down the steep path, slipping and sliding on the wet rocks. When they reached the bottom, old Dan shuffled down to the water's edge, and set the lantern down on the gravel.

*　　　　　*　　　　　*

Earlier in the evening, under cover of darkness, a platoon of British soldiers had rowed out from Ballybeg to Bonnagh Head. And now, hidden by the dense fog, they lay in ambush among the rocks on the beach. In the silence, broken only by the sounds of the incoming tide, the menacing voice in the fog chilled the men to the marrow of their bones and rooted them to the spot.

"Do not move. You are completely surrounded."

Before the men could spur themselves into action, each one was swiftly and efficiently garroted. The soldiers dragged the bodies over to a clearing behind an outcropping of rock and piled them into a heap like so much turf.

One of the soldiers peeled the sweater off a fallen rebel, removed his own red uniform jacket, donned the heavy, dark sweater, lit the lantern, walked down to the water's edge and swung it back and forth.

*　　　　　*　　　　　*

ABOARD THE *MIRAGE*

Alex stood on the rolling deck of the sailing ship, under a leaden sky. The pocket of his breeches held a fraudulent letter of safe passage, signed and stamped with an official looking seal. He was thinking of the job that lay ahead tonight, going over his instructions once more in his mind, while the big ship bucked and heaved through the rolling seas. A slap on his shoulder almost made him jump out of his skin. He turned on cat feet and swung out. Rory, the Irish navigator, looked up dumbfounded from where he sprawled on the deck.

Alex helped him to his feet. "I apologize Rory, you took me by surprise. I was thinking about what lay ahead and hoping the weather would hold when we unload the cargo."

"Aah, it's nothin' mortal sir, I been set on me arse many's a time," Rory said, shouting to make himself heard over the slapping of the sails and the keening of the wind. "I just wanted to let ye know that we are nearing the island, and we'll be dropping anchor soon." He raised his shaggy head and sniffed the air. "We're in for some bad weather, I'm afraid, though, sir. It may well blow over before we drop anchor, but if it isn't, we can look forward to a stormy ride on the way in. I've lived around these waters all my life," he continued, "and I've seen some wicked storms, furious while they are happening, but over in the blink of an eye. Sort of like the Irish temperament," he said wryly, "blowing hot and cold at the same time, like."

True to Rory's prediction, within the half-hour, the wind whipped the seas into a writhing froth that welled over the sides of the boat, buffeting the sailors as they tried to secure the ship.

Rory pointed towards the sky and shouted a warning to Alex. "Look alive, sir, you'd best secure yourself."

Alex raised his head. Black clouds rolled over them. Lightning flashed and lit up the night sky. In the distance, thunder rumbled and echoed.

Alex stood flat-footed on the deck holding onto the ropes with both hands, while the wind roared in his ears, making further conversation with Rory impossible. The gale grew teeth, a torrential rain slashed sideways into their faces and they held on for dear life.

                    *   *   *

After what seemed forever, the *Mirage* dropped anchor in the stormy sea, off the lee side of the island. The waters of the cove resembled a roiling cauldron.

Rory lowered his spyglass, yelled at Alex and pointed towards the quay. A flotilla of curraghs, bobbing like corks on the eight-foot swells, doggedly made their way towards the ship. Alex lurched to his feet and picked up a lantern. Hanging onto the ropes to keep from being dumped over the side, he held out the beacon to the oncoming boats.

The curraghs pulled alongside the *Mirage* and were lashed by twos for stability. The French sailors lowered a rope ladder and some of the boatmen scrambled aboard the ship to help lower the heavy crates and barrels into waiting hands in the curraghs below. When the boats were loaded up, Alex and Rory jumped into the lead boat. They undid the lashings and shoved off from the ship, followed closely by the second overloaded curragh and disappeared into the storm.

Blinded by the stinging sheets of spray-laden wind, the oarsmen tried in vain to stay a course through the pitching seas. A monstrous wave swelled under the lead curragh. It sprung away from its companions, and like a stone from a slingshot, careened over an oncoming wave and disappeared.

As the lead boat neared Bonnagh Head, the rope around the cargo began to unravel. Rory dropped his oar, leaned forward and grabbed onto a crate of uniforms that was in danger of sliding off the side of the curragh into the water. At that moment, the boat plummeted over a huge wave and slammed straight into the trough of the next one. The motion jerked Rory off balance, almost hurtling him into the sea. Alex grabbed at him with both hands, pulling him to safety. In doing so, he lost his own balance and a barrel of lead shot wedged his foot against the side of the curragh. Pain, like he'd never felt before, shot through his ankle as the barrel smashed repeatedly into his foot with each lurch of the wide boat. Rory shipped his oars and tried to free Alex's foot, but couldn't sustain a grip on the barrel's slick surface. With the next wave, the barrel rolled away and Alex pulled his foot free, but lost his balance and plunged over the side into the heaving waters of the bay. Rory held out an oar to him. Alex tried to get within reach of it, but didn't have the strength. Within seconds, the boat was out of sight.

*   *   *

As the curraghs rounded the headland, the waters calmed. The lead boat, followed closely by the others, veered toward the wigwagging light on the shore. One by one, the boats crunched onto the rocky beach. Rory hauled himself out of the lead boat and walked stiffly toward the man holding the lantern.

"All right then, let's get these boats unloaded."

His voice was drowned out by a volley of shots that killed him and all the occupants of the first two boats.

At the first sounds of shots, Seamus and the others came running, tripping over stones in the dark, sloshing through great pools of water they could barely see and came together at the top of the path and hid behind a large outcropping of rock. They listened helplessly, to the screams of the doomed, as the remaining men in the boats were picked off like flies.

*   *   *

When it was over, the curraghs, holding their grisly cargo, bobbed in a dance of death. The soldiers waded into the water, retrieved the cargo, and brought it to shore, leaving the dead, hanging over the boats and floating in the water.

The men behind the rocks watched helplessly, as the lieutenant gave orders to load up the appropriated carts with the weapons. He left one soldier to stand guard over the remaining carts and another to stand guard over the dead until morning when their bodies could be identi-fied. The rest of the soldiers left, pulling two of the heavy carts with them.

As the sounds of the wagons diminished, one of Seamus's men slipped up behind the sentry at the road and garroted him. Another one descended quietly to the beach, where a single lantern cast its glow on the macabre scene. He crept up behind the sentry on duty, grabbed him around the throat with his arm, and buried a knife in his chest. The sentry slumped to the ground. The rebel wiped the knife on the dead man's uniform, then picked up the lantern and waggled it towards the road.

Two of the men eased Seamus down the steep path. His heart broke at seeing the carnage, and he thanked God that he had followed his instincts and sent young Paedar home. The men, following Seamus's instructions, waded into the water and examined the hands of the dead in the boats for someone with the soft hands of an officer, but to no avail. Four of the men tied the curraghs together, loaded the dead into them and prepared to row them back to their families. One of the men left on foot for the quay to tell them of the sad news, and to prepare them for the carnage that was arriving in the boats.

Seamus was left to decide to remove the ammunition or the dead bodies of his neighbors. For him, the decision was easy. On his orders, the men slung their dead over their shoulders, struggled back up to the road and then to the mountains for a secret burial. Seamus blew out the lantern and took it with him and climbed painfully back up to the road, aided by his companions. They left the body of the soldier for the tide to take care of.

The Frenchman Alex was apparently not among the dead. Where he could be, Seamus could only guess…perhaps lost in the heaving seas; perhaps he never got on the ship in France at all. Seamus plodded down the coast road towards home, Hennessy's threat running over again and again in his mind. It will be worth your life if it fails, he'd said. He turned off the coast road and limped up the hill towards the cabin. No light showed through the cracks of the closed doors as he passed the shacks of his neighbors, but he imagined there was none asleep indoors. Though most of the men with the boats, had come from downroad from the quay and beyond, those waiting behind the doors knew only that their men were still not home and soon it would be light.

Seamus reached home and walked into the warm room. At the tragic look on his face, Siobhan rushed over and flung her arms around him. He patted her distractedly on the back and went straight to the hearth where Hennessy sat. He eased out of his sopping wet jacket, shed his wool cap, and hung them both on a peg near the fire. Although Seamus could feel Hennessy's eyes on him, he said nothing, but dropped down onto a stool in front of the hearth. Siobhan knelt in front of him, removed his wet boots and socks and placed them near the fire to dry, and sat back on her heels near the fire.

"The mission went sour. The men in the boats…murdered…all of them."

Hennessy rebuked Seamus with his eyes and inclined his head towards Siobhan. Seamus raised a weary hand. "It doesn't matter now." He ran his hands through his wet hair, looked Hennessy in the eye. The British soldiers…someone must have warned them…they were on the beach waiting for us." Seamus lowered his head into his hands, sickened at the memory of the carnage. "They garroted our lads as they climbed down to the beach and killed the others to a man as the boats landed."

Hennessy spoke quietly. "Bandy warned them…revenge for the beating he was given and because I replaced him with you. Someone saw him go into the barracks in town last night and hurried out here to tell me. I picked up one of the lads and took him to town with me."

Seamus stood up and shouted into Hennessy's face, "And so you let us all walk into a trap, and did bloody nothing to stop it?"

"You weren't here when I left and there was no time to waste. I got someone to set fire to the barracks as a diversion, so one of the lads could get Bandy out of Monahan's, in the confusion." He smacked a fist on his knee. "Something must have happened. The lad's orders were to take care of Bandy and then come directly here to warn you to stay away from Bonnagh Head, but instead, go to the quay for the pickup. Then he was to go to the quay himself, to warn the men in the boats of the change in plans."

"He hadn't arrived here by the time I left." Seamus said dispiritedly.

"So your wife said."

When he remembered Paedar's description of Bandy, Seamus had to force his next words out. "We found Bandy and another man, dead in the ditch on the way to Bonnagh Head."

"Short, stocky, man…bent nose?"

"I believe so."

"That must be where he ended up, then. Someone must have followed him from the public house. A shame, that."

"Tell that to the families of the dead, when their neighbors inform them that their husbands and sons are buried in unmarked graves in the mountains."

Hennessy spoke up, harshly. "What's done is done. What about Alex Tuillere, the Frenchman?"

"He didn't arrive either, to the best of my knowledge. None of the men in the boats had soft hands. They all had the callused hands of fishermen." Seamus folded his arms.

"Do we even know the man got aboard the ship in France?"

"Yes, he did. If he didn't come ashore, then we have to assume he's been dumped overboard and drowned or swam to shore and is waiting for someone to pick him up."

"In that case, he'll have a long wait for himself. After tonight, the patrols will be swarming all over the area, looking for survivors."

Hennessy swerved around on his stool and jerked his thumb at Siobhan, who now sat on the edge of the bed, listening quietly. "Your woman can go. The patrols won't stop her looking for shellfish for the family's supper."

Seamus stood up and turned on Hennessy. "She'll do nothing of the sort. Do you have no shame, asking a poor woman to do your dirty work?"

Siobhan stood up, stuck her hands on her hips and hissed at the men. "What am I, then…a post to be talked around?"

Hennessy glared at her. "I'm only saying…"

Siobhan cut him off in mid-sentence. She turned to her husband. "I'll go, Seamus. He's right you know. They won't suspect a woman. I go down there every day at low tide as it is. I'll leave as soon as it's light. If the man is there, I'll find him."

Chapter 13

―――――▼―――――

Ballymullian, October 1797

Reanna awoke early after a fitful night's sleep. Periodically through the night, the sound of horses' hooves on the cobbles outside and the sounds of men's voices on the street below had awakened her. Curiosity drove her out of bed, and over to the window. She looked down at Shop Street, empty in the darkness of early morning. Misty still, and the air still held the bitter odor of last night's fire.

After Liam's hasty departure from Reanna's table last night, he'd returned to give them the news that the barracks on Hill Street burned to the ground. There was not enough manpower in the barracks to put out the fire, nor was there an inclination by any of the onlookers to help. By the time it was over, he said, both the apothecary and the cobbler shop adjacent to the barracks had burned to the ground as well.

Reanna made her ablutions, dressed quietly so as not to disturb the others, tiptoed down the stairs and opened the door to the street. Something felt awry this morning, but she couldn't put her finger on it. She walked down the deserted street. Odd that she was the only person on the street this morning. Today was market day, and the streets should be filled with people by now. She looked forward to the gathering at her flat after the market closed for the day. For their tea, she would pick up some raisin buns from the bakery next door. They were Seamus and Liam's favorites.

When she arrived at the grocers, the latch was on the wooden door. She rapped insistently. When no one answered, she peeked in through the window.

The grocer's wife stuck her head out the window upstairs. "We're closed. Nothing is opened today. The soldiers were at our door before dawn, as soon as they saw the lantern lit."

That's what had felt different this morning, she realized, no smell of baking bread from next door when she'd opened the window. She turned around at the sounds of hooves on cobbles. A soldier on horseback hailed her. "Return to your homes. Everyone is to stay indoors today for an enumeration. Everything is closed. Go home."

Arriving at the shop, the closed sign was on the door. Erris, still in her nightclothes, greeted her as she walked inside. "Mam," she said, "while you were out, soldiers came and made us close the shop."

Reanna hurried through to the back. "Mae, I was just now sent home by a soldier. There's to be an enumeration today. Whatever does that mean?"

The old woman hobbled over to the side cupboard and brought back a cup to the small table. She sat down and poured some tea. "It's a house to house count of all the occupants and their whereabouts, love. They may have a suspicion that the barracks fire wasn't an accident and are on the lookout for those who might have set it."

Reanna pulled out a chair from the table and sat down. Her hand shook as she poured herself a cup of the hot brew. She had visions of soldiers leading her away to be punished for Donald's crimes. Then she remembered the soldiers on horseback that had wakened her during the night, and concern for the safety of Seamus and Siobhan's family overwhelmed her. Seamus had as much to fear from an enumeration as she did.

"The soldiers…I saw a whole troop of them heading out towards the coast road during the night. Do you suppose they'll be doing an enumeration out at the mountain as well?"

"In all probability…why?"

Reanna burst into tears. "Aah, God Mae, it's not my concern to tell you, but Seamus has his own reasons to fear exposure. A terrible thing happened to him and Siobhan just before we left Dunbury."

"Shhh, love, stop worrying yourself. Seamus is an intelligent man. If he came out of it in Dunbury, he will come out of it here as well. As for yourself, when the soldiers show up, volunteer no information, answer only what you're asked and hold your head up."

Within the hour, Reanna spied the soldiers going in and out of the doors across the street, carrying their sheets of paper. By the time they arrived at the shop and asked their questions, she was soaking wet with perspiration. She needn't have worried, Mae did most of the talking, explaining Reanna and Erris's presence as needed help for an ailing old lady.

*   *   *

THE BEACH AT INNISLOW BAY

Siobhan arose early in order to catch low tide. Mixed in with nervousness for the task ahead was a growing excitement. This French officer named Alex. Could this be the same Alex who wrote letters to Mae, making Reanna flush just by the reading of them? The same Alex that made Reanna's eyes sparkle as she talked about their times together during the year that he lived in Ballymullian?

She picked her string bag off the peg by the front door and tiptoed back to where Seamus lay in an exhausted sleep, curled up on the floor, little Troy fast asleep in the crook of his arm. She felt Hennessy's pale eyes watching her from where he lay in the cailleach. She paid him no mind, but turned around and left the cabin.

The dark sky was filled with pale gray clouds, and the air, though cold, didn't smell like rain. God willing, she'd find the man called Alex and he'd be whole, for Hennessy's instructions had been explicit. 'If he is alive, don't bring him back here,' he'd said, 'Bring him a bite to eat and send him on his way. I understand he's to make his way to Downpatrick Head in a fortnight, in any case. I suggest you tell him he'd be safer away from here until then.'

Siobhan had been horrified at the coldness of the man, 'And what do you suggest he do in the meantime?'

He'd looked at her as though she was dimwitted, 'tell him he's on his own,' he'd answered. 'He's no good to us now, is he, with no muskets to train with.'

*   *   *

Siobhan turned left onto the coast road and made her way towards Bonnagh Head. Many a morning, she'd tramped up and down these beaches and rocks in search of shellfish many times and she knew this shoreline well. If the man had made it to shore, he'd look for somewhere to hide. She knew of only one cave between here and Bonnagh Head. The entrance was disguised as a wide crack between the large black rocks, and opened into a wide tunnel. At the end of the tunnel, the trapped tides had opened the cave back into itself. In this pocket, the turgid water had worn away the earth from the roof of the cave and daylight filtered down from a hole in a field of long grass above.

She turned left onto the coast road and began her walk to the beach, the damp sea air cold on her cheeks. The gulls interrupted the calm day with their raucous screeching.

Shortly, she passed the grassy field that held the exit hole from the cave. She could see the outline of the long grass in the field as it bent and waved in the brisk wind. As she reached the beach, she heard a noise some distance behind her. She ducked behind an outcropping of rocks, and soon she spotted a platoon of soldiers in red coats, crest the hill. She left the road and slid herself down the slick grass to the beach, turned towards the rocks and was soon hidden from the sight of anyone on the road. She jumped from rock to puddle to rock, water lapping at her ankles, till she reached the mouth of the cave. Holding onto the slick rocks on either side, she stepped into the icy water at the entrance to the dank cave. She squeezed her body between the rocks, and stood inside for a moment while her eyes accustomed themselves to the darkness. She steadied herself against the slippery side of the cave and gingerly made her way a few feet into its depth, then stopped to listen. She thought she could hear breathing at the back of the cave.

Her whisper echoed in the hollow cave as she addressed the darkness. "Is anyone in here?"

She thought she heard a scratching at the back of the cave and panic overcame her. Visions of field rats scrabbling around back there made her scalp crawl. She fought to regain control.

"Alex," she said in a shaking voice, "I'm Siobhan. I'm here to help you. Are you in here?" She gave herself one more minute to stay, before panic would propel her back out into the daylight. After a moment of silence, she turned thankfully to leave, when a voice from the darkness answered her.

"Yes…I'm Alex. I'm back here."

Siobhan inched her way toward the voice at the back of the cave. In the daylight filtering from the field above, she saw a young man sitting on a rock with his back to the wall of the cave. His handsome face was pinched in pain.

Siobhan crouched beside him. "Thank God, you're safe."

"Safe maybe, but my ankle is badly broken."

Siobhan's stomach lurched as she looked at his leg below the rolled up breeches, discolored flesh bulging over the top of his boot.

"I loosened it a little, but then I figured I might not get it on again, so I left it where it was."

No matter what Hennessy's instructions had been, Siobhan told herself, this man needed help for that foot. He certainly wasn't able go anywhere on his own.

"How about the others," Alex asked, "did everything go as planned?"

She looked up at him with tortured eyes, then softly, "I'm afraid it went very badly, Alex. The British were waiting on the beach. They murdered all the men in the curraghs and confiscated the arms."

He sat silent, in shock at her words.

"Alex," she said distractedly, "I can't stay here. I saw a platoon of soldiers heading towards Bonnagh Head. If you stay here and be still, you'll be safe for the time being, for the cave is only visible from the water. Anyone finding it would have to be up to their knees in water before they'd even see it."

"I'll need to have my ankle looked after before I can make it up the mountain."

Her dismayed look gave him his answer. "There is no safety in the mountains for me now, is there?"

"Sadly, no." she admitted. "Everyone who wasn't killed has scattered, and with no muskets to train with, no one is there…" her voice trailed off.

"So," he said bitterly, "I'm on my own."

"Seamus and I won't desert you."

"Who is Seamus? I was supposed to meet a man named Bandy McFee."

"Bandy is dead. Seamus is my husband and he'll find you a safe place to stay till you're well."

"There's no need to put yourselves in danger. If Seamus can get me into Ballymullian, I have somewhere I can stay."

Siobhan's heart leapt. Now, she was sure it was the same Alex. She wanted to ask him if she was Mae Proulx's nephew, but every second she stayed here, was putting them both in jeopardy.

"We'll see that you get there." She got to her feet. "I have to leave now, before I'm seen. Just remember. Stay in the back of the cave and you'll be safe. I'll send Seamus back to get you before high tide."

She slipped out of the cave and within minutes, two armed sentries appeared around the headlands and start walking towards her from the other end of the beach. She waded out into the water and pretended not to notice them, but busied herself picking cockles out of tide pools, prying clams from the rocks, and depositing them in her string bag, all the while working her way towards them. One of the soldiers spied her and turned to his companion.

She turned away from them, tucked her shift through her legs in front of her, tied it at the waist with her string bag and waded knee deep into the cold water. Her arms tensed up with the effort as she worked her hands underneath a clod of sea grass and pulled it free of its moorings. Her bare feet slid on the moss-covered rocks as she placed the dripping clod on the nearest flat rock and broke it up with her hands. She removed the clams that nestled in its core and dropped them into the string bag around her waist. As she worked, she kept an eye on the sentries, and saw that they were keeping an eye on her as well.

They passed by her and began nosing among the rocky point that led to the cave. They maneuvered from rock to rock, avoiding the puddles, but couldn't get around the point without getting their shiny boots wet. They backed away. One sentry kept an eye on her, while the other scanned the rocks for the possibility of a dry access around the point.

She knew she had to distract them and get them to move away from the cave area before they found the entrance. With her heart in her mouth, she pretended to slip on the rocks, let out a piercing scream and went under the water with a resounding splash. The frigid water took her breath away and chilled her to the bone, but it got the soldiers' attention. They watched her walk towards the headlands; her sopping shift molded to her body and tucked up between her thighs, her backside swaying in the knee-deep water. They followed her down the beach.

When she'd led them far enough out of range of the cave, she turned around, pretending not to notice they were there. The sentries nudged each other as she unloosed her long brown hair and squeezed the water from it. Her wet shift clung to her rounded breasts. She undid her shift at her waist, lifted it high on her long legs, and wrung it out.

One of the sentries made a move towards her, but the other one took hold of his arm and shouted at Siobhan, "You there…get out of the water."

She swayed toward them, through the icy water, string bag of shellfish tied around her waist, weighing her down.

They met her at the water's edge. "What are you doing out here?"

"Same as I do every day. Gathering food for my family's supper."

"Have you seen anyone else out here?"

"Indeed I haven't," she replied, playing the innocent, and then added as if the thought had just occurred to her, "and isn't that strange, now?"

"Go back to your home. Everyone is to stay inside today."

She could feel their eyes on her as she walked back along the beach and scrambled up the steep path to the road.

             *   *   *

When Siobhan arrived back at the cabin, Hennessy was nowhere to be seen.

"Where is his nibs?" she asked.

Seamus looked put his book aside. "I have no idea. He disappeared shortly after you left. Strange, altogether."

"I found Alex," she said. "I hope I didn't speak out of turn, Seamus, but he began talking about getting to the mountain and I had to tell him that the drop had failed. He's hiding in the cave between here and Bonnagh Head, with a badly broken ankle. In spite of what Hennessy says, we can't send him on his way. The man's not able to walk."

"You're right, of course. We'll have to get him out of there to safety."

"And before high tide."

"And how do you propose I do that in broad daylight? Are there no patrols in the area?"

"Indeed there are. Two sentries were nosing around the cave. I led them away for now, but we'll need to get him out of there before they return."

Seamus muttered to himself. "Where in the name of God can we hide the man safely?"

"Well, that's the thing of it," Siobhan said excitedly, "He says he knows of a place he can hide out in town. I think he is Mae Proulx's nephew, Seamus…in fact, I'm certain of it."

"Glory be to God," he said. "There's no telling, is there?" He raised himself from the stool and walked to the door. "I'll get Paedar to help me. The tide comes in at noon. We can pull him up to the field. He'll just have to lie there quietly and take his chances till the tide goes out again."

$$* \qquad * \qquad *$$

Shortly before noon, Seamus left the cabin and made his way down the deserted road, heading for the cave. Nothing was moving, except for threads of smoke escaping from chimneys. He passed the cabins of those men he knew were never coming home again, and guilt ate at his insides for the part he'd played in their awful fate. What possible good had any of this business done? It had changed nothing for the better and everything a damn sight worse. For now, those left behind would suffer the consequences of the actions of those who had gone before. The oldest boy of the family, be he eight years old or eleven, would be forced to wear the yolk of breadwinner of the family, to take to the road for the harvest, and eke out the most meager of livings in the winter. If last winter was any indication of the type of winters to be expected around here, he thought, God help us all.

Seamus reached the cutoff and turned onto the coast road. He had gone but a short distance, when he spied a patrol coming over a rise in the road towards him. He could tell by their posturing they had spotted him, and he had no recourse but to continue on his way until they met up on the road. His brain spun in a frenzy, fashioning a plausible story of what he was doing out here. The closer they got, the more his knees shook.

One of the soldiers curled thin lips back over rotted teeth and snarled at him, "What are you doing out here? Don't you know everyone is to stay in their homes today."

"I'm only on me way up the road," he said, acting the dolt. He pointed to the side of the road. "Me wee lad is itching something terrible from the worms in his backside, d'ye see, and his mammy sent me out to pick some comfrey root fer to boil up fer to cure it." He waggled his finger at a patch of weeds growing in the ditch. "She insists it come from that patch right over there." He shrugged his shoulders helplessly.

The soldier screwed up his face in disgust. "Well...get it quickly then and get back to where you live and stay there."

Seamus limped over to the side of the road, congratulating himself on his quick thinking. Now, what in hell does bloody comfrey look like, he wondered, and he pulled up one of the green things growing by the side of the road. As luck would have it, it had a bulbous root. He held it up to show the soldiers, then shoved it in his pocket, aware that they waited impatiently for him to leave. They followed him back to the cutoff. He thought he could feel their eyes on his back as he walked up the road to the mountain.

He walked into the cabin. Siobhan sat beside the fire, nursing Troy.

He held the weeds over the fire. "Tell me," he said, "does comfrey cure arse worms?"

"Seamus, watch your language, and no, not that I'm aware of, why?"

He dropped the weeds into the fire. "Because," he said, "now there are two soldiers in the world who think it does." He chuckled to himself and lay down on the bed.

"Soldiers?" She said in exasperation. "Soldiers? Did you find Alex?"

His mood turned serious. "I couldn't get to him, could I? I met up with the patrol and they sent me home. We'll just have to wait until dark."

"But Seamus, he'll drown when the tide comes in. The water goes all the way to the back of the cave."

"Well then, we'll just have to hope it's a low tide and the water doesn't get all the way to the back of the cave, or that he has the strength to climb up out of the hole into the grass. In any case, there is nothing else we can do for the time being."

$$* \qquad * \qquad *$$

Later that night, Seamus creaked open the top half of his cabin door and looked up into the sky. Not a cloud in sight, and a full moon shone diamond bright out of a cold autumn sky, lighting up the countryside.

Closing the door, he muttered, "Where is the cursed rain when you need it?" He shrugged into his jacket, wrapped a scarf around his neck, picked up a walking stick and left the house. He saw not another soul till he got to Fergus's, where Paedar waited, lolling up against the side of the rundown cabin. The two of them walked down the road, with the moon for company. They stayed in the shadows as much as possible, until they reached the coast road. They moved cautiously from gorse bush to rock until they reached the field.

Seamus hobbled through the tall grass to the hole, "Alex," he whispered, "this is Seamus. Can you hear me, lad?"

A voice answered him in Mayo Irish. "Yes, I can hear you, but I'll need help to get out of this hole. My ankle is badly hurt, broken I think."

"Yes…hold on, I've a lad with me…" Seamus directed Paedar to get into the hole and give Alex a boost. He stretched his arm into the hole. "Give a hand up here to me, and use your good foot to push yourself when I say go." With Paedar pushing from the back and Seamus pulling with all his might, Alex scrabbled up out of the hole onto the grass.

Seamus lifted up the leg of Alex's breeches. "Let me take a look at you, son."

What he saw sickened him. Alex's foot swelled over the top of his loosened boot.

"I didn't dare take the boot off for fear I'd never get it on again."

"It's well you didn't." The boot would have to be cut off, but in the meantime it was a mixed blessing, for it would be keeping the ankle in place. Seamus touched the bruised flesh with gentle fingers.

Alex grimaced with pain. "It got caught between a barrel of shot and the side of the boat."

Seamus removed the scarf from around his neck and tied it in a loop under the knee and threaded the other end through a belt loop, raising Alex's foot off the ground.

"I'm sorry son, that'll have to do till we get you into town to a doctor. Will you be able to walk using my stick if I support you?"

"I'll try." He leaned on Seamus to try it out. Paedar crouched down and ran to the road to scout for patrols. When the boy waved the all clear, Alex limped across the field on Seamus's stick. The two men hobbled off toward town, keeping close to the gorse bushes that lined the sides of the road, while Paedar sped ahead to keep watch.

"Where is it you're going in Ballymullian?"

"I have an aunt who owns a millinery shop there."

"Would you be talking about Mae Proulx then?"

"You know her?"

"I do, and I also know the danger you'll be putting everyone in, by your arrival."

"I know it as well, but I have need of a doctor. Later, perhaps, I can find somewhere else to hide out."

Further conversation became impossible. Although Seamus and Paedar supported him as best they could, Alex's pain increased with every step, and he abandoned the use of the stick. As for Seamus, even with the use of his stick back, the extra burden of Alex was making Seamus's body scream out in protest. He wanted nothing more from life at this moment than a good night's sleep on Reanna's floor.

By the time they'd reached the halfway point to Ballymullian, Alex's pain got the better of him and he sagged unconscious between them. Seamus and Paedar eased him behind some roadside bushes and laid him on his back. There was nothing to be done except to wait for him to revive and then push on.

Shortly after they settled themselves in the bushes, Paedar offered to run up ahead and check for patrols.

Seamus cut him off in midsentence with a finger to his lips. The sound of men's voices could be heard in the silence.

He whispered to Paedar, "Keep a close eye on Alex. If he wakes, tell him not to make a sound."

Seamus crept forward and parted the bushes. Two soldiers armed with muskets came into sight around a rocky bend in the road, from where they themselves had been not ten minutes before. They stopped, lowered themselves to the ground and rested their backs against the rocks. A few moments later, they were joined by another patrol approaching from the Ballymullian side, presumably, Seamus thought, their turnaround point.

Seamus listened as the soldiers discussed the previous day's events among themselves.

"Were you able to save any of your belongings from barracks fire?" one of the soldiers asked the other.

"None at all. I was out patrolling the streets, keeping an eye out for 'the big Irishman'. I heard the explosion from four streets away."

"Did they sentries ever catch up with him?"

"No, but they know he's behind setting the fire. He leads a bloody charmed life for now, but some day his luck will run out."

"I believe it's about to run out now, with this latest fiasco," said another. "Another detachment from Castlebar has arrived in town, and tomorrow they are doing a mass enumeration of the countryside to make sure everyone is accounted for. We'll check all names against our list of troublemakers. We'll find him, never fear."

At this news, Seamus said goodbye to his dreams of a good night's sleep. I'll have to make the trip back home before daylight, he fumed…to give Hennessy time to escape.

Rest time over, the soldiers got to their feet and marched back they way they came. Seamus waited until they were out of sight and then returned to the others. Alex was awake and resting. A worried Paedar sat beside him, looking like a mother hen with her chick.

They gave the patrol time to get far away before they made their move to follow them into town. By traveling cautiously, and staying to the side of the road, they arrived safely into town. Once there, Paedar went ahead of Seamus and Alex, keeping close to the buildings. By the time they reached the millinery shop, Seamus could barely walk himself.

*   *   *

Paedar and Alex slipped into the shadows while Seamus rapped quietly on Mae's door. He rapped again, not wanting to frighten her, but still fearful that they might be discovered.

The little woman, nightcap awry, peered through the glass.

"Mae…it's me, Seamus. Please open the door."

She fumbled a bit as she opened the shop door. "Seamus…what on earth…!"

Alex and Paedar emerged from the shadows.

Mae put a hand up to her mouth. "Alex, mon cher," she exclaimed as she recognized her nephew. "Come in.come in!"

Seamus pushed Paedar in the door after Alex and latched the door after them. They hurried through the curtain to Mae's quarters in the back of the shop. She motioned Alex toward her chair by the hearth. He sank gratefully into it and Paedar lifted his injured foot onto the footstool.

Mae's hand shook as she gently smoothed his dark hair back off his forehead. "What has happened to you, my dear? You're hurt. Are you in some sort of trouble?"

He caressed her withered cheek. "It's a long story, ma tante. I will tell you what I'm able, tomorrow. I need a place to stay for a time, if I may impose on you."

"Of course you may, no need even to ask. I wouldn't hear of you going anywhere else."

Seamus cut in, "He needs a doctor Mae…One who knows how to keep his own counsel."

Mae raised her eyebrows at the request. "That would be Doctor McCabe. He lives on this side of the street, next door but one to the house on the corner. It has small panes of glass in the window and a brass knocker on the door."

"If it's all the same to you, I'll go round to his place now and see if he'll come straight away to have a look at the lad. His ankle needs tending to."

Shortly after he left, Seamus returned with a short, square man in tow, medical bag bulging from underneath his cape. He bent to examine Alex's foot.

Seamus whispered to Mae; "We're not needed here now, so we'll say goodnight. We have to get back before daylight."

*   *   *

Two hours later, Seamus said good night to Paedar and humped up the last hill towards home. He stumbled in the door. His knees began to give way and Siobhan caught him and led him over to the hearth and eased him onto a stool, then turned back and closed the door.

She knelt beside him and removed his boots. "You'll be all right, Seamus, love." She felt his forehead with her hand and fetched him a dipper of water and watched him while he drank. "For the love of God, what took you so long? I was jumping out of my skin with worry."

"We had decided to stay overnight at Reanna's and come home in the morning because of curfew and all, but we overheard a patrol discussing an enumeration that's to take place out here in the morning to find out which people are missing. At the same time there will be a house-to-house search for survivors from the boats. I came back to warn Hennessy to get away, but I see he's anticipated me."

"Indeed he has," Siobhan answered, "he came roaring in about two hours ago, and informed me that he was leaving the country and he wouldn't be back."

Seamus huffed in disgust. "…looking after his own skin, as usual."

"You'll never guess what he did before he left though. He went through the trunk." She shook her head in amazement. "You wouldn't believe what was in there, Seamus." She started counting off the contents on her fingers. "There was a complete set of clothing, which he put on over the clothes he had on his back, a purse of money, that he counted and then stuffed everywhere into his pockets, a bottle of real whiskey that disappeared into his bag, a pistol, which he hid in his coat. I tell you, Seamus, the man was prepared for the next coming of the very Christ himself."

Seamus shook his head and clucked his tongue at her irreverence.

"…And that's not the end of it. Then he pulled out some papers from the trunk and went through them. Then he set fire to them."

"Look over there on the dresser and see what he left behind for you." Siobhan had lined up the booty in a straight row. A stick of red sealing wax, complete with an official looking metal seal, a writing quill and a bottle of ink.

She continued, "He sat down and wrote a letter giving himself safe passage and signed it with some hoity-toity Lord's name. Then he folded it in three, melted some of this red wax onto the seam, pushed this metal thing into it, blew on it till it was cool and put the letter in his vest pocket. And then he did a nice thing."

She ceremoniously handed Seamus an official looking document "He signed over this cabin to us, dated last October, with the understanding that we know nothing of him or his activities. He said he wouldn't be needing the trunk anymore either, and that it would make a nice bed for Troy." She walked over to the trunk where Troy was snuggled up in a brown blanket, fast asleep with half of his fist in his mouth. "Can you believe our good fortune, Seamus?"

"A nice thing is it? Good fortune, is it?" Seamus snorted suspiciously, "I'd trust that bugger about as much as I'd trust an Englishman." He got up from the stool and limped across the room. He lifted the sleeping child, blanket and all from the trunk and deposited him on the bed, then carried the trunk over by the light of the hearth.

He tapped around inside the bottom of the trunk until he found what he was looking for. Cursing Hennessy, he smashed his fist into the false bottom. The wood splintered. He ripped off the remaining slats with his bare hands. He removed a folded slip of paper, read it, then waved it angrily at Siobhan.

"D'you see this? This is a list of men's names, among which are some who died last night." He held the paper over the flames until it caught fire and then dropped it. Then he broke up the false bottom into small pieces and fed them into the fire as well. "As usual, he's covered his own tracks and left someone else to take the blame. May the man's immortal soul rot in hell for the terrible things he's done." He held the paper over the flames till it caught fire and then dropped it. He shook his fist in the air. "He wasn't satisfied until he put my whole family in jeopardy, down to the wee baby. Shame on him."

Siobhan rubbed ashes into the wood of the trunk to disguise where the false bottom was. Then she made up Troy's bed again and tucked the sleeping baby back into it. Seamus wrapped the seal and the sealing wax in a cloth, took an iron spoon from the hearth and went outside to bury the evidence. He dug a hole in his patch of garden, buried the cloth bundle and stamped the earth back into the hole. Then he smoothed it over, swiped it back and forth a few times and walked over it again. By the time he'd cleaned off the spoon and replaced it, Siobhan had scattered the ashes in the fireplace, thrown another clod of turf over the coals and placed the quill and bottle of ink beside the book on the dresser. They checked around once more and then crawled wearily into bed.

*   *   *

Early next morning, before daylight, the door was thrown open and two armed soldiers burst into the cabin and yanked Seamus and Siobhan out of bed. Troy woke up at the commotion and crying, put his arms out to his mother. Siobhan ran over to him and picked him up out of the trunk.

"Is your name Hennessy?"

"It isn't. My name is Seamus O'Dowd and I'm the schoolmaster."

"Where is the man called Hennessy?"

"I have no idea. I've not seen the man since I purchased the cabin from him last year."

The soldier looked at the paper he held in his hand. "It says here that a James Hennessy owns this cabin."

Seamus rummaged in the dresser drawer, picked up the deed to the cabin and handed it over to the soldier.

"Why wasn't the change registered at the barracks in town?"

Seamus ran his hand through his unruly hair. "Well, I guess I'll have to plead ignorance on that one. I wasn't aware that it had to be."

While he interrogated Seamus, the other soldier ransacked the cabin. He pulled everything out of the little dresser, upended it and threw it in the middle of the room and examined the dirt floor underneath it. He lifted the cailleach up to the wall, examined the floor underneath it and let it fall with a loud bang. Troy started in fright and began to scream. Siobhan rocked him up and down against her shoulder trying to comfort him. The soldier continued his search, pulling the blanket out of the trunk and throwing it on the ground. He examined the trunk from all sides and checked the fireplace for loose stones. Then, the two men left abruptly, stating that everyone was to remain indoors for the rest of the day. Seamus and Siobhan listened to their receding footsteps and then fell into each other's arms in relief.

Chapter 14

▼

Ballymullian, October 1797

The commotion of Alex's arrival had awakened both of them last night, but before Reanna had finished explaining to Erris who he was, her daughter's eyelids had drooped and she'd fallen asleep again. A grand thing it was to be young and innocent and free of the encumbrances of adulthood, Reanna marveled. And so, she had stood by herself at the top of the stairs, straining the hear the quiet conversation from downstairs, wanting with all that was in her to see Alex again, but mortally shy at the prospect of it, after the way she had deserted him so many years ago. Besides which, it was not her place to interfere in Mae's reunion with her beloved nephew. As well, there'd been no mention from downstairs of the fact that she was even in the house. There would be time enough in the morning for a reunion. Right now, the important thing was to get Alex's injuries looked after. She'd almost wept when she heard him cry out in pain. She heard the doctor reassure him that now the ankle was set, the worst was over. She tiptoed back to her bed, where she lay awake for a long time, questions spinning around in her head…what was Alex doing here in any case? How did he get hurt? And how was it that he was with Seamus?

The murmur of hushed voices from downstairs filtered up to her sleeping room and lulled her to sleep. The last thing she heard was Dr. McCabe's soft voice wishing Mae and Alex a good night and the tinkle of the bell as he left the shop.

Reanna awoke from a fitful sleep, well before dawn. She shivered with anticipation. Alex was back and he was downstairs. Sometimes, good things do come out of bad, she told herself and got up out of bed. She reached over to Erris's bed, pulled the bedcovers up over her sleeping daughter's shoulders and closed the door so as not to disturb her. She checked the water level in the three-legged pot, poked the fire to life under it and laid down some fresh clods of turf on the embers.

Until now, she'd made a practice of creeping down the stairs, before she got dressed, to tend to Mae's fire, so the room would be warm and toasty by the time she brought down the old woman's breakfast. Mae had insisted that she could tend to the fire herself, but Reanna had countered that; 'I'm fixing my own, anyway.' However, with Alex downstairs, she in her nightclothes wouldn't do at all. She scooped some of the still warm water out of the bastible and made her ablutions. Her fingers fumbled the buttons closed on her navy blue dress. She hastily ran a brush through her long hair, coiled it into a coppery twist on the back of her head, and on second thought, left it to tumble gracefully around her shoulders. She picked up her skirts and crept down the stairs.

Mae slept on her back, nightcap in place, open mouth emitting a soft purr, dainty hands folded primly on top of the bedcover. The sight of Alex asleep in Mae's chair beside the hearth, took her breath away. He was still handsome. Dark eyelashes, the envy of any girl, fanned out against his cheeks. The watercolor glow from the hearth played on his gypsy features.

Blushing furiously, she quietly added fresh turf to the fire and poked it to life. She stole another peek at him. He looked so uncomfortable, reclining in Mae's chair, legs stuck straight out in front of him, supported by a footstool. His left leg was held straight with flat sticks and swathed loosely in bandages. His head lolled upright, supported by one hand, and his bandaged arm lay against his chest.

Mae's reedy voice broke the spell. "Reanna, do you see who's here...Alex!"

Alex yellow eyes snapped open. "Reanna...Reanna O'Neal?" He turned his gaze immediately to her eyes, those intelligent eyes that he had never forgotten. "You came back!" A broad smile lit up his face. He tried to rise, and gave up in dismay.

Reanna stood in embarrassed confusion at the frank admiration in his eyes, twisting her dark red hair into a coil over her shoulder. "Reanna Campbell, now."

His eyes clouded with disappointment. "You're married, then?"

Her heart leaped in hope at the sorrow in his voice, but this moment called for solemnity. She lowered her head. "I'm a widow, since last September." Then hesitantly, she took the plunge. "And you Alex, are you married?" She held her breath for his answer.

Mae spoke up from her bed. "No, he's not. Isn't that right, Alex?"

He nodded.

Heat suffused Reanna's face. She felt fifteen again. She smiled shyly. "And how is your ankle this morning?"

"Sore as a boil," he replied. "I guess I won't be galloping around for awhile."

"I'm sorry to hear that," she offered, feeling the hypocrite, knowing full well she was not sorry at all to hear that he might be staying around for a while. She spun around so he wouldn't see the flush on her cheeks. Mae, looking like a cat with a dish of cream, watched the proceedings with glee.

Reanna gave her a tremulous smile and kissed her wrinkled cheek. "I'll be bringing breakfast down shortly," she whispered, and escaped up the stairs, touching her burning cheeks and berating herself for acting like a giddy schoolgirl instead of a respectable widow.

Reanna stirred the breakfast porridge, mind in a whirl, absently watching Erris brushing her long dark curls in front of the mirror.

"Mam, who was that man came to Aunt Mae's last night?"

Reanna was at a loss for an answer. The fact that Seamus had brought Alex here in the middle of the night, could mean only one thing. It was not an open visit and the less said the better. When in God's name would the need for secrets end, she wondered bitterly. The child had spent almost her whole life under one kind of strain or another. Now she had another secret she had to live her life around.

She cut slices of oaten bread and arranged them on a plate. "He is Mae's nephew, from France. I'm not aware of why he is here, but you mustn't mention it to anyone."

She looked at her mother with solemn eyes. "I promise. I won't mention it." She brought the bowls over to her mother to be filled with porridge.

They brought breakfast downstairs on a tray to the table. Reanna introduced Erris to Alex and she greeted him in French.

Reanna's mouth dropped open in surprise. "Where did you learn that?" she asked, impressed.

Mae raised her hand in the air. "Guilty." When Reanna turned away, she waggled a finger in mock rebuke at Erris. "That was supposed to be a surprise for later."

Erris hung her head in embarrassment. "I'm sorry," she mouthed.

Reanna could contain her curiosity no longer. "Are you able to tell us why you are here, and how you got hurt, Alex?"

He shook his head. "I regret that I'm not able to, Reanna, and at the risk of sounding flippant, it's best for all your sakes that you know nothing." He looked at Erris. "Is it safe to speak in front of the child?"

Reanna nodded. "Indeed it is, for hasn't she had to keep secrets all of her life?"

All eyes were on Alex as he began his litany, speaking in rehearsed tones.

"Suffice to say, I am here by chance. My name is Sean McNally and I'm a salesman of woolens from Sligo. If anyone asks, I've been here for a week recovering from a fall from my horse." He turned his gaze to Reanna, surprised at his giddiness at seeing her again. "As long as we are asking questions, madam, wherever did you disappear to ten years ago? We thought you were dead."

Reanna shot a distressed look over at Mae. The little spinster returned her look with a steady noncommittal gaze.

Reanna took a deep breath and answered shortly, "I moved to Dunbury."

"But…in the middle of the night? Why would you do that, Reanna?"

Reanna hung her head in confusion.

Erris spoke up. "Because that's where my Da was and where you married and had me, right, Mam?"

Relief washed over Reanna's face. "Yes, that's right, love, right indeed. Some day if you like, Alex, I'll tell you more of the details, but now is not the time." She picked up the teapot and poured a refill of tea around the table.

Alex turned a questioning look to Mae. She returned his gaze, and then to lighten the mood, she changed the subject.

She took Alex's good hand in her own. "I've kept your letters, mon cher. I hope you don't mind, but I've allowed Reanna to read them as well."

He nodded his agreement. Reanna buttered a slice of bread and placed it on Alex's plate. He smiled his thanks.

Mae released his hand and picked up her china cup. "They were very impressive letters, Alex, learning so many languages and all. Your mama would be so proud of how you've grown up." She turned to the others. "You know, Alex's mother could speak many languages as well. She was the bookish one in our family. I was the beauty." Mae struck a ludicrous pose, and laughed at her own good humor.

When everyone had finished breakfast, Reanna placed a hand gently on Erris's arm.

"Would you take the dishes upstairs and clean them up, lovey? The adults need to talk."

When Erris was out of earshot, they discussed Alex's safety. They agreed that Mae's small room didn't afford enough security in the event that a curious millinery customer made it her business to peek around the curtain. Alex's presence would surely be discovered, as the hearth was in line with the curtain. To this end, it was decided that he would hide out upstairs in Reanna's flat.

Reanna went upstairs to forewarn Erris, while Alex eased himself up the stairs on his backside. Reanna slid her arm around his waist and helped him over to the twin of her chair in front of the hearth. The feel of Alex's firm body awakened feelings in Reanna that she thought had disappeared forever. Flustered, she slipped a footstool underneath his foot, gathered up some blankets and made a pallet on the floor nearby for him.

"Alex, you can sleep in my bed," Erris offered. "I don't mind sleeping on the floor. I sleep on the floor at Uncle Seamus's all the time."

With an embarrassed look at her Reanna, he replied. "Thank you kindly, Erris, but the floor will do just fine. It will be easier for me if I need to turn over during the night, you know."

*   *   *

Late in the afternoon, Doctor McCabe arrived. He called Reanna over to the stool where he was examining Alex's ankle. "D'you see this here?" he said, cleansing the swollen mass of discolored flesh, "You need to keep it clean and dry." He sprinkled some yellow powder on Alex's wounds and handed her the tin. "Sprinkle some of this on the wound after you clean it, and be sure to watch for any red streaks on his leg." He swaddled Alex's leg loosely in bandages and fastened a slat onto each side of his leg to immobilize it "That'll do for now. I can't put a proper

splint on the ankle until the swelling goes down and the pain eases off."
He fastened his black bag, and got up from the stool. "Good day to you.
I'll be back to look at it in a few days."

$$*\qquad\qquad*\qquad\qquad*$$

The next evening, Reanna sat on the stool in front of Alex, with his
injured foot in her lap, and cleaned around the cuts on his leg, taking
care not to let the water touch the bandages around his ankle. Then she
took care of his arm. She had not touched a man so intimately since her
marriage to Donald and the warmth of Alex's skin made her realize how
much she missed a man's touch. They locked eyes in apprehension at
the tinkle of the doorbell downstairs. They heard Mae's cane hitting the
slate floor as she went to answer the door.

They heard her greeting Liam, then a rap at the bottom of the stairs.

"Reanna," Liam's raspy voice called happily from down below, "can I
come up and see the prize pig?"

Reanna thought Alex's grin would split his face wide open as Liam's
head appeared around the corner of the stairwell.

Liam knelt beside the chair and wrapped Alex in a bear hug. They
pounded each other on the back for good measure. "I heard you were
coming," the older man said.

Reanna continued happily tending to Alex's wounds, as he brought
Liam up to date. They were so easy with each other, and Alex speaking
the Irish like he was born to it. Liam turned his rheumy eyes on Reanna.
"It's really a grand thing you are doing for Mae to take care of Alex and
let him stay up here away from prying eyes."

"I'm happy to do it," Reanna said fervently, "If I live to be a hundred
I can never repay the dear woman for all the kindness she's shown me."

$$*\qquad\qquad*\qquad\qquad*$$

After Liam left, Reanna lit the candle and picked up her sewing basket. "I hope you'll forgive my rudeness Alex, for I still have some finishing up to do before tomorrow."

She arranged his blankets on the floor. "Be sure and let me know when you're tired and I'll help you get settled."

"I'm not ready for sleep. We have some catching up to do."

She sat in her chair, threaded her needle and began to carefully baste some matching grosgrain ribbon into the felt crown of a forest green hat. "Can you guess where this hat is going?"

He shook his head noncommittally.

"Crofton House."

"So, you've seen Lady Evelyn since you've been back? What did she have to say to you when she saw you again?"

Reanna smoothed the ribbon flat underneath her fingers. "Oh, I didn't see her. She's bedridden I understand…suffers from the same thing that her poor mother did. This hat is for her daughter, Lady Ellen."

They sat in silence for what seemed forever. As Reanna stitched, she felt Alex's eyes on her. Then he broke the silence with the question she knew was coming.

"Why did you run away, Reanna? I waited for you until almost midnight before I set out to look for you."

Reanna said not a word, but kept her head down, eyes intent on her work.

"When I arrived at Crofton House," Alex continued, "I could see no lights in the front of the house, so I walked around to the scullery and peeked in the window. Mary was scrubbing pots, and let me in. She told me the party had gone on late and everyone had left long ago. She said that about eleven o'clock, you bolted into the scullery from the back stairs, looking like you'd seen a ghost. Mary'd yelled at you, but you went like a shot out the back door. Then she'd gone upstairs to see what made you run and found the master unconscious on the floor in Lady Margaret's room, with his head all bloody and his trousers in disarray."

Reanna dropped her work in her lap and covered her face in shame.

Alex reached over and took her hands away from her face. "Don't hide your face. You've done nothing wrong." He smiled wryly. "Mary told me that she figured he'd been up to his old tricks and got to you. So after she made sure he was still unconscious, she gave him a kick for good measure and left him there."

In spite of herself, Reanna felt the beginnings of a smile.

"Was he the reason you ran away, Reanna?"

She sat silently stitching for a long time before answering. "He was. I thought I'd killed him, and I drove myself to distraction for years, fearing I would be found and punished. When I arrived here, Mae told me that one of his own horses had thrown him and he had broken his neck...two years ago it was."

He laid his hand over hers. "Did she tell you I never forgot you, Reanna?"

Flustered, she slipped her hand out of his. "No, she didn't Alex, but she gave me your letters to read." Her fingers guided the needle methodically through its paces. Finally she spoke, "What are you mixed up in, Alex? And what has Seamus got to do with it? I'm that worried for Siobhan and her family, with all these strange goings on."

He shook his head. "I can tell you nothing about Seamus, except that he has come through the worst of it in safety. Things will settle down soon, and they'll tell you themselves, I am sure."

"And your own part in this? I don't understand how a wounded French soldier ends up hiding in Ballymullian."

He sighed deeply. "All right, but I think I'd better start at the beginning. He shivered. Reanna arose from her chair, picked up a blanket from the floor and tucked it around him.

"You read my letters, so you understand what is going on at home?"

"Somewhat."

"And you have the gist of what I do for a living?"

"Travel to foreign places and translation of foreign languages, isn't it? It sounds an exciting life to me."

"So it was in the beginning, because I was a boy, and caught up in the adventure of it all." His eyes clouded over with pain. "But when Pierre and his family were killed, along with thousands of other innocent people, grief turned me into a man." He blinked his eyes rapidly. "And I began to see past the adventure into the cesspool that was war."

Reanna set aside her work, reached out and took his hand between hers. "What a terrible thing to see. I'm so sorry, Alex."

He told her of his experiences in a monotone voice as though he were alone in the room with his thoughts. Afterwards, he shook his head, "The saddest part was, that nothing seemed to improve after all the killing. Just different sets of people doing it."

Reanna nodded.

"And now, for some reason of which I was never informed, but think I've since figured out, I was sent here to help train the Irish with French weapons." In a voice heavy with disillusion, he concluded, "I wonder, is this maneuver to help the Irish reclaim their country, or is it France advancing her own ends by using Irish lives to help Napoleon invade England. It's like a sick chess game, with the rich as the players and the poor as the pawns."

Reanna sat still as a stone. A glamorous life turned into a nightmare, she thought.

"And your ankle? What about that?"

"I was in a curragh, coming into the bay during the storm two nights ago. My foot jammed between a barrel and the side of the boat. When it released, I was thrown out into the bay."

Reanna gasped and covered her mouth with both hands, her blue eyes widening in dismay. "Poor you!"

"When my foot hit the salt water, I thought I would die with the pain. By the time I regained my senses, the boat had disappeared from my sight. The storm still raged. It was all I could do to keep myself afloat. I had to fight to remain calm."

Reanna took his hand. Her voice broke, "God love you, Alex."

"From the top of a wave," he continued, "I saw a dim light in the distance. My lungs were ready to burst from the exertion by this time, but I swam toward it. As I got closer into the bay, the wind eased off, and the fog rolled in. I headed toward where I thought I'd seen the light."

He shivered and pulled the blanket closer around his body. "A half hour later, the tide spit me out onto the rocks. I hung on and when the tide went out, I found the cave and crawled into it. That's where Siobhan found me."

Reanna's mouth fell open. "Siobhan found you?"

He held up his hand. "She did. But she can tell you her part in all this if she wishes. I don't know anymore than that."

Chapter 15

―――――▼―――――

Ballymullian, December 1797

With few exceptions, the cold winter rain fell daily from a leaden sky as Christmas approached. The people still struggled in the grip of hardship. In retaliation for the attempted arms drop and the burning of the barracks in September, Ballymullian and the surrounding countryside had been placed under a dusk to dawn curfew. The cruelest hardship visited on them, however, was the rescinding of their privilege to attend Mass and educate the poor. This hurt their hearts and minds a great deal more than it hurt their pockets, for this was the greater part of who they were.

As for Seamus, being forbidden to teach was tantamount to cutting off his blood supply. This outward expression thwarted, he poured his heart and his soul onto paper by candlelight in his cabin. Every night, he and Siobhan said the rosary on their knees. Of a Sunday, Siobhan insisted they say it in the morning as well, to take the place of Mass, after which they bundled Troy up against the downpour and made the trek into Ballymullian to visit at the millinery shop.

It was on one of these visits that Alex confessed to them of his deep concern for Mae's health.

'She scarcely eats enough to keep a bird alive and she's losing weight at an alarming rate,' he'd said. 'She insists on helping out after supper, so I slide downstairs on my backside and read to her in French while she stitches. But, eyesight aside, she seems unable to sustain the energy needed to complete the simplest task. Lately, on these cold dark nights, she's begun to take to her bed as soon as supper is over. I read to her until she dozes off. It's a great worry for all of us.'

      *   *   *

In the weeks before the troubles at Bonnagh Head, business at the millinery shop had almost doubled. Word of Reanna's millinery prowess had reached the surrounding towns, and the gentry from as far away as Westport and Castlebar had traveled to *La Modiste* to order their Christmas hats from the two women. However, since the curfew, the shortened hours had caused a decline in local business and a number of townspeople who'd ordered hats hadn't the money to pay for them. This in turn caused Reanna no amount of grief, for she'd had to order millinery supplies from Dublin and had scarcely enough funds to pay for them.

Now, for the last time that evening, she trudged wearily up the narrow steps, her arms piled with half-finished hats that Mae had been working on. Her fingers ached, her arms ached and she felt overcome with sorrow about her dear friend's worsening health. She dropped her burden beside her chair. She sighed and massaged the knots in her neck. Her weariness wasn't born of ingratitude, she told herself. She was indeed grateful for the new business, but the truth of it was, there seemed no end to the labor. She gazed at Alex as he slept, head resting against the back of the chair. He looked so right, somehow, sitting there in front of the hearth. She didn't want to imagine life without him. But the facts were, the time was fast approaching when he would have to return to France. Recalling all the recent events in their lives, she broke and tears fell unbidden down her cheeks. She fumbled her handkerchief out of her sleeve, held it up to her streaming eyes and escaped into her bedroom. When she'd composed herself, she returned to Alex's chair. He reached out, took her hand and drew her down to the arm of his chair.

"Why were you crying?"

She made as if to get up. "I'm fine now, really. It's only that I'm worn out."

"Then you must let me help."

"You need to get well, Alex."

"I am well. My arm has healed and I don't use my ankle to sew."

"But it's woman's work."

"Nonsense, I've been sewing since I was seven years old. Just show me what you want me to do." He grinned at her. "I'm really quite adept at it, you know."

*   *   *

In the next few weeks, Alex proved to be as good as his word. In the evenings, he and Reanna sat in front of the fire stitching in comfortable silence, or in quiet conversation. Hearing Reanna tell of her life from the time she left Ballymullian, deepened Alex's regard for her. She had grown from the frightened adolescent he had known to this sure and selfless woman. But he knew that each day of his recovery brought him closer to the day he must leave her and return to his unit in France. Neither one mentioned this, but the unspoken fact of his departure lay like a ticking clock between them.

*   *   *

A few days before Christmas, Alex sat alone in front of the hearth, and stared across the room at the window. Doctor McCabe had just left and the news was discouraging. After almost three months confinement,

Alex's foot was still unable to bear any weight without excruciating pain, a condition that might continue for some time. The doctor had insisted that Alex's splints had to stay on for at least another fortnight.

The portly man had shaken his head sadly. "I'm sorry, lad. I've done all I can. There are a lot of small bones in the foot, you know, and in all probability, they've been smashed to smithereens. The fact is, I can't repair what I can't see, so you'll just have to wait it out till the bones heal of their own accord and see what happens."

"How long a wait will that be, do you suppose?"

The cold comfort of his words still hung in the air. "I can't tell you that, lad. All in God's time, I expect."

*   *   *

Alex, heart heavy with despair, slumped back into his chair and closed his eyes until he heard Reanna's footsteps approaching. She stood beside him; hands clasped tightly together, brows drawn together in concern. "What did the doctor have to say? Will you be returning to France then?"

"It doesn't look like it, at least for a while."

Reanna's eyes glistened in relief, and she put her hand to her mouth to hide its trembling. Alex drew her down onto his lap and enfolded her in his arms. He brushed her lips gently with his own.

"Would you have me go, Reanna?"

"God in Heaven, no," she confessed. "I dread the day you must leave."

He stroked her cheek with the back of his hand. "I dread it as well. I've given it considerable thought and I've come to a decision. I'm not going back."

She drew back in dismay. "Wouldn't that be desertion?"

He looked down at his useless foot. "Yes, it would be…and then I wonder if they haven't already written me off as dead."

Reanna caressed his neck and nestled further into his arms, feeling that she was home at last. Alex raised her face to his and kissed her slowly and tenderly on the mouth. "When it's safe to do so, cara, will you be my wife?"

"With all my heart," she whispered softly.

*   *   *

Sunday morning, thick snowflakes fell and covered the ground with a soft white blanket. Reanna agonized over what she was going to feed everyone for the double celebration of Christmas and Erris's eleventh birthday the next day. Although she and Alex together had completed the Christmas orders, money was slow coming in. She had decided it would have to be black pudding and colcannon, what with money still being so tight and all.

At mid-morning Liam burst through the door and hollered upstairs at her. "Reanna, come down here and see what I found!"

Reanna appeared, wiping her hands on her apron. "What is it?"

"Look here!" He pulled two plump hens from underneath his loose jacket and held the wriggling birds up by their feet. They flapped their copper wings frantically and tried to escape from his grasp.

Reanna put her hands on her hips and glared at him. "They look suspiciously like hens from Crofton House, Liam."

"Aren't you the trusting soul," he replied in an injured tone and went straight away with his booty out the back door to the little enclosed yard and wrung their necks.

Later, Erris sat on the doorstep and plucked the shiny coppery feathers from the plump bodies and placed them carefully in a bag. Her head buzzed with Christmas plans. If she had enough feathers, she would ask Mam for a square of red velvet from the shop and fashion a small feather pillow for Alex to rest his foot on. Mam would be so excited when she got her present this year. Mae and Alex had secretly been teaching Erris to speak French as a present to Mam and Seamus. She was to recite the *Our Father* in French at dinner.

When she'd finished her chore, she handed the plucked birds to Reanna, who gutted them and rinsed them clean in a tub of water. Liam buried the entrails in the small yard. Reanna plunged the cleaned birds into a bath of steaming water to loosen the pinfeathers and then brought them to Mae and Alex, who armed with paring knives, removed any large pinfeathers from the loose, pink flesh. When Mae's knife slipped and cut her thumb, Erris offered to take her place. Alex showed her the technique of holding the blade behind the pinfeather and scraping it frees against her thumb. It was then that he noticed her spatulate thumb and remarked that a boyhood friend of his had one of those and had considered it to be good luck.

Reanna recalled how upset she had been at Erris's birth, believing that the thumb was a curse for not admitting her fears about Erris's parentage to Donald. Somehow, whether her precious daughter's birth was the result of Lord Dalton's rape or whether Erris was Donald's daughter, seemed so far away now, and really not important at all.

          *   *   *

Christmas day dawned clear and bright. The shop door opened and Seamus with little Troy in his arms, stamped the snow off his boots and entered, followed by Siobhan who carried a pot of mixed shellfish she'd cooked at home. Clams there were and cockles, periwinkles and mussels. Liam arrived shortly after, carrying a jug of poteen, from which he poured a measure into the adult's cups to take the chill off their bones. He picked Mae up bodily as though she were a feather, and carried her upstairs to join the others. Seamus brought up the small table from Mae's room and they placed it beside Reanna's table. Siobhan covered them both with linen cloths. The men brought all the chairs from downstairs. The hens cooking in the large black pot emitted a savory smell that permeated the flat. Alex peeled turnips till he thought his fingers would fall off, then Siobhan carried them downstairs to cook with the potatoes in Mae's fireplace.

Reanna had arisen before dawn, and made some oaten bread. Due to the fact that she hadn't had to spend money for black pudding, she splurged and sent Erris next door to the bakery to purchase a cream cake for dessert. The warm room shook with laughter as Siobhan related Seamus's incident with the British soldiers and the comfrey root.

When they all sat down at the table to eat, Erris performed her recitation. When she'd finished, Reanna wiped her eyes, rose from her chair and embraced pupil and teachers.

Seamus was impressed. "I think this one would do well to go away to school, Reanna. She is a clever girl and there is only so much I can teach her here."

"But Seamus, we don't have that kind of money. Besides, she's a girl. It's not really done, is it? Only boys get further education."

"Nonsense. She's eleven years of age and is brighter than any two boys I know. If she's going to make something of herself, now is the time to start." He sat up straighter in his chair. "Lack of money aside, there are always provisions for the gifted, you know. If you can see your way clear to have her go, I'll write the letter to the Wolford Academy in Roscommon and tell them of her capabilities. If she's accepted, I'll take her there myself"

Reanna looked over at Erris, who leaned forward in anticipation. "Would you like to go away to school, love?"

Erris jumped up and hugged her mother. "Oh Mam, that would be so grand."

"Well then," Reanna smiled, "we'll certainly give it some thought."

Chapter 16

───────▼───────

Rathskill Mountain, April 1798

On a soft April morning, the O'Dowds left their cabin at first light, to ensure a squatting place at market for the day. Seamus limped down the path, carrying one-year-old Troy, who dozed against his chest. Siobhan carried Seamus's stick over her shoulder, on which she'd hung her bundle of knitted goods. Seamus's learning sign hung on a string around her neck.

Throughout the night, a warm rain had washed down the surrounding countryside, and now the azure sky with its fast disappearing skiff of gray clouds, promised a warm, sunny day. But, the best news of all was that after six long months, the curfew and the restrictions had been lifted. On Sunday they'd attended Mass with their neighbours and Seamus had resumed his classes the following day.

Paedar, an expectant smile on his face, hailed them from the path. "Have you had a reply from the school in Roscommon, yet?"

Seamus shook his head in disappointment. "No, I haven't," he replied. "I would have thought I'd have heard by now. I suppose I'd better write another letter in the event the first one went astray."

Troy awakened at the sound of his cousin's voice and stretched out his arms to be taken.

Paedar waggled his fingers. "Hand that big lump over here to me."

Seamus gratefully turned his son over to Paedar who hoisted the child up onto his back, and galloped with him down the trail towards the coast road. Troy's squeals of delight floated back to them.

Siobhan handed Seamus his stick, then stretched and breathed in the fresh air. "Aah, God, Seamus, doesn't it feel grand to have things back to normal again?"

Seamus didn't answer, just picked his way down the road, lips pursed in thought.

"Did you hear me?" she demanded.

"I did."

"Well then...?"

He rubbed a hand thoughtfully over his face. "It's just that I'm not so sure as you that things are back to normal...and if they are, what makes that so grand?"

"For God's sake Seamus," she retorted, "pick yourself up! Conditions are a damn sight better than they've been for a long while."

"And still a damn sight worse than they should be." He raised his stick in salute to Paedar and Troy who waved at them from the coast road. "It's only that I have a sneaking suspicion that it's not over yet."

"Why is that?"

"For the simple reason that my classes, although larger than before, are now made up of children, women and old men. There's not one able bodied man to be seen."

"Well, a lot of them died in the troubles in September, and perhaps the others have taken to the road to find work to feed their families."

Seamus shook his head. "I'm not convinced. On the other hand, perhaps it means that the men have already made up their minds which way they're going. And I should just concentrate on the people who come to be taught. If women, children and old people it is, so be it."

"Do you imagine you'll ever have a proper place to teach in?"

"Now who's dreaming?"

They walked along, each wrapped up in their own thoughts, till Seamus broke the silence.

"It's peculiar you asked that question, for you know, Donald asked me that same thing almost twenty-seven years ago. I don't see that we're any closer to realizing it now than we were then."

Siobhan stopped short. "How do we know that, if we don't ask? The Anglican Bishop seems a reasonable man. He's been agreeable to the saying of Mass and your teaching in the fields. I can't imagine why he'd object to the addition of a roof to keep us dry in the process."

Seamus walked along in silence, then muttered as if to himself. "They certainly wouldn't give us any money to build it, but if they gave us a little plot of ground, and supposing we did it ourselves..." He walked along in silence for a few steps. "I'll ask."

Chapter 17

▼

Ballymullian, August 1798

August arrived unseasonably hot and bright. Alex picked up his walking stick and hobbled down the stairs to Mae's room. He hadn't regained the full use of his ankle. It had set stiff and was still catchy when he put any weight on it. He despaired of ever being able to walk again without the support of a stick, but he was walking, and for that he was grateful. It allowed him to lift some of the burden from Reanna and Erris.

After Christmas, Mae's health had begun to fail. She'd been bedridden for almost a fortnight now, and they'd all been taking turns sitting up beside her these nights, sponging her forehead, and giving her sips of poteen for the pain.

Alex crossed over to the chair where Reanna slept beside his beloved aunt's bed. He picked up the candle from the small table and looked at the old woman's sleeping face. Bushy brows over sunken eyes, face yellow, cheeks drawn with pain. A moan escaped her lips. Tears gathered in his eyes. He placed a gentle hand on her forehead. He replaced the candle on the table and shook Reanna gently.

She rose to her feet at the distressed look on his face. "What is it, love?"

"Would you take a look at her, cara? She's really ill, I'm afraid."

Reanna took one look at Mae, and then picked up her skirts and hurried up the stairs and into the sleeping room. "Erris," she whispered, urgently, "wake up now."

Her daughter sat up in bed and saw her mother's tear-filled eyes. "What's wrong, Mam?" she cried.

"It's Mae. I'm afraid she's very sick, darling."

Erris threw her covers off and put her arms around her mother. Sobs shook her body. "Shall I go for Seamus and Siobhan?"

Reanna took her handkerchief out of her sleeve and passed it to her daughter. "No, love, I need you to run for the doctor. Tell him that Mae is very sick and will he please come. The others will be here after Mass, in any case."

Erris threw on her clothes, and flew out the door. In a few minutes, she was back with Doctor McCabe.

After he examined Mae, he closed his bag without a word. He looked up at the worried faces in the room and motioned them out of earshot of the bed. They followed him into the shop.

He shook his head. "There is nothing else to be done, except to keep her comfortable."

Reanna buried her head in Alex's chest and sobbed. "I can't stand to see her like this." Alex motioned to Erris, who stood alone. She stumbled over to him in tears and joined her mother into the circle of his arms.

Alex looked over the heads of his loved ones at Dr. McCabe. "There must be something stronger we can give her for the pain."

The doctor picked up his black bag. "What have you been giving her thus far?"

Reanna pushed her hair back from her face. "Poteen, but since she's had to take to her bed, it's not helping anymore. That's why I sent Erris to fetch you. The amount we need to give her now only makes her sick to her stomach, and it still isn't strong enough to dull the pain."

He shrugged his shoulders. "The only other thing I can suggest, is an opiate called laudanum, but, it's that expensive, only the wealthy can avail themselves of it."

Laudanum, Reanna thought, a familiar word, but she couldn't remember where she had heard it. "Where would we be able to get it if we had the money?"

"At the apothecary in Castlebar, but unfortunately, being Sunday, nothing is open." On the way to the door, he patted Reanna on the shoulder. "She's sleeping now. Just pray to God that she stays that way. I wish I could do more, but unfortunately I can't."

*   *   *

Shortly before noon, Seamus and Siobhan arrived with Paedar and Troy. The toddler immediately wriggled out of Paedar's grasp and toddled over to Erris's outstretched arms. She and Paedar took him outside to play in the sun. Liam made an appearance a short time later. Reanna tearfully told them of Dr. McCabe's diagnosis.

"Laudanum," Liam said. "That's the name of Lady Evelyn's sedative medicine. Since the apothecary was never rebuilt after the fire last year, haven't I had to travel all the way to Castlebar for it."

"Of course," Reanna said aloud. "Laudanum. That's what it was I gave Lady Margaret for her pain that day. And if Lady Evelyn has the same sickness as her mother before her, naturally she'd have some."

The men stayed downstairs sitting watch beside Mae as she slept, while Reanna and Siobhan went upstairs to prepare food for everyone and a special broth for Mae in the event that she woke up and was able to eat something.

When the food was ready, the women brought it downstairs to Mae's room, where they all gathered around a kish of potatoes and another basket containing hot India bread. Reanna placed a dish of salted buttermilk on the small table and poured the tea.

Liam speared a potato with his knife. "I saw something out of the ordinary out by Crofton House Friday night," he began. "I was mending harness in the stable, when a rat darted into one of the stalls. One of the horses went mad with fright and kicked down the stall door. Then he bolted towards the road." He peeled the steaming potato and deposited the peel back into the basket. "There I was, trying to corner him out by the gate, and who do you suppose rode past?" He dipped his potato in the dish of buttermilk and took a bite. "Soldiers…from Ballymullian… all of them, so far as I could tell."

Alex straightened up in his chair. "How could you tell they were from Ballymullian?"

Liam chewed thoughtfully on his potato. "I recognized the captain…skinny little bagger with poppy-eyes." He reached for a cut of India bread and buttered it on three sides. "The fact of the matter is, they were riding towards Castlebar. And, to add insult to injury, weren't their horses hitched up to Irish carts. More than likely the very ones they stole from us. Loaded up, they were, and with the devil knows what."

"What do you think that was in aid of?"

"I had no idea at the time, but on my way here this morning, I made it my business to take a close look when I passed by the new barracks on Hill Street. No signs of life at all. Windows closed, even the porte cochere is barred. It looks to me like they've closed shop."

*   *   *

At the sounds of pandemonium in the street, everyone jumped to their feet and headed outside to find out the cause of the excitement.

A bareheaded lad on horseback clattered up the street, shouting, "The Frenchies are here! The Frenchies are here!" The man's horse reared and bucked, as the crowd of people, firing questions at the rider, closed in on it.

"Have you not heard the news?" he asked, reining in his horse and beginning the litany he had repeated many times in the past few days. "Last Wednesday, I chanced to be up north in Killalla, minding my own business. Suddenly, I seen three big ships come sailing into the bay at Kilcummin Strand…flying the English colors they were. Then, the town mucky mucks put themselves into a fishing boat and rowed out and climbed aboard one of the ships. The next thing I knew," he said, warming to his subject, "the English colors were hauled down, a grand sight to see, and the French colors were raised!"

The people on Shop Street roared their approval. The messenger's horse reared in panic at the uproar. When his rider got the animal under control, he continued. "By then, a large crowd had gathered on the dock. When they saw the French colors being raised in place of the English colors, they went mad, yelling and laughing, and jumping up and down. Then the next thing I see, is the rowboats coming ashore. Aah, it was a lovely sight, all them blue uniforms." He paused for breath. "And in the first rowboat, sat they that rowed out to the ship. Under arrest they were." He stood upright in his stirrups to better see his audience and shouted so all could hear. "The French soldiers are on their way, fillin' up the roads. Hundreds of our own lads are walking alongside them, dressed in French uniforms, carrying pikes." He reined in his horse and shouted. "Clear the way!" The crowd parted in front of him and he galloped off towards the coast road to spread the news.

*   *   *

When the horseman disappeared around the corner, everyone returned to the shop. Siobhan sent the children upstairs. "Play quietly," she reminded them, "don't forget there's sickness in the house."

She went over and straightened the covers on Mae's bed, then wrung out a cloth in water and held it to her lips. There was no response. She sponged her face tenderly and returned to the chair beside the bed and picked up her knitting.

The men sat down together in front of the hearth. "Well," Liam said, "that clears up that mystery. I guess the Ballymullian troops were privy to a faster horseman than we were."

Seamus nodded his agreement.

Alex and Reanna stood in the corner of the room, whispering urgently to each other.

She clutched his arms. "What are we going to do, Alex?"

His face contorted in pain. "I hate to leave, but I must."

Reanna cried out, "No Alex. You can't leave."

Alex tried to soothe her. "I must, Reanna. Giving sanctuary to a deserter is a crime. My staying here will put you all in jeopardy."

She stuck out her chin determinedly. "I don't care, Alex. I'm not living my life in fear anymore. You've been safe here so far. Besides, I can't think of any reason why the French Army would be interested in a millinery shop. And if they did come in here, you have your Sean McNally identity papers you can use."

Liam threw up his hands in amazement. "You mean you've not tested out your new identity yet?"

"Of course I have, Liam. Haven't you noticed me out on the road. I'm the one with the big stick, hopping away from two armies." He shook his head in frustration.

"Would you be any safer out at our place?"

Alex patted his bad leg. "Thank you kindly Seamus, but I'd never be able to make the walk."

Liam spoke up. "I'd hide you out in my own room, son, for no one ever comes into the stables except us as works there, but Crofton House is the first place the French will commandeer. As well, there'll be plenty of Irishmen with them only too happy to get inside the works and see how the other half lives. There isn't a corner in the whole place won't be looked into." He scratched his head. "Have you given any thought to turning yourself in?"

"Yes, I have, but I've decided against it."

"And why would you do that," offered Seamus, "when you've a perfectly good reason not to have attempted to return so far."

"My injury wouldn't be reason enough for the Army. I could have written a letter to General Forget and at the very least, let him know I was alive."

"Then, why didn't you?" Liam asked dispassionately.

"Because, Liam, I've been struggling with my conscience as to whether I should go back to France at all, and just recently made up my mind." He put his arm around Reanna's waist. "And you, Liam, why didn't you write to the general?"

"My guess is that my conscience isn't as prickly as yours, my friend." He chuckled. "And what did you decide?"

"I decided," said Alex emphatically, "that I've had enough of it. It's no better in France, and here at least, I'm with my loved ones. I'm not going back. I'll take my chances as Sean McNally." He kissed Reanna on the cheek. "Can we tell them now, love?"

"I suppose we'd better." She smiled shyly.

"Reanna and I are betrothed."

Siobhan jumped to her feet, knocking her knitting flying to the floor. She emitted a squeal of delight. She threw her arms around Reanna and Alex, nearly knocking Alex off his feet.

Liam pounded Alex on the back and kissed Reanna. "I thought it would come to this. I only wondered when you'd get around to giving us the news."

Reanna went upstairs to tell the children.

Seamus turned to Alex, his face serious. "It pains me to think of you spending the rest of your life looking over your shoulder, Alex. If you gave yourself up, they'd probably leave you where you are, wouldn't they, for you're no good to them now, are you?"

"The Army doesn't like loose ends, Seamus. In any case, they would-n't leave me here. I'd be made to return to France, where I joined up."

"All right, I'll give you that."

"Suppose you go back with them and get your discharge," said Liam. "Why couldn't you then return to Ballymullian."

"They wouldn't give me a discharge, they'd stick me behind a desk forevermore."

"Why not a desk in Ballymullian?"

"To use your own words, Liam, keeping me here would be a waste of my talent for languages. They'd never do it." He folded his arms. "I'll stay where I am and take my chances as Sean McNally."

*   *   *

Shortly after dinner, Troy fell asleep on Erris's lap, and as they had over an hour's walk to home, the visitors hugged everyone, said their good-byes and set out for the coast road and home. Reanna and Alex convinced Liam that Mae would probably sleep through the night. He left shortly after the O'Dowd's departure to return up the hill to Crofton House.

*   *   *

A few evenings later, Reanna and Alex had settled themselves to stitching in their chairs. Erris stayed below on watch with Mae, who'd been waking and sleeping by turns. Just before dark, Erris rushed upstairs, eyes wild with concern. "Mam, Aunt Mae…she's groaning and thrashing her head from side to side on the pillow."

Reanna ran down to check on her and was soon back upstairs, beside herself with anxiety. "I can't stand to see her like this any longer Alex. I have to do something." She yanked her shawl off the hook at the head of the stairs. "Erris love, please go downstairs and sit with Mae."

Alex rose himself to his feet and reached for his walking stick. "Where are you going, Reanna?"

"I'm going to get her some laudanum," she said over her shoulder, "...from Crofton House."

"Reanna, wait."

He was answered was the slam of the downstairs door. By the time he struggled downstairs to the door, there was no sign of her on the sun-drenched street.

                    *   *   *

Within a short time, Reanna approached the iron gates of Crofton House for the first time since her return to Ballymullian almost two years ago. Her eyes widened in shock at the appearance of the mansion. The front windows were broken out; the granite pots of red flowers that had fronted the entrance doors, now lay smashed to pieces among the soil they had once contained. Red fuchsia spilled out among the carnage, dying, their roots exposed to the sun. The entrance doors gaped open. Boisterous men carried out gold candelabra, rolled up carpets, casks of wine, hams and other household goods. They loaded them into a wagon, jumped in the seat and flicked the reins at the sorrel mare. The frightened animal bolted down the drive, pulling the careening wagon behind it, through the gates and out onto the road toward town. Reanna stole a look at them as they passed through the gates, supposing that they must be French, but when they got closer and she heard their voices, she discovered they were her own people.

She looked straight ahead and walked through the gates with a purposeful stride as though she belonged there. She had no story prepared if someone stopped her to inquire about her business, she only knew that somewhere in that house there was laudanum and she would get it for Mae. She edged left toward the fuchsia bushes as she walked toward the back of the house. She spotted Liam bending over, shoeing a mare.

Outside the stable doors, a man standing on a wagon, tossed bales of hay down to a lad who was stacking them inside the open doors of the stable. She skirted the wagon and headed towards the clanging sound emitting from behind the black jaunting cart.

Liam lifted his head at her approach. "What in God's name are you doing here, Reanna? Don't you know Crofton House has been taken over. It's not safe."

She gestured frantically at him. "I don't care. I must talk to you."

"Follow me," he said and led her into the stables. The two lads working the hay didn't give them a second glance. Liam led the way. Reanna kept her head averted anyway. She followed him into the stables and picking up her skirts, climbed the ladder up to his room in the loft

"What is it, love?" he asked worriedly.

Her control broke and she sobbed into his chest. "It's Mae… She's dying Liam. I just know it. She's thrashing around in so much pain. I have to do something."

He held her away from him and searched into her face. "What is it you want me to do?"

"Nothing…I'm going inside the house myself to get Mae some laudanum from Lady Evelyn's room."

He put a restraining hand on her arm. "You can't do that. She's under house arrest. There'll surely be a guard outside her bedroom." He started toward the ladder "Let me get it."

Reanna's voice was soft in its insistence. "You've never been upstairs, have you, Liam?"

He turned around. "No, that I haven't, but I can talk my way in."

"I worked up there, remember?" Her voice brooked no argument. "And, I know right where to look. I'll be fine…Please don't worry."

He held her at arm's length. "If you are determined to go up there, listen to me closely. The Frenchies arrived a few days ago, stayed only a short time, and then moved on, leaving a captain in charge, with three of our own under his command. I would imagine that the Frenchie has taken over the master suite, so you'll have to find out where they've moved Lady Evelyn."

"In that case, I know right where she'd want to be...her mother's room."

"There'll surely be a guard outside her door."

"They haven't been here long enough to recognize all the staff. I'll pretend to be her nurse."

Liam looked admiringly at Reanna as though seeing her for the first time. "Well, I'll be damned," he said.

"Please, go to Mae, Liam," she pleaded. "I'll be there as soon as I can."

"No...I'll not leave until you're safely back here. So hurry...but keep a close eye out," he warned as she hurried toward the ladder.

"I'll be careful," she promised.

Liam climbed down after her and watched as she left the stable.

Reanna crossed the yard to the servants' entrance. She let herself in the vestibule door and closed it quietly behind her. Judging from the large amount of mobcaps and uniforms in disarray in the cubbyholes, it appeared that very few staff were in the house. She wondered if they'd all taken flight when the takeover occurred. There was not a pair of shoes to be seen. She chose a cap and apron from one of the cubbyholes. The years fell away as she tucked her hair once more under the cap, tied the apron around her waist.

She opened the scullery door and stood in the dim light streaming in from the small window above the sink, shocked at the chaos in front of her. In the kitchen, a cask of wine sat on its side on the long wooden table, droplets from its unsecured tap, pooled among the empty whiskey bottles, half eaten food and dirty dishes.

A mouse climbed out of one of the pots, darted down a leg of the table, across the slate floor in front of her and disappeared under the heavy door of the pantry. She jumped back startled against the sink. The sharp smell of yellow soap still clung to it. She recovered her wits and crossed to the door leading to the main part of the house. She leaned her ear against it. At that moment, a bell on one of the pulleys began an insistent jangle, summoning a member of the kitchen staff to one of the rooms in the house. Reanna's eyes darted to the board, noting that the call was coming from the master suite. She'd better check it first. Perhaps Lady Evelyn hadn't been moved after all.

Almost immediately, hurrying footsteps approached the kitchen. Reanna whirled towards the pantry and closed the heavy wooden door behind her. She cringed in the blackness and felt every hair on her body stand up in terror. She knew that somewhere in this dark, enclosed space, lurked a mouse that was bound to run up her skirts. She gathered her clothing in folds around her ankles and tried not to scream as she hopped from one foot to another in the dark. She heard footsteps in the kitchen, the clinking of glass and then the slam of the kitchen door. She fled from the pantry, opened the servants' door, and felt her way upstairs in the dark. Lanterns had always lit up the hallways until bedtime, and she knew that once in the bedroom, she'd only have to open the heavy drapes to get the last of the early evening light from outside.

She stood at the top of the stairs, listening, and heard nothing. She cracked open the door, and peeked down the empty hall. She sped past Lady Margaret's room towards Lady Evelyn's suite. She put her ear to the double doors and listened. Hearing nothing, she slipped quietly inside. She stood in a wide parlour, the end of which was graced by a large window. The heavy wine drapes were pulled aside to admit the natural light, which filtered down on an enormous fern that sat between two tapestry chairs. Against the wall, sat a highly polished table with curved legs, which held a wilted bouquet of flowers in murky water.

Reanna poked her head through one of the doors into a dressing room whose hooks held all manner of clothing. Shelves held stacks of shirts and nightclothes. Another closet held hunting and riding attire, including riding boots and crops. She peeked into the adjacent sleeping room. It was unoccupied. Reanna then realized that she was probably in the deceased Lord Dalton's suite. She shivered and left quickly.

She walked across the hall to Lady Evelyn's rooms and grasped the latch. It moved under her hand. She stiffened in fear, and turned and fled back into Lord Dalton's bathroom. She didn't have time to close the door completely, but slipped in behind it, heart pounding. Through the crack, she spied Hester coming out of the other suite. Reanna listened to her footsteps cross the marble floor of the parlour. When she heard the outer door close, she waited a minute more, then hurried into Lady Evelyn's rooms once again.

She tiptoed into the bathroom, through the dressing room and entered the sleeping room. It looked very much like Lady Margaret's room had been, except that it was larger and more elaborate. A double bed dressed in sapphire blue, sat against a draped wall. It was unoccupied and turned down for the night. A lantern emitted a dim light from a draped table across the room. Beside it on a silver tray, sat a dusty bottle of wine and a crystal glass on a tray. Liam was probably right about the Frenchman occupying the master suite, Reanna thought to herself. Hester had been summoned to turn down the bed. The call came from this room. Where had the Frenchman gone? Maybe he was on his way back to the room at this moment.

She ran over to the bedside table, opened the small drawer and fumbled inside. It was empty. She swallowed, breathed deeply and knew that her next stop was the room in which she'd been raped so many years ago.

Reanna closed the double doors quietly behind her and was making her way carefully down the hall towards Lady Margaret's room, when the servant's stair door opened. Trapped, she caught her breath and stood rooted to the spot as the door swung open. A rough looking man, carrying a mug and a pasty, stepped into the wide hall. He closed the door with his foot, spotted her, and eyed her up and down. He walked toward her. Reanna raised her head and stood her ground.

"Who are you then, my girl?" he asked in Mayo Irish. "And where is it you think you're going at this time of night?"

In a stern voice, she replied, "I'm Lady Evelyn's nurse and I've come to take care of her…that is, if I can find her. As it happens, she is not in her suite. Would you be so kind as to tell me where she's been trotted off to?" She stood, arms folded, foot tapping, waiting for an answer.

The man took a huge bite of his meat pie, then waved his thumb at the Lady Margaret's room behind him. "She's in there," he said and wandered off down the hallway.

She opened the door quietly and stood beside the wardrobe. The room looked smaller than she remembered it. Her eyes swept inadvertently to the carpet where Lord Dalton had raped her. She firmly directed her attention away from the past and concentrated on the present. Lady Evelyn lay in the same bed her mother had suffered in twelve years before. Though only middle aged, her illness made her appear much older. Her eyes were closed and her face, pudgy no longer, but wasted and gray in color. Reanna tiptoed to the bed, hid behind the lantern on the table and reached around to the front of the bedside table and opened the drawer. She fumbled around until she felt a familiar sized bottle, lifted it out, extracted the stopper from the brown bottle and sniffed the cloying smell. She replaced the stopper and dropped the laudanum in her apron pocket.

The drawer stuck when she tried to close it. She moved around to the front of the small table to slide the drawer in straight. It squealed in protest. Lady Evelyn's eyelids quivered open and her drugged eyes met the stranger's gaze. The sick woman reached in panic for her bell-pull. Reanna moved it out of her reach, then turned and fled from the room. She forced herself into a walk until she closed the door of the back stairs. Then she fled blindly down the stairs to the scullery, ripping off her cap and apron as she went. She tossed them into a cubbyhole in the vestibule, slipped the bottle of laudanum in the bosom of her dress and walked quickly out of the door of the servants' entrance. Liam, who had been watching from the stable, moved quickly towards her and they walked out of the stable yard and down the drive to the gate.

*   *   *

Light faded from the evening sky, as they made their way to town.

"I stole her pain medicine, Liam!" Reanna cried in anguish. "What if that's all she had?"

He put his arm around her shoulder. "She's well able to get more," Liam said comfortingly. "She has the means, you know."

She reached for her handkerchief. "But she isn't able to call anyone to tell them that she's in pain," she insisted, "for I moved the bell-pull out of her reach."

"The staff will keep an eye on her."

"That's the thing of it. It looked to me like most of them had left, taking their shoes with them, although I did see Hester."

"Well, then, she'll be fine. Stop worrying, Reanna, just remember you did it for Mae."

They reached Hill Street and began the descent into the town.

Reanna pointed down the hill. "Sparks! Oh, God, Liam, I think there is a fire on Shop Street."

They took off like a shot down the hill towards the barracks. They heard shouts and the sounds of breaking glass from inside. Through the open doors, by the light of a lantern, they saw men inside the building, riffling through desks and breaking up floorboards. The courtyard gates yawned open.

Down the road towards Shop Street, they spied a group of men with sticks, shattering the grocer's window. The grocer stuck his head out the upstairs window and swiftly withdrew it. The men broke open the shop door. A few minutes later, they ran back into the street, arms loaded up with bags and boxes of food, chased by the grocer and his son. Reanna and Liam looked at each other in alarm, then broke into a run. They turned into Shop Street and couldn't believe what they saw. Groups of their own people with torches and sticks looting the shops and setting fire to the buildings.

Alex and the other shopkeepers stood outside on the street armed with sticks ready to protect their property.

Alex supported himself on one stick and had another at the ready. He shouted at the hooligans.

"These are Irish businesses, you ignorant bastards."

One of the rowdies shouted back in defiance, "These buildings are Lord bloody Dalton's holdings, and we don't want them in Ballymullian!"

In time, other levelheaded citizens, who outnumbered the rowdies, joined the ranks of the shopkeepers and chased them off.

Chapter 18

—▼—

Ballymullian, September 9 1798

It was well after dark by the time Liam answered the summons. He came through to the back and joined the others beside Mae's bed.

He turned to Reanna and Alex, an unspoken question in his eyes.

Reanna's face collapsed in sorrow. She shook her head. "Not long now, I'm afraid," she whispered. "The priest just left. He gave her the last rites."

Liam gazed into his old friend's face. He smoothed Mae's hair back with a knotty hand, and kissed her on the forehead. Then he turned to face the others.

"I'm afraid I have some more bad news," he said, quietly. "It seems the British defeated the French forces at Ballinamuck over to Longford, yesterday." He raised his eyes to Alex, "I guess it's back to business as usual," he said, dejectedly.

Alex stiffened, stunned at the news. "When did you find this out?"

"This afternoon," Liam said. "A French soldier pulled up to the stables. His horse was half-dead, the poor beast was that lathered. He instructed me to saddle up two fresh horses and to be quick about it. Then he ran into the big house. I barely got the second horse saddled, when he and the French Captain who was left in charge of Crofton

House, came flying out of the house, jumped on their horses and left. I was on my way to the scullery door to see could I find out anything from the two Irishmen who were left, and don't I meet the two of them buzzing off. They weren't hanging around to be the welcoming committee when the British returned. They stayed around just long enough to tell me of the defeat."

Alex took Reanna's shaking hand in his own. She looked from one to the other. "What happens now?"

Liam shook his head. "There'll be hell to pay when the British get back and Lady Evelyn's agent gets their ear about the condition of Crofton House. He's been released by the French and is back there now, frothing at the mouth. All the rent money he collected has been confiscated and Crofton House is in disgraceful condition. Everything of any value that isn't nailed down has been stolen and what hasn't been stolen has been trashed."

Alex clenched his fists. "Do they know who the ringleaders are? I'd like to get my hands on the bastards myself."

Liam shook his head. "I don't know about that, but I'll guarantee you there'll be no rest until somebody pays for it."

                    *   *   *

Early the next morning, Reanna woke to the sound of voices outside on Shop Street. Hoofbeats clacked erratically on the cobbles below. She jumped out of bed and ran to the upstairs window. Two British soldiers on horseback, trotted slowly up the street, through broken glass and burned out torches. They appeared to be assessing the damage done to the buildings and making notes in a black notebook.

She jostled her daughter awake. "Erris…wake up, darling. There are British soldiers out on the street. Stay up here and don't come down until I call you."

Erris sat up in bed, rubbing her eyes. She nodded sleepily, then lay back down again.

Reanna grabbed her shawl off the hook and tiptoed down the stairs. She roused Alex, asleep in the chair beside Mae's bed.

"Alex," she whispered, "wake up." She motioned him to follow her. They stood behind their door and watched the soldiers dismount in front of a limestone building across the street. They examined the burned out window and the scorch marks. One pounded on the shop door; it opened and then disappeared inside.

Alex and Reanna returned to Mae's room. She took one look at Mae, fell to her knees and began to wail. "Mae," she pleaded, leaning over the old woman, and trying vainly to rouse her. With tears in his eyes, Alex laid his hand on his aunt's chest. He could detect no heartbeat.

Reanna raised tortured eyes to Alex.

He shook his head and said in a choked voice; "She's gone, Reanna."

"No," she cried, and leapt to her feet, almost knocking over the small bedside table in the process. Alex made a grab for the lantern and righted it, as it slid toward the edge of the table. He tried to take Reanna in his arms.

She jerked away and ran out the shop door, leaving it ajar. "I'm going for Doctor McCabe," she called over her shoulder.

"You can't, Reanna. Wait!"

Alex limped to the door to stop her, but he was too late. She was halfway down the street. At that moment, across the street, the shop door opened and the soldiers stepped out onto the street. They spotted a distraught Alex in the doorway, and made their way across the street to confront him.

One of the soldiers, peered at Alex over the top of small wire rimmed spectacles, and jerked his thumb towards the shop.

"Inside," he said.

Alex walked into the shop and they followed him.

"What's going on here?"

Distraught with grief, Alex almost answered that his aunt had just died, but caught himself in time. He motioned to the back room, and said in his best British accent, "A woman has just passed away."

With that, a weeping Reanna, with Doctor McCabe in tow, burst through the door, glanced distractedly at the soldiers, and then hurried into the back room. Alex and the soldiers filed in after them. The soldiers peered down at the motionless form, satisfied themselves that it was not a ruse, then stood back while Doctor McCabe conducted his examination. When he pronounced Mae dead and covered her face with the bedcover, Reanna collapsed in Alex's arms.

The spectacled soldier motioned to the doctor to join him. After answering a series of questions about Mae, Doctor McCabe shook his head sadly. "She was a grand woman...but very ill for over a year." He gestured to the bed. "We'd been expecting this for some time."

The soldier nodded. "You can go now for now, but we may need to ask you further questions later." He marked down the doctor's address in his black book, and saw him to the door.

The soldier opened the curtain. "Come in here. We need to ask you a few questions."

Alex took Reanna's arm, gave it a comforting squeeze and propelled her into the shop area.

Reanna's knees grew weak with the certainty that their lives were at an end. She sat down on the bench, anxious fingers twisting her handkerchief into a knot.

The soldier stood with his back against the door, pencil poised over his black notebook. He turned toward Alex, who stood by the curtain. "Did you have anything to do with all this," he said, jerking his thumb across the street at the damaged building.

Alex's steady gaze met the soldier's own. "I did not."

"Where were you when it was going on?"

"Standing outside trying to keep this shop from going up in flames."

"Is this your shop?"

"No."

"Then, who might you be?"

"My name is Sean McNally."

"Where are you from?"

"Sligo," Alex replied, leaning on his stick, looking for all the world as though he had nothing to hide.

The soldier turned to Reanna. "And your name?"

Reanna stood up and looked at him with steady eyes. "Reanna Campbell."

"Who is the dead woman?"

Reanna's composure deserted her. She put her hands to her face and burst into tears again.

Alex started over to comfort her. The soldier waved him back to the curtain.

Reanna regained her composure. "Mae Proulx," she answered calmly. "We were partners in this shop."

He put his hand out to her. "Show me the lease."

Reanna left the room and returned in a few moments with a slip of paper and handed it to the soldier.

He read it and looked at Reanna over his spectacles. "This lease only has one tenant's name on it, Mae Proulx."

She took the lease from his outstretched hand. "I'll be sure to get it changed."

"See that you do."

He turned back to Alex. "What is your business here?"

Alex gave him a wan smile, "I came to ask the widow Campbell for her hand in marriage, but I didn't expect to encounter such sadness."

Reanna looked at him aghast, afraid he was telling more than he should.

The soldier jerked his head toward the stick that Alex was leaning on. "What's wrong with your foot?"

"My horse fell on me," Alex answered.

"When?"

"A year ago." Alex shrugged. "It never healed."

The soldier looked around the shop. "Do you have anything here belonging to Crofton House?"

"No, we do not."

"We'll see," he said. He jerked his head at the other soldier. "Search the premises for any of the missing items on your list."

The other soldier saluted and went through the curtain. Reanna's mind screeched a warning. Lady Evelyn's laudanum was on the table beside Mae's bed. Shaking, she followed the soldier into the back. The little brown bottle was gone from the table. Only the lantern remained. Heart pounding, she swept her eyes casually over the floor near the bed. She spotted it on the floor, where it had fallen when she had nearly upset the table. It was barely visible in the dim light. She slid it underneath the bed with her foot.

Fortunately, the soldier seemed disinclined to place himself too close to Mae's body and was folded in half looking up the chimney. Finding nothing, he stood up, wiped his trousers and headed toward the stairs.

Reanna barred his way. "Please," she said, "my daughter is sleeping upstairs. She knows nothing about the old woman's passing yet. May I go to her?"

He moved her aside. "I'll go first, you follow me."

Reanna followed him up the stairs, hoping that Erris would be wise enough not to speak.

Reanna walked into the sleeping room behind the soldier. Erris lay on her side, face to the wall, Pegeen by her shoulder. Reanna watched her child's back rise and fall with each breath, and she knew she was feigning sleep.

The soldier completed his search and pounded back down the stairs, with Reanna following after. They returned to the shop. Reanna moved to Alex's side.

"No missing items here," the soldier reported.

Without warning, his superior jerked a billy out of his belt and aimed it directly at Reanna's face. Alex jumped in front of her and made a grab for it. His stick clattered to the floor, his leg buckled and he sprawled face down after it.

"I guess you do have a bad foot," the soldier acknowledged.

Alex picked himself up off the floor, ears burning in anger.

The soldier picked up his billy where it had landed harmlessly on the slate floor, deflected by Alex's body.

"I guess you're not fast enough to have been mixed up in any of this business."

He turned to Reanna, nodded his head towards Mae's room and said, "My condolences on your loss." At the door he turned back. "Change the name on that lease," he warned and closed the door after him.

Reanna and Alex collapsed in grief in each other's arms. A tearful Erris flew down the stairs, and they opened their arms to her.

"I heard it all," she cried, "but I was too afraid to come down."

"You did the right thing, love," Reanna assured her, "we're so proud of you."

*   *   *

Shortly after the soldiers left, Reanna hung a black ribbon on the door of the shop, and lit candles at the head and foot of Mae's bed. Erris left to walk the four miles to fetch the O'Dowds and Paedar. The baker's son was pressed into service to run to Crofton House and inform Liam of Mae's death. He came back with the message that Liam was unable to come right away, but that he would arrive sometime in the evening.

For the rest of the day, the other shop owners on the street, each in their turn, arrived to pay their respects, and bring a gift of food. Reanna introduced Alex as Sean McNally, her fiancé from Sligo, and accepted their best wishes. Everyone had many good things to say about Mae's kindness in times of trouble. Reanna knew more than most, how kind she had been.

In the afternoon, Erris arrived back with Paedar and the O'Dowds.

That night, after they closed the doors to the neighbours, they put Troy to sleep in Reanna's bed, then all sat with Mae throughout the night, for a last visit, reminiscing about all the good times they'd had together. The adults toasted her with poteen.

In the morning, Liam, Seamus, Paedar and the baker from next door, hoisted a plain box onto their shoulders and carried Mae from the shop. Reanna, Erris, Alex and Siobhan, with Troy in her arms, accompanied by a priest, walked behind them as they carried their beloved Mae to her final resting place in the stark Catholic graveyard on the outskirts of Ballymullian. After some prayers and a few words by the priest, amid their own tears, they said their good-byes and walked slowly back to Shop Street.

*   *   *

SEPTEMBER 17, 1798

Reanna yawned and opened her eyes. She gazed heartbroken at the sleeping face of her beloved child across the room. Since last Christmas, Erris had spoken of little else but going away to school and someday becoming a teacher. Reanna had not realized how deeply she, herself, was caught up in the idea of Erris's acceptance into the boarding school. But the fact of the matter was, Seamus still had not received a reply to any of the letters he had sent to the Wolford Academy in Roscommon, slamming the door shut on any hope they might have harbored for furthering Erris's education there. In Ballymullian, opportunities were bleak indeed as there were no schools, Catholic or otherwise. Those who could afford education, were sent elsewhere. In light of British recriminations against Catholics for the part they played in the French invasion, the O'Dowd's permission to build a schoolhouse had been withdrawn. What a pity, she thought, to get that close to realizing their dream and then having it taken away. Siobhan herself had looked forward to teaching the girls to knit and sew.

Reanna wracked her brain. There had to be some way to get the money to send Erris away to school. A germ of an idea seemed intent on pushing its way to the front of her consciousness. But the panicky feeling in the pit of her stomach accompanying it, impelled her to smother it again and again. She closed her eyes, and without warning, the answer surged forward to be recognized. And all at once, she knew what must be done to get the money.

She threw off the quilt, determination and fright competing for dominance. Ten minutes later, she was dressed in her finest and hurrying up Shop Street in the early morning light on her way to Crofton House.

*   *   *

Reanna let herself in the familiar black iron gates and walked down the curving lane between tall banks of purple asters, toward the double doors of Crofton House. Once more, order had been restored. The warming sun shimmered off new panes of glass in the windows. Temporary wooden boxes, overflowing with bright yellow and orange zinnias and marigolds, stood in place of the stone urns on the wide verandah. Heart pounding, she climbed the wide steps to the front door. She rubbed the dust off her shoes onto the backs of her stockings, straightened her hat and knocked firmly on the door. She stood weak-kneed, like a condemned prisoner on her way to the gallows, and straightened the folds of her navy dress with perspiring hands. The door opened and an ancient liveried butler stood in front of her. She recognized him from the time she worked here and hoped that he didn't recognize her. She sent a gambler's prayer heavenward and drew herself up to her full height.

"Good morning John. I'd like to speak with Lady Ellen, if it's convenient."

His old eyes tried in vain to recognize this stranger that stood before him and called him by name. He took measure of her, and couldn't decide whether she fit or not. "And who may I say is calling?"

"Reanna Campbell."

He looked at her down his spectacles, shook his head in confusion and asked her to step in. She followed his shuffling footsteps inside and once more gazed up the familiar wide staircase that led to the family rooms. She clasped her hands together to still their shaking. He led her through double doors into the drawing room. After he left, Reanna nervously paced the length of the room, her shoes echoing on the marble floor (devoid now of rugs). She ran her hand over the wine velvety draperies, pulled tight against the morning sunlight and bent to breathe in the fragrance of yellow and red blossoms that graced an ornately carved side table against the wall.

*   *   *

A tall, imperious woman in her thirties, entered the room. Her mousy hair was gathered into a severe pompadour and her rusty hued no-nonsense dress, swished about her ankles as she approached the woman who stood warming her hands over the fire in the marble fireplace. She looked vaguely familiar. A familiarity that was unsettling, somehow.

Her dark, snapping eyes bore curiously into the other woman's. "Do I know you?"

The redheaded woman answered in a calm voice. "My maiden name was Reanna O'Neal, and I used to work here twelve years ago."

Lady Ellen raised her eyebrows. She shook her head impatiently and strode across to the bell pull that hung on the wall. Her sharp words cut back across the room over her shoulder. "Then it must be obvious to you that Hester is the one you need to speak to about employment."

The clear voice stopped Lady Ellen in her tracks. "I used to do for Lady Margaret."

Lady Ellen felt her back stiffen. Now she knew who she was. Memories of that shameful night, and its implications, were written all over her pale face as she turned slowly and walked back to her.

"Reanna O'Neal...yes...what is your business here?" she asked in a chilly voice.

"There is a child," Reanna answered calmly.

Lady Ellen's lips tightened. "...And...?"

"She is very bright and my hope would be to send her off to boarding school in Roscommon."

Lady Ellen pursed her mouth. Her eyes were riveted on Reanna's face, but her mind was elsewhere. Her father's scurrilous actions had been the cause of family shame for many years. His death some years ago, had finally given the family the peace of mind they craved. With her mother, Lady Evelyn, on her death bed, the last thing she intended to have happen was for a bastard from her father's seamy past to return to haunt them and fill their last days together with renewed pain.

Her decision made, she walked over to a writing desk. Retrieving a small key from her pocket, she opened one of the drawers and withdrew a packet of bills.

"Take this," she said, thrusting the bills into Reanna's hands. "I want you to know that the reason for this money is a thank you for the excellent care you took of my Nan while she was alive. Do with the money what you will. If you choose to spend it to send **your** child to school, that's your affair. Just don't ever return here again for any reason." She turned on her heel and left the room.

Reanna stuffed the packet of bills in the bosom of her dress as a knock came to the door. She followed the shuffling old butler to the front door.

As she walked exultantly towards town, with enough money to see Erris through all the schooling she could ever wish for, she justified to herself that she didn't really lie to Lady Ellen about her child's parentage. She couldn't in any case, because she herself didn't know for sure.

*   *   *

OCTOBER 22, 1798

Excitement ran high in the Campbell flat this particular morning, for it was the day that she, Reanna Campbell would wed Sean McNally. Reanna listened to the happy voices of her family and friends, gathered downstairs to be with Alex and her when they would exchange their vows.

Since Mae's death, Liam had drawn even closer to all of them. He and Alex had opened up the back room and turned it into a tailor shop. They installed a counter and constructed a high stool with a cross bar, on which Alex could rest his foot.

Reanna slipped into the mustard colored frock that she and Siobhan had made, along with a new shift for herself and Biddy. Erris fastened it up the back for her. The O'Dowds and Paedar and Biddy had arrived early in the day, with news that Seamus had received an answer to his letter from the Wolford Academy in Roscommon. Although classes had already begun, Reanna had been accepted and would leave within the week. Reanna had smiled to herself. She knew what had turned the tide for Erris's acceptance was not Seamus's entreaty on her behalf, but the fully paid up two year tuition that Reanna had sent by special messenger herself. Erris would miss Paedar terribly when she went away to school, since he was more like a brother than a cousin, but, she'd promised to teach him every new thing she learned as she'd done in the past.

Reanna sat on a chair and slipped on her shoes. Erris ran a brush through her mother's thick red hair, with its threads of silver. Reanna twisted it loosely up into a knot on the top of her head and fastened it with an amber comb. She secured her wide matching hat carefully behind her pompadour with an amber hatpin and arranged the veil in a cloud around her face. She heard the jangle of the front bell, heard Liam greeting the priest and then footsteps coming up the stairs.

Siobhan stood at the landing, tears in her eyes. "You look elegant, love."

Reanna rushed over to her, threw her arms around her and kissed her flushed cheeks.

"I couldn't have done any of it without you. I love you, Siobhan."

Siobhan, flustered by Reanna's display of affection, stammered, "The priest is here, you'd best hurry," and flew down the stairs, and Erris after her.

Reanna stood by herself in reflection, then walked alone down the narrow staircase where Alex waited for her, a broad smile on his handsome face.

Waving to get her mother's attention, Erris held up a hand written sign. It read; McNally's Millinery and Tailor Shop, closed for a wedding. Back at four.

The end

Epilogue

NOVEMBER 1798

Wolfe Tone, one of the originators of the Society of United Irishmen is captured after an aborted invasion in Northern Ireland. He is thrown in prison, and sentenced to be hung, drawn, and quartered.

When his request to be shot like a soldier is denied, he slits his own throat with his penknife.

*   *   *

1801

Britain establishes the Act of Union in retribution for the Irish uprising of 1798. This Act of Union abolishes the presiding Irish Parliament and installs a hand picked British Government, thereby firmly squashing any hopes that Ireland may have harbored towards ever having total control over her own destiny.

In ensuing years, her rights and privileges would be doled out with a stingy hand and not without a price.